AMERICAN MACHIAVELLI

F. YEW

MACH XXI

ISBN Paperback: 979-8-9935427-0-6
ISBN Hardback: 979-8-9935427-1-3
ISBN eBook: 979-8-9935427-2-0

Edited: Dawn Baca: fiverr.com/dawnbaca
Formated: Dawn Baca: fiverr.com/dawnbaca

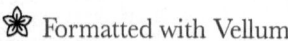 Formatted with Vellum

To my wife, who changed my life in the most unexpected and beautiful way.
To my children, who bring light and joy into my days, every single day.
To my Nonno, who introduced me to philosophy and whose life and spirit became the spark for this series.
To my Noni, who helped raise me with wisdom, humor, and care well into adulthood.
To my Papa, whose example gave me the role model I needed growing up.
To my best friend and his wife, thank you for being the family I always wanted and always needed.

Good examples arise from good education, good education from good laws, and good laws from those reforms that were made by good men.

—Niccolò Machiavelli
Discourses on Livy, Book I,
Chapter 18

DISCLAIMER

This thriller is a work of fiction and political satire. It is intended solely for the purposes of commentary, criticism, parody, and public discourse, and is protected under the First Amendment of the U.S. Constitution.

Any names, likenesses, or references to real individuals, particularly public figures, are used fictitiously and satirically. No factual claims are being made about any actual person, group, or organization. The inclusion of real names or figures does not imply endorsement, approval, or involvement.

Any resemblance to private individuals or real-life events is purely coincidental. Where such resemblance may appear, it is unintentional and incidental to the broader satirical narrative.

PRELUDE: MAN IN THE SHADOWS

Y ou will never know my name. That is by design. I have walked between two worlds, standing at the intersection of power and rebellion, watching history bend under the weight of corruption. I am a high-ranking official in the Plump administration, at least, that's what they think. But in the dimly lit corners of a decaying democracy, I am also a voice in the resistance, a whisper in the storm, a keeper of secrets too dangerous to expose, until now.

America is crumbling. You can see it in the hollowed-out towns where factories once thrived. You can hear it in the frustration of workers who labor endlessly yet remain trapped in a cycle of poverty. You can feel it in the growing divide between the billionaire class and the rest of us, the forgotten, the silenced, the expendable.

It did not have to be this way. We were promised prosperity. We were promised leadership that would put the people first. Instead, we have been handed a system rotting from within, driven by the failures of an Executive branch, ruled by ego, a Legislative branch paralyzed by greed, and a Judicial branch compromised by political puppetry. The foundation of this nation was supposed to be unshakable, yet here we stand, on the precipice of collapse.

Oligarchy is no longer a warning; it is our reality. The billionaire class has manipulated our economy to ensure its endless rise while the rest of us remain tethered to stagnation. Sixty percent of Americans live paycheck to paycheck. Eighty-three percent of households struggle financially. The average worker today earns less in real wages than they did half a century ago. The American Dream has become a mirage dangled before us, but forever out of reach.

Our political system, once an institution of governance, has mutated into a grotesque marketplace where elections are bought, and democracy is auctioned to the highest bidder. The Supreme Court's Citizens United decision ensured that Super PACs and billionaires could drown out the voices of ordinary citizens. More than 90% of House elections and 80% of Senate elections are determined not by merit, but by who spends the most money. Our representatives do not represent us; they serve those who paid for their campaigns, their power, and their silence.

Meanwhile, America is dying, literally. Life expectancy has plummeted to 77.5 years, the lowest among developed nations. Healthcare is a luxury, not a right. Birth rates have reached historic lows, and for the first time, our future looks smaller than our past. The land of opportunity has become a wasteland of broken promises.

And the future? Artificial intelligence and automation loom over the workforce, threatening to replace millions. Jobs that once defined the American middle class are vanishing, and the question is not whether we can adapt. It is whether those in power will allow us to. Will AI be used to uplift society, or will it serve only to further enrich the elite while discarding human labor as obsolete?

This is the reality they do not want you to see. But James Machiavelli saw it. And he did something no one else had the courage to do. He wrote The People's Awakening: A New American Era. A thesis so damning, so disruptive, that the President of the United States ordered his assassination. Not exile. Not imprisonment. Death.

I was there the night the order was given. I was there when the classified directive passed through secure channels. I was there when the plan was set in motion.

I was also there when James Machiavelli survived.

I have seen both sides of this war. I have walked among the powerful, listened to their whispered fears, and witnessed their desperation as they cling to their crumbling empire. And now, I am here to tell you: the revolution has begun. The people have awakened. And there is no turning back.

This is the story of the man they tried to erase. This is the story of America's reckoning.

1

CHECKMATE

PRESENT DAY

JULY 2028 — 7:00 P.M.

Houston, TX.

The air inside the convention hall crackled with anticipation. The Republican Party had gathered in full force, its elite dressed in designer suits and red ties, basking in the glow of what they believed was their inevitable victory. Plump 2028: Making History Again flashed across every massive LED screen as confetti and patriotic banners cascaded from the ceiling. Delegates, donors, and die-hard supporters waved their flags in euphoric celebration.

Plump strode onto the stage, his usual smug grin stretching across his face as the deafening cheers reached a fever pitch. He raised a hand, basking in the crowd's adoration before approaching the podium. The teleprompters lit up; the cameras zoomed in, and just as he opened his mouth to speak.

His microphone cut out.

The sudden silence was jarring. The cheers died down as confusion rippled through the hall. Staffers rushed to the sides of the stage, frantically signaling to technicians. Plump tapped the mic, his face twitching in irritation.

Then, the speakers crackled back to life, but it was not Plump's voice that echoed through the convention center.

It was a recording.

A deep, unmistakable voice filled the hall. "Sir, are you sure about this? Eliminating an American citizen… along with his family?"

A hush fell over the crowd.

Plump's eyes widened as his voice responded, dripping with casual cruelty. "Take him out. And his family. No mistakes. No survivors."

Gasps erupted from the audience. Some gaped at the speakers, unable to process what they had just heard. Others whipped out their phones, capturing every second of the revelation. The high-ranking officials in attendance—senators, governors, corporate backers—exchanged panicked glances.

Then, on the massive screens behind Plump, an image flashed—the headline of a news article.

JAMES MACHIAVELLI AND FAMILY KILLED IN TRAGIC CAR ACCIDENT.

—The New York Times

The timestamp showed it had been reported over a year ago.

The room remained frozen in shock, all eyes darting between the screen and the man standing at the podium. Plump, for the first time in years, looked genuinely afraid.

"Get this under control!" he bellowed, slamming a fist on the podium.

But the moment he spoke, another recording played.

"Mr. President, it's done. Machiavelli and his family are dead."

Plump's voice responded. "Good. No loose ends."

The room erupted into chaos. Reporters scrambled, broadcasting the moment live to millions of viewers across the nation. Secret Service agents moved in, their hands at their earpieces, desperately trying to locate the source of the hack.

Then, from the middle of the crowd, a single voice rang out through the silence.

"My name is James Machiavelli."

Gasps turned into outright pandemonium.

There he stood, alive, very much alive, flanked by a small but unarmed security team. His presence sent shockwaves through the room. The impossible had happened: a man declared dead had returned to confront his executioner.

"That coward-ass bitch," Machiavelli continued, his voice reverberating through the stunned silence, "ordered my family and me assassinated because I wrote a thesis detailing the corruption within our decaying political system and provided solutions that would benefit the vast majority of the American people."

Plump turned red with fury, pointing toward his security. "Get him out of here! Arrest him!"

No one moved.

The room had shifted. The power dynamic had changed. For the first time, it was Plump who was on the defensive. The people, the delegates, the donors, even members of his inner circle stood frozen, waiting to hear what Machiavelli had to say.

"I stand before you tonight," Machiavelli continued, his voice growing stronger, "not just as a candidate on this year's ballot, but as a representative of a greater movement, an alliance of everyday Americans from all walks of life, united in our mission to restore the true American dream for the vast majority."

Plump's lip curled in a sneer, his fists clenching. "You're nothing but a fraud!"

"I'm the fraud?" Machiavelli roared, his voice cutting through the tension. "The fraud is you! The fraud is every corrupt politician, justice, operator, lobbyist, donor, CEO, and bureaucrat who has manipulated this country for personal gain while the rest of us suffer. And to all of you, I say—CHECKMATE!"

The room held its collective breath.

"We own the greatest trove of compromising information, incriminating evidence, damaging secrets, or quite simply… dirt," Machiavelli continued, scanning the sea of stunned faces. "This information also includes all of your personal and financial account information. And what's particularly damning is that it wasn't stolen; it was handed to us by your own people. The ones who smile to your face, pledge their loyalty, and then quietly orchestrate your downfall."

A murmur swept through the audience. Paranoia took root. Who among them had betrayed the others?

"If we were to release this entire trove today, the American people would rip you out of your homes and build a bonfire with your bodies," Machiavelli said coldly. "Your screams would sound like a lullaby to them as you burned slowly. But that's not what we want. Blood will not rebuild this country. Vengeance will not feed the hungry, educate the young, or heal the sick."

Machiavelli took a step forward, his voice steady. "Instead, we are going to use this information to extort you, not for money, but for the American people. You will now start putting their well-being above your own greed. You will learn very quickly what that means."

Plump trembled with rage. "You think you can threaten me? You think you can threaten us?"

"Oh, you misunderstand," Machiavelli said, smiling faintly. "This isn't a threat. It's a promise."

The screens behind him flickered again.

"For those of you who need a little more convincing," he continued, "we will be releasing a new scandal at the top of the hour from 9 p.m. until 11 p.m. tonight. Just to give you a taste of what we can do. If you don't start working for the American people, we will destroy you."

Machiavelli let the words sink in, then tilted his head slightly.

"Enjoy your party," he said. "The world you've grown comfortable in, the world where you get richer while the rest of America suffers. That world ends tonight."

Then, he turned and walked out, leaving behind a room full of the most powerful people in America, all suddenly aware that they were no longer in control.

2

AFTERSHOCK

PRESENT DAY

JULY 2028 — 7:30 P.M.

Houston, TX.

The silence inside the convention hall didn't last long. It never does in politics. What began as stunned disbelief quickly unraveled into chaos. A chorus of shouts, gasps, and frantic whispers filled the air. Delegates clutched their phones, rapidly typing out messages, calling aides, or livestreaming the moment. The donors, the ones who had spent millions to ensure another Plump presidency, turned pale as the implications settled in. The man on stage, the one who had always commanded the room, now looked like a cornered animal.

President Plump gripped the podium, his knuckles whitening. His usual bravado wavered for a fraction of a second before returning in a fit of rage.

"FAKE! This is FAKE NEWS!" he bellowed, pointing at the screen behind him. "Deep state lies! AI-generated garbage! They're trying to steal this election with a hoax!"

Secret Service agents moved onto the stage, whispering urgently into their earpieces. The president ignored them; his face contorted with fury. Plump jabbed a finger in his direction.

"Arrest that man! He's a fraud, a criminal! A deep-state puppet! GET HIM OUT OF HERE!"

But no one moved. The weight of the moment had paralyzed everyone.

For the first time in decades, Plump had lost control of the room.

The White House in Crisis

Within minutes, the situation at the convention escalated into a full-blown national emergency. The White House communications team scrambled, pulling advisors from dinner tables and red-eye flights. An emergency strategy meeting was called in the Situation Room.

Inside the West Wing, the Chief of Staff was already shouting into his phone. "How the hell did this happen? Who got hacked? And why weren't we warned?"

The intelligence officials on the other end of the call scrambled for answers. The cybersecurity team at the NSA was already tracing the breach, but the attack had been precise, clean, and devastating. The recordings had not only been played inside the convention hall but had simultaneously been broadcast live on every major network and social media platform.

It was a catastrophe.

The president stormed into the Situation Room minutes later, red-faced and seething. His legal team, intelligence chiefs, and closest advisors were already seated, waiting for direction.

"We have to shut this down. Now," Plump barked. "Tell the networks it's fake. Tell them to stop running it!"

The Chief of Staff cleared his throat nervously. "Sir… that's not how this works. We don't control independent media."

Plump glared at him. "Then find a way to control it!"

One of the intelligence directors spoke up. "Sir, we're working on tracing the source of the recordings. It's possible they were deep-faked, but if they weren't?"

"They were," Plump snapped. "No question. We don't even need to ask."

A communications officer cautiously interrupted. "Mr. President, our base will believe that, but the rest of the country is in shock. We need a statement."

Plump turned to his press secretary. "I'll tell you what the statement is. This is a coup. A leftist hoax. Deep-state actors are trying to rig this election." He pounded the table. "I want every Republican official to be saying the same damn thing. This is fake. This is an attack on democracy. And anyone who believes it is a traitor."

His press secretary nodded, already crafting the narrative in her mind. "We'll flood the networks with talking points. Call it an AI hoax, disinformation, foreign interference, whatever sticks."

Plump smirked, regaining some confidence. "Good. And someone get the FBI looking into this Machiavelli guy. If he faked his death, he's a criminal. I want charges."

Media Firestorm

As Plump's orders took effect, the propaganda machine roared to life. Within the hour, every right-wing news outlet was echoing the same talking points. The recordings were AI-generated. Machiavelli was a fraud. The Democrats had staged the entire thing to frame the president. The deep state was at it again.

But the damage had already been done.

Major networks, unable to ignore the biggest political scandal in modern history, ran the story nonstop. Experts dissected the recordings, analysts speculated on the implications, and legal scholars debated whether the evidence was enough to launch criminal proceedings. The internet exploded with theories, videos, and memes dissecting every frame of the convention footage.

As more people watched the clips, something unexpected happened; doubt crept into Plump's own base.

Some die-hard supporters refused to believe it, dismissing the scandal outright. But others, particularly those already wary of the establishment, asked questions. Had Plump really gone too far? Was there a line even he wouldn't hesitate to cross?

Meanwhile, social media platforms were in turmoil. Hashtags like #PlumpExposed and #JusticeForMachiavelli trended worldwide. The Machiavelli Movement, which had existed in the shadows for months, exploded overnight. His message of anti-corruption and reform resonated with millions who had long felt disillusioned with both parties.

3
ERASURE PROTOCOL
18 MONTHS AGO
JANUARY 2027 — 6:00 P.M.

Silicon Valley, CA.

J ames Machiavelli came home late that evening, exhausted from another monotonous day at the office. His nine-to-five had been as uneventful as ever, just another cog in the machine of corporate America. As he pushed open the door of his modest suburban home, something felt off. The air was thick with an unnatural stillness, as if the house itself was holding its breath.

The scent of fresh coffee lingered in the air, but James hadn't made any. That's when he saw him. A man in a crisp suit sat calmly at the kitchen table, a steaming mug in hand. Around him, three other figures stood strategically, their stances firm but non-threatening.

"Please, Mr. Machiavelli, have a seat," the man in the suit said, his voice measured, controlled.

James hesitated, his mind racing. Fight or flight? But there was no fight to be had, and flight was pointless. His family—where were they?

"Where is my wife? Where are my children?" he demanded.

"They're safe," the agent assured him. "For now."

James clenched his fists, but he complied, pulling out a chair and lowering himself into it. The man in the suit leaned forward slightly, locking eyes with him.

"I need you to listen very carefully, James. Because after tonight, the world must believe you and your family are dead."

James's pulse quickened. His mouth went dry. "What the hell are you talking about?"

The agent reached into his coat and placed a small recording device on the table. A click, a brief static hum, and then a voice. A voice James knew too well.

"Take him out," the voice of Ronald Plump said, casual, almost indifferent. "His book, his stupid thesis—it's getting into the wrong hands."

Another voice responded, hesitant. "Sir, with all due respect, assassinating a U.S. citizen."

"Then take out the whole family," Plump interrupted. "Make it look like an accident. No loose ends."

Silence stretched as the agent stopped the recording. James felt as if the air had been sucked from his lungs. His book, a niche political critique, a call for reform that barely sold enough copies to be considered a small success, had somehow drawn the ire of the most powerful man in the world.

James swallowed hard. "Why am I still alive?"

The agent sat back, regarding him with an almost amused expression. "Wrong question. The real question is: why are you and your family still alive?"

James said nothing, his mind struggling to process the impossible reality he was now living in.

"I was sent here to kill you," the agent continued. "By direct order of the Director of the CIA, who, in turn, was following Plump's orders. But you got lucky."

James's hands shook beneath the table. "Lucky?"

The agent nodded. "There are those of us who still believe in the Constitution. That's why I'm here. That's why you're still breathing. But you can't stay James Machiavelli anymore."

James's voice was barely a whisper. "What are you saying?"

"I have a team outside ready to stage your family's deaths. It will be quick, clean, and convincing. As far as the world will be concerned, James Machiavelli and his family will have died tonight."

James's mind whirled. He thought of his wife, his children. "You expect me to just disappear? To let my kids believe their father is dead?"

"They already know," the agent said, softening slightly.

"We extracted them hours ago. They're safe, waiting for you. But we have to make this look real. Once we are sure that we have convinced the President of your death, you'll get to see your family."

A lump formed in James's throat. "And then what?"

The agent leaned in, lowering his voice. "Then, in a few weeks, you'll meet the CIA Director and a few others who want you to understand exactly what's going on. You'll go into hiding, with no contact with the outside world. You will receive new resources, and you will have a chance to fight back."

James exhaled sharply, rubbing his temples. His life, his family's lives, were being erased in real time. But what choice did he have?

He looked up, meeting the agent's gaze. "Alright. Let's do it."

The agent nodded. Outside, the night was about to swallow James Machiavelli whole.

4

THE FIRST EXPOSURE

PRESENT DAY

JULY 2028 — 9:00 P.M.

Los Angeles, CA.

The nation remained transfixed on their screens, gripped by the shocking revelation that the President of the United States had ordered the assassination of American citizens. Even more astonishing, the attempt had failed. The target, now very much alive, had not only survived but emerged with a stunning declaration: he was running for president. And this was just the beginning. He promised to expose even more damning scandals in the coming days.

As the clock struck nine, television screens across America flickered to the highly anticipated evening news. The usual anchors, typically composed and measured, now sat before their cameras, their faces taut with disbelief.

Tonight's lead story was unlike any before—scandal, murder, and corruption woven into a harrowing tale of political power spiraling out of control. The broadcast began with a deep-voiced introduction:

"Breaking news from California: A sitting United States Senator, long considered one of the most powerful figures in the Democratic Party, has been implicated in a stunning murder case involving his pregnant mistress. Even more shocking evidence suggests that he successfully orchestrated the wrongful conviction of her husband, using bribery, extortion, and outright corruption to cover his tracks."

The camera cut to a polished anchor, her expression grave as she continued, "The evidence, which has been leaked to several major news outlets, includes damning financial records, incriminating emails, and even the real murder weapon, thought to be destroyed but hidden by one of the senator's closest aides for leverage. The revelations paint a harrowing picture of political influence subverting justice, with implications that could shake the foundations of the United States Senate."

Unraveling the Cover-Up

The story had broken in waves throughout the evening. First came whispers of scandal, hushed, vague murmurs about a major political figure caught in a moral quagmire. Then, just as speculation reached a fever pitch, the flood-gates burst. A trove of leaked documents hit journalists' desks simultaneously, painting an irrefutable portrait of deceit. Senator Shift murdered his pregnant mistress and framed her husband.

Emails directly linked the senator to the cover-up, exposing his threats to the district attorney investigating the case. The digital trail of intimidation was clear: withdraw charges, divert attention, or face political and personal ruin. Even more damning were the financial records: a six-figure sum funneled into an offshore account belonging to the presiding judge of the case. The judge, it appeared, had been bought.

And then came the weapon.

A once-loyal aide, growing wary of his employer's increasing volatility, had secretly kept the murder weapon, the very thing the senator had ordered disposed of. Instead of eliminating it, the aide had stored it in a safe deposit box as an insurance policy, a failsafe in case the senator ever turned on him. It was the final, inarguable nail in the senator's coffin.

Immediate Fallout

The news exploded like an atomic bomb across media platforms, dominating headlines and social media feeds. Within minutes of the story airing, a frenzy of reactions flooded the internet:

"Unbelievable! A sitting U.S. senator not just implicated,

but orchestrating a murder? This is beyond corruption. It's evil."

"How many innocent people have been framed before? If this could happen to one man, how many others have been victims of powerful politicians?"

"This is why we need real oversight. If an aide hadn't saved that weapon, we might never have known the truth."

Protesters gathered outside the senator's Los Angeles office, wielding signs demanding justice. "RESIGN NOW" was the dominant chant, punctuated by cries of "FREE THE INNOCENT!" as crowds called for the immediate exoneration of the wrongly convicted husband.

Official Reactions and Political Tremors

By 9:30 p.m., prominent politicians from both parties had issued statements, eager to distance themselves from the scandal. The White House press secretary held an emergency briefing, though the administration remained cautious in its response.

"The allegations against Senator Shift are deeply concerning. We urge a full and independent investigation, and justice must prevail," the press secretary stated, avoiding outright condemnation but acknowledging the gravity of the situation.

Republican Leaders Were Far Less Reserved

"This is exactly what unchecked power looks like," Senator William Harding of Texas declared in a fiery press conference. "A man who used his office to kill, cover up, and then destroy an innocent life, this is the absolute worst of Washington. The American people deserve better."

Meanwhile, Democratic lawmakers scrambled to contain the fallout. Some allies of the senator remained silent, hoping to assess the full extent of the damage before making public statements. Others, recognizing the inevitability of political carnage, swiftly turned against him.

"If these allegations are true, then Senator Shift must resign immediately and face the full force of the law," said Congresswoman Maria Delacroix of California, one of the first within the senator's party to call for his resignation.

The Legal Reckoning Begins

As the public outcry swelled, so did legal action. The district attorney, now revealed to have been coerced, held a stunning press conference of his own. Voice shaking but resolute, he laid out the extent of the senator's intimidation tactics and confessed to bowing under immense pressure.

"I failed in my duty to uphold justice," he admitted. "But I will do everything in my power to rectify my mistake. Effective immediately, I am reopening the case. The innocent man who was convicted will have his day in court again, with full transparency and fairness this time."

The FBI, already investigating in light of the new evidence, announced an official probe into corruption at multiple levels. Federal agents were reportedly en route to the senator's homes in both Washington, D.C., and California, with warrants in hand.

The Senator's Response, or Lack Thereof

For the accused senator himself, silence was the only response. As reporters swarmed outside his estate, cameras caught only drawn curtains and heavily guarded gates. His press team, previously quick to issue denials for lesser scandals, refused to comment. The senator's legal team, however, was another story.

"These are baseless allegations," his attorney stated in a hastily arranged press conference. "Senator Shift has been the victim of a vicious smear campaign orchestrated by political enemies. We will fight this with every legal avenue available."

Few believed him. The evidence was too overwhelming, too damning. Even among those who had once staunchly defended the senator, confidence was rapidly crumbling.

The Nation Watches, Waiting

As the hour ticked by, the nation remained glued to their screens. What would come next? Would the senator be arrested? Would the innocent husband finally be freed?

Could such a high-profile politician truly be held accountable for such heinous crimes?

It was only the beginning of what would surely be a historic unraveling of power and corruption.

The headlines would write themselves for weeks to come. But on this night, this explosive, unbelievable night, one fact remained indisputable: the truth had finally come to light, and the American people were watching.

5

THE SECOND EXPOSURE

PRESENT DAY

JULY 2028 — 10:00 P.M.

Savannah, GA.

The clock struck ten, a nation on the edge of their seats, already trying to come to terms with two huge political scandals. The usual calm, professional demeanor of the news anchors had been replaced with visible tension. Their eyes betrayed a mix of shock and disbelief as they prepared to deliver what was sure to be one of the most explosive revelations in modern political history.

The broadcast continued with the network's signature breaking news alert, the dramatic tones underscoring the gravity of the moment. Then, the lead anchor took a deep breath and began.

"Breaking news from Georgia: A Republican congress-woman, long known for her incendiary rhetoric against the

LGBTQ and minority communities, has been exposed in a stunning scandal. That is right, Congresswoman Lime. Newly released evidence reveals that she was born a man, underwent gender reassignment surgery decades ago, and was married to a man for over twenty years, without him ever knowing the truth."

The Evidence Unfolds

What had started as an unverified rumor on the internet quickly escalated into a full-blown political crisis when a cache of damning documents was released to multiple media outlets. The evidence was overwhelming: an authentic birth certificate listing her original male name, detailed medical records documenting the gender reassignment surgery, and, perhaps most damning of all, the testimony of the now-retired surgeon who had performed the procedure.

"This is not speculation. These are verified documents, authenticated by multiple sources," the anchor continued. "The Congresswoman's birth certificate clearly states that she was born male. The medical records confirm the procedures undertaken to transition. And the testimony from the doctor who performed the surgery leaves no doubt, this is the same individual who has built a political career attacking the very community she was once part of."

As the shocking details scrolled across the screen, the reaction online was immediate. Social media platforms exploded in a frenzy of disbelief, outrage, and, for some, vindication. Within minutes, hashtags like #HypocrisyExposed, #LiarInCongress, and #TruthHurts were trending worldwide. The revelation sent shockwaves through both the political and social spheres, igniting a firestorm of debate.

Public Reaction and Immediate Fallout

Outside her Georgia office, a crowd had already gathered. Protesters and counter-protesters clashed as emotions ran high. Some carried signs denouncing her hypocrisy, while others, loyal supporters, stood in stunned silence, struggling to reconcile the person they believed in with the truth now laid bare.

Inside the congresswoman's inner circle, panic set in. Statements were hastily drafted, advisors debated damage control strategies, and calls were made to political allies in desperate attempts to contain the fallout. But the damage was done. Every major network, newspaper, and online news outlet was running the story. There was no way to spin the truth.

The congresswoman herself had yet to make a statement. Her official social media accounts had been deleted, and reporters camped outside her residence saw no sign of activity.

Meanwhile, former allies in the Republican Party distanced themselves at breakneck speed. "This is a personal matter," one senator remarked when pressed for a comment, but his reluctance to defend her spoke volumes. Others, especially those within the more extreme factions of the party, were outright condemning her, calling for her immediate resignation.

The LGBTQ community, which had long been a target of her vitriol, responded with a mixture of justified outrage and bitter irony. "This is the height of hypocrisy," said one prominent activist in a live interview. "For years, she demonized us, called us unnatural, and voted against our rights. And now, we find out she was one of us all along?"

As the story continued to unfold, another stunning revelation came to light. The same congresswoman who had fought against LGBTQ rights and same-sex marriage had secretly entered a surrogacy agreement with a gay couple. Legal documents and financial transactions provided irrefutable proof that she had accepted money to carry a child for two men, a direct contradiction of the very values she publicly championed.

The Road Ahead

As the night stretched on, speculation turned to the inevitable question: what would happen next? Would she resign? Would her party force her out? And what about her marriage? Reports indicated that her husband had been blindsided by the revelation, his world shattered by the realization that the woman he had loved for decades had been hiding such a fundamental truth.

Political analysts debated the long-term consequences. Some argued that this was a death blow to her career, while others suggested that in an era of extreme partisanship, even a scandal of this magnitude might not be enough to unseat her.

One thing was certain: America had never seen anything like this before. And by morning, the entire world would be watching to see how it all played out.

6

THE THIRD EXPOSURE

PRESENT DAY

JULY 2028 — 11:00 P.M.

New York City, NY.

The nation sat in stunned silence as the latest bombshell dropped. At 11 p.m., the major networks, already on overdrive, interrupted their current coverage to reveal another unprecedented scandal, one that exposed the very foundations of the news industry. The CEOs of the two top competing news stations were caught conspiring with leaders of both the Republican and Democratic parties to manipulate information, bury the truth, and profit off political division. The evidence, an overwhelming trove of leaked emails, financial records, and testimony from insiders, painted a damning picture of a media landscape built on deception.

. . .

A Web of Lies

The leaked documents, released simultaneously to independent journalists and watchdog groups, left no room for doubt. The emails showed executives actively strategizing how to suppress stories that exposed corporate and political corruption. One particularly damning exchange detailed how a report on a pharmaceutical company knowingly distributing a harmful drug was buried after a multi-million-dollar advertising deal was reached with the network. Another revealed how a state governor's involvement in an election fraud scheme was deliberately sidelined to protect political allies.

In one shocking email thread, an executive bluntly stated, "People don't want the truth. They want entertainment. Scandals that reinforce their own biases keep them coming back." Another replied, "Partisan division is the golden goose. The more they hate each other, the more they watch."

But the emails were just the beginning. Audio recordings surfaced, revealing newsroom meetings where top executives discussed how fueling political animosity led to skyrocketing ratings. In one recording, a senior executive is heard laughing as he states, "Outrage equals engagement. If we keep them angry, we keep them watching." Another recording captured a CEO dismissing concerns about journalistic integrity, declaring, "The truth is irrelevant if nobody's tuning in."

. . .

Follow the Money

Perhaps the most incriminating piece of evidence was the financial trail. Bank records proved both networks received backdoor payments from political figures and corporate entities to suppress damaging reports. One exceptionally egregious transaction showed a seven-figure payment from a defense contractor to kill a story about overbilling the government for faulty military equipment. Another revealed several direct payments from a billionaire tech mogul to prevent coverage of unethical data collection practices. A comprehensive list of stories that were buried or manipulated in exchange for financial gain accompanied the leak. Among them:

- A detailed exposé about voter suppression efforts, squashed days before a critical election.
- Evidence of a Fortune 500 CEO's direct involvement in offshore tax evasion schemes, never aired despite full verification.
- A police brutality case with overwhelming evidence, pulled from the airwaves after a police union threatened to withdraw advertising dollars.

Immediate Fallout

As the revelations spread, a crisis of credibility engulfed the media landscape. Viewers across the country felt betrayed, their trust shattered by the institutions they once relied on for truth. Social media exploded with outrage, with hashtags like #MediaBetrayal and #FakeNewsExposed trending within minutes.

Within hours, high-profile anchors resigned in protest, distancing themselves from the growing scandal. Some delivered scathing on-air statements before walking off set, condemning their own employers for betraying journalistic ethics. Others, however, scrambled to defend their network, claiming the leaks were exaggerated or taken out of context. Their reassurances fell on deaf ears.

The crisis was not limited to the networks alone. Political leaders caught in the conspiracy rushed to issue statements denying involvement, yet their names were unmistakably linked to the evidence. Public confidence in both major parties plummeted, fueling an already growing sentiment of distrust toward government institutions.

The Rise of Independent Journalism

As the traditional media burned, a new wave of independent journalists seized the moment. Leveraging online platforms, they vowed to expose the "next wave" of lies, promising uncompromised, unfiltered truth. Citizen journalism surged as people turned to alternative sources for news, wary of corporate-backed outlets. Streaming platforms and social media became the battleground for an information war. Where trust was no longer granted, it had to be earned.

In the days following the scandal, newsrooms were in chaos. Corporate sponsors pulled funding. Advertisers distanced themselves. Stock prices for major networks plummeted as investors panicked over the uncertainty of the industry's future.

By morning, the landscape of American journalism had changed forever. The illusion had been shattered. The people now knew the truth. The news had never been about informing them. It had been about controlling them. And they would never see the media the same way again.

7
OPERATION TRANSPARENCY
PRESENT DAY
JULY 2028 — 12:00 A.M.

New York City, NY.

As the nation reeled from the night's revelations, a new message broke through the chaos. A deep, measured voice echoed across screens and airwaves, its presence undeniable, its intent chillingly clear.

"I hope we have your attention."

The message came from Machiavelli, the shadowy figure behind the leaks, the architect of the night's reckoning. His tone was calm but unwavering, each word carrying the weight of absolute conviction.

"To those who seek to deny, distort, or discredit the truth we have revealed, you have been warned. Any attempt to combat, lie, attack, mislead, or dismiss this information will be met with the exposure of your transgressions. We possess far more than what has been shown tonight. The corruption runs deeper than you can imagine, and we will not hesitate to bring it all to light.

To those who believe they can silence us, who think they can intimidate, threaten, or harm our people, my family, or the great citizens of the United States—know this: We are prepared. Any move against us will trigger the release of the darkest truths that those in power have fought desperately to keep hidden."

A pause. A moment of quiet, heavy with implication. And then, the final declaration:

"Tomorrow at 8 p.m., I will reveal myself to America and the world. An hour-long video will be released detailing who I am, why I am here, the crises facing our nation, and the solutions we must pursue. This is only the beginning."

8

THE ARCHITECTS

18 MONTHS AGO

JANUARY 2027 — 10:00 A.M.

Undisclosed Location

A heavy steel door groaned open, its sound reverberating through the sterile corridors of the secure facility. The air was thick with antiseptic and the dull hum of fluorescent lights. Machiavelli's breath hitched as he stepped forward, his pulse quickening with anticipation.

And then he saw them.

His wife stood there, her eyes brimming with emotion, and behind her, their children. Their youngest son held on to the caretaker's hands, while their older son stood there stunned. For a moment, he hesitated, afraid that if he blinked, they would vanish like ghosts in a dream. Then, his wife rushed forward, her arms wrapping around him in a desperate embrace. His fingers tangled in her hair, his body shaking with the force of his relief.

"I thought I lost you," he whispered.

"We're here. We're safe," she murmured, pulling back just enough to cradle his face in her hands. The touch was tender, yet her composure carried the strength he needed. This was the moment she had waited for through endless nights of fear—finally close enough to steady him. Her eyes held his, gentle but unwavering, willing him to draw on her calm.

"We've been cared for. There's nothing to fear now."

A soft throat-clearing reminded them of the presence of the CIA agent standing by. "I'm sorry for keeping you apart. We had to be sure Plump believed the assassination was successful. It was the only way to keep you alive."

Machiavelli's gaze darkened, but he nodded, understanding the necessity. "I need her with me," he said firmly.

The agent hesitated for only a moment before nodding. "She can accompany you to the meeting. The children will be escorted out by the caretaker."

His wife kissed the tops of their children's heads before they were led away, her fingers lingering against their small hands. Then, with squared shoulders, she took Machiavelli's hand in hers, and together, they followed the agent down the corridor.

The meeting room was an unremarkable space, with steel-gray walls, a long table at the center, and harsh overhead lighting. The air crackled with tension as Machiavelli and his wife entered. Seated around the table were some of the most powerful and enigmatic individuals he had ever encountered. The Director of the CIA, two senators, several congressmen, and a pair of hackers whose reputations preceded them. Their eyes bore into him, unreadable yet expectant.

The CIA director, an older man with a hawkish expression, spoke first. "Machiavelli, it's good to see you in one piece."

Machiavelli crossed his arms. "I'd rather not be here under these circumstances."

"None of us would," one of the congressmen muttered.

The Director continued. "We brought you here because you need to see what your words have set in motion."

A senator slid a thick dossier across the table. Machiavelli flipped it open, scanning the reports and surveillance images. His stomach tightened as he saw the numbers. Over ten million people had joined the resistance in the past year, their ranks filled with everyday Americans who believed in the ideas he had laid out in his book.

"Your work was the inception," the Director said. "The resistance has taken those ideas and built something bigger, something real. And now, it's time to take the next step."

Machiavelli glanced up warily. "What step?"

A congressman leaned forward, his voice steady but intense. "You run for President of the United States."

Machiavelli barked out a laugh, more from shock than amusement. "You can't be serious."

The senator beside him met his gaze. "We're dead serious."

Machiavelli shook his head. "I'm not a politician."

"That's exactly why you're perfect," the Director said. "The American people don't want a career politician. They want someone who will actually fix the system. They want an outsider."

A hacker, a young woman with piercing eyes, leaned in. "They want you."

Machiavelli exhaled slowly, his mind spinning.

The senator elaborated, "People's dissatisfaction with the government fueled Plump's rise. But he was a symptom, not the cure. The system is still broken. We need someone who isn't tied to the establishment, someone with no special interest affiliations. Someone who speaks for the people."

A congressman nodded. "We've analyzed the data. People are more disillusioned now than ever. They don't trust politicians. But they trust you."

Machiavelli turned to his wife, searching for her reaction. Her gaze carried the struggle of processing it all, but her hand spoke the certainty her lips could not.

The director pressed on. "We can also expose Plump's attempt on your life."

Machiavelli's jaw clenched. He had almost died because of that man. His family had nearly been taken from him. But now, they wanted him to step into the political arena? To fight a battle that could destroy them all?

"This is insane," he muttered.

The Director sighed. "You want the truth? You don't have much of a choice. We saved you, yes. But that put a lot of good people at risk. And as long as Plump and his allies believe you're alive, you will always be a marked man. You can't hide forever."

Silence settled over the room.

Then, the director pushed back his chair and stood. "We'll reconvene tomorrow morning. Hopefully, with your support."

One by one, the council members rose and filed out of the room. The last to leave was the young hacker, who shot him a knowing look before disappearing through the door.

Machiavelli sat there for a long moment before turning to his wife. "Tell me this is crazy."

She smiled faintly. "Oh, it's crazy."

"Then tell me we shouldn't do it."

She reached for his hands, holding them firmly between her own. Her voice was calm but resolute, carrying the certainty she had already accepted. "James… they're right. You were already marked for death. You can either keep running, or you can fight back."

He closed his eyes. Exhaustion settled deep in his bones. When he finally spoke, his voice was quiet but resolute.

"If I do this… I do it on my terms."

His wife nodded. "Then we'll do it together."

Machiavelli exhaled, fortifying himself for the battle ahead. Because now, the real war was about to begin.

9
ALLIES AND OATHS
18 MONTHS AGO
JANUARY 2027 — 12:00 P.M.

Undisclosed Location

James Machiavelli sat on the edge of the hotel bed, his hands clasped together, his head hanging low. The weight of the past two weeks pressed down on him like an unbearable burden, crushing his spirit and filling him with guilt. The room was dimly lit, with the soft glow from the bedside lamp casting long shadows across the walls. The silence between them was heavy, filled with unspoken fears, doubts, and the haunting echoes of the life they had left behind.

"I'm sorry, Paola," James murmured, his voice barely above a whisper. "I'm so sorry for putting you and the boys in this position. None of this was supposed to happen."

Paola, sitting beside him, placed a gentle hand on his knee. Her touch was warm, reassuring, and full of the love that had carried them through the years. "James, stop. None of this is your fault," she whispered. "You wrote the thesis because you wanted to help people. You wanted to make a difference in the lives of children who, like you, grew up in impossible situations. You wanted to give them hope, resources, and a fighting chance to survive and thrive. This isn't just about politics or power; it's about change. Actual change."

James shook his head, rubbing his face with both hands. "But this? What they're asking of me? It's not who I am. They want me to stand in front of millions of people and pretend to be someone I'm not. That's fraud, Paola. I would be a fraud."

Paola turned to face him fully, her dark eyes fierce with conviction. "They want you to be you. That's the whole point, James. You have an enormous heart. You've always wanted to help people, and now, you actually have the power to do it. Think about what this means. A room full of high-ranking officials, an entire network of over ten million people who believe in you. You've already inspired them. People have sacrificed so much for this cause, for you. We've sacrificed. They all sacrifice for you because they know you will sacrifice for them."

She paused, taking a deep breath before continuing. "Our families and friends think we're dead. I can't even imagine what my mom and dad are going through. I do my best not to think about it, but I know she must be devastated. But at least with this, this plan, her pain, their pain, is only short-term."

James swallowed hard, his throat tight with emotion. "These past two weeks... knowing that you and the boys were alive was the only thing keeping me from losing it." He exhaled sharply and ran a hand through his hair. "I hadn't even thought about your mom and your dad. They are the best parents I have ever had. Giovanni and Rachele... they were the only family I had after my grandparents died. We were close. So damn close. I can't imagine what they must be going through."

Paola reached for his hand and squeezed it. "James, we will make this right. But you have to see that this isn't just about us anymore. You started something bigger than yourself, and now you have a choice. You can walk away, or you can embrace it and fight for what you believe in."

James let out a bitter chuckle. "And what if I fail? What if I'm not strong enough for this?"

Paola gave him a small, sad smile. "You are strong enough. I've seen you at your worst, and I've seen you rise again and again. You've been fighting your whole life, James. You know what it's like to struggle, to suffer. That's exactly why you're the right person for this. People will see themselves in you. They'll know you're real."

James turned away, staring at the window, at the reflection of a man he barely recognized anymore. "I would understand if you and the boys don't want to be part of this," he said finally, his voice raw with emotion.

Paola didn't hesitate. "We're with you. No matter what."

10

THE BLUEPRINT

18 MONTHS AGO

JANUARY 2027 — FOLLOWING DAY
9:00 A.M.

Undisclosed Location

The meeting the next morning was tense, yet the air crackled with an unspoken energy. The assembled council members, senators, strategists, former bureaucrats, federal intelligence agents, and Anonymous members, sat in a semicircle, waiting for Machiavelli to speak. Every person in the room had, at some point, played a role in shaping the very system they were now preparing to dismantle.

Machiavelli took a measured breath before addressing the room.

"I accept the council's proposal. But before we move

forward, I want to thank each of you. I know it couldn't have been an easy decision to be in this position. Most of you, at some level, bear responsibility for the way our government functions today. I see men and women who have spent years building and upholding this system, and yet, here you are, willing to tear it down to save it. That is no small thing."

A murmur of acknowledgment passed through the room. Some exchanged glances. Others looked down, reflecting on the weight of his words.

"The greatest leaders recognize that they are but one spoke in the wheel, no greater than those around them. They understand that leadership is not about power but about fulfilling a role in service of a greater purpose. True leaders lead by example, placing the well-being of their people above their own.

I am eternally grateful for the chance to serve, indebted to you for saving my family and my life, and deeply humbled by your trust in me as your candidate."

Machiavelli leaned forward, his expression sharp and expectant. "Now, what is the plan?"

The Strategy Unveiled

A senator from Vermont, a veteran of the political landscape, cleared his throat. "You've already given us the plan, years ago, before Plump was elected for a second time. I was among those who dismissed you then. I regret that now. But

I have been listening for a while, and I will continue to listen."

Machiavelli nodded, his gaze unwavering. "A strategy alone will not be enough this time. We are past the point of gradual reform. The only way this works is through absolute, unrelenting exposure. We need to compile as much compromising information, incriminating evidence, damaging secrets, or quite simply 'dirt' on every corrupt politician, justice, operator, lobbyist, donor, CEO, media personality, media network, and bureaucrat."

The room fell into a charged silence.

"This includes personal and financial accounts, the playbooks they used to manage scandals, and the contacts they rely on for damage control. We will execute a blitzkrieg campaign. No mercy, no hesitation. We will unmask them before they can spin the narrative."

The Information War

A Republican congresswoman from a deep-red state raised a hand. "How do we ensure this information reaches the public without manipulation? Without being buried by counterpropaganda?"

"Extortion. They will release the truth because if they don't, we will release the truth about them. We open new channels of communication and hold the media accountable. No more filters, no more editorialized distractions."

. . .

The Plump Dossier

"Our first and most crucial target is Plump. His grip on his base is strong, but it is not invincible. The key is contrast, laying bare the vast chasm between his life and that of his followers. We inundate his supporters with details of his inherited wealth, his failures, the privileges he has squandered, the betrayals he has committed, and his dependence on undocumented labor. His supporters revere him because they believe he speaks for them. We will show them he never has and never will."

The senator from Vermont interjected, "That might work for some, but his most ardent supporters will reject any information that challenges their perception of him. We need a messenger who reflects them, someone from their own ranks."

Machiavelli nodded. "Precisely. The information itself is not enough. It must be framed and delivered by an outsider who resonates with his base. Someone who understands their struggles, their fears, and their disillusionment. The message must come from within their own circles, not from establishment figures they already distrust."

The Corruption Files

"Next, we compile dossiers on every corrupt figure in the political, corporate, and media landscape. No distinction between party lines, this is about unearthing the rot in its entirety. The public must see how both parties have weaponized narratives, controlled opposition, and manipulated perceptions."

A data analyst from the intelligence sector leaned forward. "We will need to sift through financial records, leaked correspondence, insider testimonies, and confidential legal documents. This isn't just about individual corruption; it's about the networks that enable it."

"Agreed," Machiavelli said. "Every donor, every lobbyist, every media conglomerate that has shaped public discourse to serve the few at the expense of the many; we expose them all."

The Political Illusion

"Finally, we must dissect the strategies employed by both parties to manipulate public opinion. Every manufactured crisis, every diversionary tactic, every psychological manipulation laid bare."

A former campaign strategist from Washington spoke up. "This is where it gets dangerous. Once we reveal the playbook, they'll adapt. They'll create new distractions, new enemies. How do we stay ahead?"

"By anticipating their responses and exposing them in real-time. The moment they attempt to shift the narrative; we highlight the manipulation as it happens. Think of it as a live autopsy of political deceit."

A younger member of the council, a professor in media studies, smiled. "Like Vincent Gambini in My Cousin

Vinny. Calling out the contradictions in real-time, breaking down their defenses on the spot."

Machiavelli smirked. "Exactly. The candidate we put forward must be relentless, charismatic, and unafraid to humiliate those who twist the truth. Every time they attempt to gaslight the public, he or she must be ready with an irrefutable counterpunch."

The Blitzkrieg Approach

"Our greatest advantage is anonymity. With everybody in this room, we have eyes and ears in every part of the government. We will maneuver behind the scenes until we launch at the RNC."

James Machiavelli continued, "After we launch, we must appear to be on opposite sides. Some of you will come out after me, some of you will play quiet or nice publicly, and then work with the schemers on the down low. Some of you will be wary of me and will choose to stay neutral, and some of you will jump on board shortly after we launch."

He looked around, making eye contact with everyone in the room.

"Once we launch, I will draw as much of our enemies' attention as possible, keeping them focused on me, assertively confronting Plump at every public and private event, making our opposition unmistakably clear through vocal and persistent challenges. I will stir them up into a frenzy so that they continue to make mistakes. You will continue to work in the background, driving divisions within the political parties, within the business leaders, within the justice system."

He paused and took a deep breath.

"We will gain favor with the military because when our plan eventually works, Plump will, at some point, attempt or succeed in declaring martial law. I don't like deceiving the American people, and we will come forward with the truth after we are in office. I wish we could be straight up from the start about our network, but we are in dangerous territory, and you're all putting your lives on the line for this cause, for America as a whole."

11

THE BROADCAST

PRESENT DAY

JULY 2028 — 11:00 P.M.

Undisclosed Location

[T]he video begins with darkness. A single spotlight flickers on, casting a sharp contrast against the void. Machiavelli stands at the center, his expression unreadable, his posture unwavering. His eyes lock onto the camera, steady and unafraid. The silence lingers just long enough to build anticipation before he speaks.]

Machiavelli:

"In one hour, every piece of dirt on me will be released to the public. Every mistake, every failure, every flaw, will be laid bare for the world to see. I will not run from my past, nor will I ask you to. I am no saint, nor do I pretend to be. Like you, I have stumbled. Like you, I have regrets. But unlike those who stand behind closed doors, insulated by wealth and privilege, I do not fear the truth.

I will never ask for blind trust. Blind trust is the currency of tyrants. I will never demand loyalty without question. Loyalty without scrutiny breeds corruption. I will err again, as all humans do. But my promise to you is this: I will answer every question to the best of my ability. If ever I withhold information, it will not be to deceive, but to strategize. Because what we are fighting for demands it.

I will not shield myself behind half-truths or convenient lies. The foundation of this movement, this new era is built upon four unshakable pillars: Accountability. Honesty. Education. Integrity. And today, I stand before you to uphold those promises."

[He pauses, allowing the weight of his words to settle.]

"Over the coming months, you will learn a great deal about me, who I am, what I have done, and what I stand for. But understand this: I do not matter. My name, my face, my existence—they are insignificant. I am a single thread in a vast tapestry, one of millions working together to reclaim what is rightfully ours. This is not about me. It is about you.

We are not building a campaign. We are not seeking an office. We are building a revolution. Not through violence, not through chaos, but through the one force they cannot withstand: truth. We will be the path clearers, the architects, the weapon forged in the hands of the American people. And together, we will take back our country."

[He takes a breath, steadying himself before delivering the next revelation.]

"Eighteen months ago, Ronald Plump tried to have me assassinated."

[The words hang in the air like a death knell. The silence that follows is deafening.]

"You may ask, why? Why would a sitting U.S. President view me as a threat? Why would a man with nearly unlimited resources and global influence consider me, one man, a danger? The answer lies in a single document."

[He reaches off-screen and lifts a worn book, its cover weathered and marked with annotations.]

"This thesis, The People's Awakening: A New American Era, was self-published with little fanfare. It should have faded into obscurity, dismissed as the musings of a dissenter. But it did not. Because within these pages lies a vision that the elites fear more than any foreign adversary, more than economic collapse, more than even their political rivals. This document exposes the machine, the gears of control that they have operated for generations. It details how they have weaponized our government against its own people. And it reveals how, once armed with knowledge, the American people can dismantle their stranglehold on power."

[He flips through the pages, pausing briefly before looking back at the camera.]

"They saw this thesis as a declaration of war. And so, they responded in kind. The attempt on my life was not hidden. It was an open secret among those in power, a whispered certainty in their circles. They believed that by erasing me, they could snuff out the movement before it took root. But they underestimated us.

A coalition formed in the shadows, rogue government officials, whistleblowers, Anonymous operatives, military defectors, and corporate leaders who still believed in democracy. These individuals risked everything to protect me and my family. When the attempt on my life became imminent, they acted prudently. My death was staged, a deception necessary to buy time. And for the last eighteen months, we have not been idle.

We have prepared."

[His voice steadies, his conviction unwavering.]

"Seventy million Americans—patriots, workers, students, veterans, everyday citizens—have formed a network unlike anything in history. Together, we have assembled the most damning collection of evidence ever compiled. We have documented crimes at the highest levels of government. We have traced the flow of illicit money. We have uncovered the fraud, the manipulations, the lies that have kept us divided, subjugated, enslaved.

And soon, so will you."

[The intensity in his voice rises, his passion undeniable.]

"This is not a conspiracy. This is not a fantasy. This is reality. Their reality. The one they have fought desperately to keep from you. But no more.

You will see the evidence with your own eyes. You will

read their signatures, hear their voices, trace the money trails they thought were invisible. And when you do, you will understand why they fear us."

[He leans forward, his voice dropping to a near whisper.]

"They fear us not because of violence. Not because of rebellion. But because of the one weapon they cannot disarm:

Truth."

[He straightens, his expression resolute.]

"And here is the ultimate truth: I am not your leader. I am not your savior. This movement belongs to you, to every American who has ever been unheard, every worker who has been exploited, every soldier sent to fight wars for profit, every family who has struggled while the rich grow richer. This is your fight.

We are not asking for permission. We are not waiting for change. We are the change. And they cannot stop what has already begun."

[He lifts his chin, his final words an unshakable declaration.]

"To those in power who hear these words, know this: Your time is up. Your days of unchecked rule are over. We do not seek revenge. We seek justice. We do not seek destruction. We seek rebirth.

The People's Awakening is here. And it will not be stopped."

[The screen fades to black. A single phrase appears in

bold, white letters.]

'Truth Will Set Us Free.'

[End of video.]

12

FOR ALL TO SEE

PRESENT DAY

JULY 2028 — 11:00 P.M.

Undisclosed Location

James Machiavelli's decision to release his personal history to the public was unprecedented. In a world where politicians carefully curate their images, Machiavelli took the opposite approach, laying bare his past before the media, ensuring that no scandal could be used against him. He understood that trust could not be demanded; it had to be earned through honesty, accountability, and transparency.

Owning His Past

Machiavelli's revelations were met with mixed reactions. Some admired his candor; others saw it as reckless.

But no one could deny that his approach was different. At twenty-one, he had fathered a son out of wedlock with an ex-girlfriend, a fact that many would have hidden. At twenty-four, he was arrested for assault and battery, an incident that was later reduced to an infraction when it was revealed that the person he attacked was his ex-girlfriend's abusive husband, a man who also physically abused his son. Two speeding tickets and a single layoff completed the so-called "dirt" that he disclosed.

His message was clear: No man is perfect, and no leader should pretend to be. Mistakes were not the problem. Hiding them was. In contrast with politicians who spent their careers dodging scandals, Machiavelli wanted to show that his imperfections made him relatable to the very people he sought to represent.

With his past laid bare, he turned the spotlight toward the future, a future shaped by the radical yet necessary policies outlined in his thesis, *The People's Awakening: A New American Era.*

Education as the Foundation of Power

"If knowledge is power, then education is everything." This was Machiavelli's core belief, and his educational reform proposals reflected this philosophy. He argued that the traditional K-12 system was outdated, failing to prepare American youth for the challenges of the modern world.

His solution? A federally optimized K-15 system that would overhaul education by implementing:

1. **Classroom Restructuring**–Reducing class sizes nationwide to no more than eight students per teacher to ensure personalized education.
2. **Extending Education to K-15**–Incorporating three additional years focused on military education (without mandatory service), governmental studies, and financial literacy, preparing students for responsible adulthood.
3. **Year-Round Schooling**–A transition to a balanced academic calendar that maximizes learning opportunities while reducing burnout.
4. **Elevating Educators**–Increasing teacher salaries and resources to attract top-tier professionals, giving educators the same level of respect and support as military personnel.

He envisioned a nation where education was not a burden but a gateway to a prosperous society, where young Americans entered adulthood with the skills and knowledge necessary to thrive.

A Family-First Nation

Machiavelli understood the importance of strong family structures in building a stable society. His *family-first policy* focused on ensuring that federal education mandates did not encroach upon personal and family time. The key components included:

- **No-Homework Policy**—All federal education requirements would be completed within school hours.
- **After-School Programs**—Programs that encouraged family participation rather than extended academic workloads.
- **Stronger Parent-Teacher Communication**—Clear channels to bridge the gap between schools and families, ensuring education aligned with familial values.

This proposal mirrored the separation of church and state but applied to culture and education. By protecting family time, he believed America could foster both stronger personal bonds and a more effective workforce.

Winning Trust Through Transparency and Accountability

One of Machiavelli's most ambitious policies was his approach to governmental transparency. He asserted that simply doing right by the people was not enough. Leaders needed to *show* their work. His vision included:

1. **Public Accountability Logs**–A centralized system documenting every action of elected officials from proposal to completion, akin to a public blockchain ledger accessible to all citizens.
2. **Stricter Ethical Standards**–Government officials would be held to higher standards than ordinary citizens, with severe penalties for misconduct.
3. **Military Investment**–Prioritizing fair compensation, educational opportunities, and better benefits for military personnel, ensuring those who served were adequately supported both during and after their service.

Machiavelli saw these policies as essential to rebuilding trust in a system where partisan politics often shielded corruption. By making every action transparent and holding officials accountable, his government would set a new standard for integrity.

Restructuring the American Electoral System

Machiavelli recognized that America's political infrastructure was outdated and ineffective. His electoral reforms sought to address three key problems: citizen engagement, candidate selection, and the efficiency of governance.

- **Expanding Government Participation–** Increasing the number of elected positions and standardizing all legislative and judicial term lengths to a single five-year term with no re-elections, ensuring fresh ideas and minimizing corruption.
- **Eliminating Partisan Primaries–** Overhauling the candidate selection process to focus on qualifications and merit rather than party affiliation, encouraging capable leaders to step forward.
- **Limiting Campaign Seasons–**Restricting campaign activities to a set timeframe, allowing officials to focus on governance rather than constant electioneering.
- **Government Performance Analytics–** Introducing a system to measure legislative impact similar to sports analytics, providing voters with clear, data-driven insights into a candidate's effectiveness.

These policies would transform American governance into a system that rewarded competence rather than political survival, ensuring that individuals committed to public service rather than personal gain filled leadership positions.

. . .

Hardening and Streamlining Government Operations

Machiavelli's final pillar of reform centered on the justice system. He proposed a radical restructuring to remove political influence from the judiciary, ensuring that justice remained impartial and uncorrupted. His reforms included:

1. **Independent Justice Department**– Prohibiting political officials from appointing judges, prosecutors, and Justice Department officials, removing partisan influence from the judicial system.
2. **Judicial Ethics Committee**–Establishing a non-partisan body composed of legal experts and ethicists to oversee judicial appointments, ensuring that candidates were selected based on merit rather than political alignment.
3. **Transparent Selection Process**–Requiring public disclosure of evaluation criteria for judicial candidates, preventing backroom deals and partisan favoritism.
4. **Accountability Measures**–Holding judicial appointees to the highest ethical standards, with mechanisms in place to investigate and discipline those who abuse their positions.

By severing the ties between politics and justice, Machiavelli sought to restore faith in the legal system and ensure that every American, regardless of status or influence, was treated equally under the law.

Conclusion: A Movement, Not Just a Campaign

James Machiavelli's radical transparency and bold policy proposals were unlike anything seen in modern American politics. He was not just another politician seeking office; he was a movement challenging the very foundation of the current system. By releasing his personal history, he demonstrated he had nothing to hide. By presenting his policies with unwavering clarity, he proved he had nothing to fear.

His message was simple: America needed change. Not incremental adjustments, but a complete restructuring of education, governance, and justice to reflect the realities of the 21st century. Whether the nation was ready to embrace his vision remained to be seen, but one thing was certain, Machiavelli had already changed the conversation. And in politics, that was the first step toward revolution.

13
HOMECOMING
PRESENT DAY
AUGUST 2028 — 5:00 P.M.

Silicon Valley, CA.

The sun had set over Silicon Valley, casting a golden hue over the quiet, secluded estate where the long-awaited reunion was about to unfold. Paola Machiavelli stood still at the threshold of the grand room, her heart pounding in her chest as she heard the approaching footsteps of her family. Her sons, Luciano and Angelo, stood beside her, equally tense and overwhelmed with anticipation.

Inside the estate, Maria Rossi, Paola's mother, paced anxiously, unable to steady her trembling hands. She had spent what felt like years grieving the loss of her daughter, son-in-law, and grandchildren. The day she had received the devastating news of their deaths in a car accident, a part of her had died as well. She had clutched Paola's childhood photos, sobbing uncontrollably, unable to fathom a world without her only daughter. Every day had been a battle against the weight of that loss, a loss that had reshaped her very soul.

Then, the impossible happened.

Maria had been watching television when James Machiavelli, the quiet, reserved man she had known as more than her son-in-law, but as her son, stood before the entire country at the Republican National Convention. He had never been one for the spotlight, yet there he was, standing before the world, revealing the shocking truth, Paola and their children were alive. The supposed accident had been a cover-up for an assassination attempt. Maria had gasped, clutching the arm of her husband, Paolo, as tears streamed down her face.

"They're alive! They're alive!" she had cried, the anguish of years melting into overwhelming relief. Paolo had stood motionless, his normally composed demeanor shattered. He believed he had buried his daughter. That he would never see her again. Her return, even through a television screen, was beyond comprehension.

Now, Maria and Paolo stood together, gripping hands as the door before them slowly creaked open. The air was thick with anticipation, every second stretching endlessly. And then, there she was.

Paola took a hesitant step forward, tears brimming in her eyes as she met her mother's gaze. The room fell silent, the weight of lost years and unspoken words hanging between them. Then, with a sudden, desperate cry, Maria rushed forward, enveloping Paola in a crushing embrace. The dam of sorrow and longing broke, and sobs wracked their bodies as they held each other.

"Mia bambina!" Maria wept, pressing her hands against Paola's face as if to ensure she was real. "I thought, I thought I'd lost you forever!"

"I know, Mamma," Paola choked out. "I know. I wanted to come back to you. I wanted to tell you, but we couldn't."

Her father, Paolo, stepped forward, his stoic expression faltering as he pulled his daughter into his arms. He held her tightly, his body trembling with the force of his emotions. "My Paola," he murmured. "They told us you were gone. They told us we had lost you."

Luciano and Angelo stood watching, emotions warring on their young faces. Maria turned to them, her heart swelling with love and sorrow. "Luciano, Angelo!" she cried, reaching for them. They rushed into her embrace, feeling the warmth of their grandmother's love for the first time in what felt like an eternity.

"Nonna," Angelo whispered, his voice thick with tears. "We missed you so much."

"Oh, my sweet boys," Maria sobbed, kissing their foreheads. "You are here. You are safe. That is all that matters."

With the rest of the family having gathered, the news of Paola's return spread like wildfire. Her brother, Antonio; his wife Lora, her aunts, uncles, cousins, and closest friends stood in stunned silence, taking in the sight before them. Then, questions erupted all at once.

"How did this happen?"

"Where have you been for the last eighteen months?"

"How could they have lied to us like this?"

Paola felt the weight of eighteen months of fear, grief, and exhaustion pressing against her chest, threatening to spill out in a torrent of emotion. For a heartbeat, she wanted to collapse under it all, to finally let go. Instead, she drew in a steadying breath, reminding herself of what was still at stake, and that this was the moment when she had to embody calm for everyone else. Lifting her hands to quiet them, she steadied her voice.

"I know you all have questions. I wish I could answer them, but there are things I cannot say right now. Just know, we had to stay hidden. It was the only way to keep us alive."

Then, inevitably, the questions turned to James.

"Paola, what is going on with James?" Antonio asked, disbelief in his voice. "We saw him at the RNC. That is not the James we knew."

"He was always so modest, so private," her uncle added. "And now he is standing before the entire country, making speeches, taking on the world."

Paola smiled, glancing toward her children, who were embracing their Nonno, filled with joy watching the reunion unfold.

"James has always been a deep thinker. He has always been great at what he does. This… this is just another part of his journey. We all have our roles to play, and this is his. It is the hardest thing he has ever had to do, but he is doing it because he believes in a better future for all of us."

Paolo studied his son-in-law's eyes when watching the video released days earlier, recognizing something new in his eyes. He was still James, but there was a fire in him now, a determination he had never seen before.

"And you?" he asked Paola. "Are you safe now?"

Paola nodded, though the weight of uncertainty pressed heavily against her heart. She knew they weren't safe; she knew her family wasn't, but she also knew she could never let them see that fear. For now, they needed hope. She drew a steady breath and said softly but firmly, "For now, we are together. That is all that matters."

Maria reached out, taking Paola's hand in hers. "Then that is enough. We have you back. We have Luciano and Angelo back. Whatever comes next, we will face it together."

The room erupted in another round of embraces, tears, and laughter. The past could not be changed, the pain could not be undone, but in this moment, love triumphed overall. Paola was home, and for now, that was all that mattered.

14

THE INFERNO

PRESENT DAY

JULY 2028 — 11:00 P.M.

New York City, NY.

T he events at the Republican National Convention sent shockwaves through the political landscape, igniting a media firestorm that quickly consumed the 24-hour news cycle. The last 48-hours since the unprecedented revelation of President Plump's alleged assassination orders and the subsequent political scandals dominated television screens, radio waves, and digital headlines. Every major news outlet and political commentator scrambled to provide their spin on the seismic event, exposing the deep divides within the media ecosystem.

Plump was furious. He had always thrived on chaos, but this was different. This wasn't just an attack. This was an existential threat.

The White House issued a full-blown call to arms. Plump took to Truth Social, posting an all-caps rant:

```
"THE DEEP STATE IS TRYING TO
STEAL AMERICA! THESE
RECORDINGS ARE 100% FAKE! WE
WILL NOT LET THEM WIN!!! STAY
STRONG, PATRIOTS! WE FIGHT
BACK TOMORROW!!!"
```

```
"Another LOSER trying to make
a name for himself. FAKE NEWS,
TOTAL HOAX. Nobody tried to
kill this clown. He's just
looking for attention! SAD!"
```

Fox News: Damage Control and Deflection

On *Fox & Friends*, the hosts tried to downplay the impact of the revelation, speculating that the audio was a "deepfake," and a "leftist conspiracy." Brian Kilmeade suggested that the recording was a product of the "radical deep-state," hastily changing the subject to the scandal involving Senator Shift. "This is the most egregious abuse of power we have ever seen." Ainsley Earhardt emphasized, "We have to question the source here. Who really benefits from this?" Only Steve Doocy, who was more hesitant to address the scandals, said, "I get what you're saying about considering the source, but these documents... they're damning. If even half of it is true, it means that viewers on both sides have been played. That's not just a left-wing or right-wing problem. That's an American problem."

Jesse Watters, on his Primetime show, immediately pivoted to an alternative narrative: "Even if this were true, let's not forget that James Machiavelli is a known radical with an agenda to tear down the America First movement. Let's be real here, folks. This guy drops a bombshell like this, claims Plump tried to have him killed, and expects us to just believe him? Where's the real evidence, and I am not talking about that obvious AI-generated recording? Sounds like a deep-state stunt to me."

Meanwhile, Sean Hannity took a more aggressive approach, calling the incident a "blatant attempt by the leftist media to interfere with democracy." He defended Plump as a "target of an elaborate smear campaign," drawing comparisons to previous attacks on conservative figures. "This is a clearly dangerous man. Not only is he trying to smear President Plump with baseless accusations, but he's also talking about a 'revolution'? That's not democracy, that's anarchy!"

Laura Ingraham took it a step further, declaring, "This is a coup attempt, plain and simple. The elites are desperate to remove Plump by any means necessary."

MSNBC and the Liberal Response

On *Morning Joe*, Joe Scarborough opened the show with

an incredulous shake of the head. "You can't make this up," he said. "This is a level of corruption and criminality that we haven't seen in modern American politics."

Mika Brzezinski speculated on the potential fallout: "This isn't just a scandal; this is a national crisis. If these tapes are real, we are looking at an administration built on deception and violence. Of course, because of Senator Shift, the right is going to use this to paint all of us as corrupt."

Rachel Maddow took a deep dive into the logistics of the leak, connecting it to broader concerns about authoritarianism. "For years, we've warned about the dangers of unchecked executive power. This is what it looks like," she warned. "The question now is: Will Republicans finally turn on Plump, or will they fall in line again?" Without touching the Senator Shift scandal, Rachel continues, "the real story here isn't just the hypocrisy, though it is *astonishing*. The real story is that the Republican Party has created a culture where people feel they must hide who they are in order to succeed. Congresswoman Lime's entire career was built on a lie, but the reason for that lie was the fear of being rejected by the very people she tried so hard to please."

The Talk Show Circuit: Comedy and Shock

The late-night hosts had a field day. On The Late Show, Stephen Colbert opened with, "Ladies and gentlemen, we finally have proof that Plump is the villain in every bad action movie." He then mimicked Plump's voice, adding, "'Take him out. No mistakes. No survivors.' I mean, come on, could you be more on-the-nose?"

Jimmy Kimmel was equally biting. "We always knew Plump thought he was a mob boss. But it turns out he actually thinks he's Thanos." The audience roared as Kimmel continued, "Look, we've heard some crazy things from this guy, but straight-up assassination orders? At this point, I wouldn't be surprised if he had a death ray."

On the more politically diverse Real Time with Bill Matter, the host took a pragmatic view. "The problem here isn't just Plump," Matter argued. "It's the entire culture of unchecked power in Washington. We've allowed this to happen. This isn't the first assassination order, folks; it's just the first one that got caught on tape."

Harold Stern, never one to hold back, reacted with characteristic bluntness. "Holy shit. Plump actually said it out loud? Like, is he even trying to hide it anymore?" He then addressed his longtime listeners, saying, "You know, I had the guy on my show years ago. We all knew he was crazy, but damn, ordering a hit? That's next level."

Stern also took aim at Plump's loyalists. "I wanna know what the MAGA crowd is thinking right now. Are they just gonna pretend they didn't hear that? Are they gonna be like, 'Nah, he was just joking about killing an entire family'?"

Stern continues, "We have to get this Machiavelli guy on this show. Can someone get ahold of his people? Does he have people? He shows up out of nowhere and disappears like Keyser Soze. Anybody listening who is able to get a hold of this guy, let him know we want him on the show. Wait, Joe Brogan has already booked this guy for a live stream this week. Okay, at least we know he has people. We will get him on the show next."

15

COLLATERAL DAMAGE

PRESENT DAY

AUGUST 2028 — 5:00 P.M.

San Antonio, TX.

T he neon glow of *The Joe Brogan Experience* studio pulsed with an electric energy as millions of viewers tuned in. The night's guest had ignited a firestorm across the nation, and for the first time since the explosive revelations at the RNC, James Machiavelli sat down for a live, unfiltered discussion.

Joe Brogan leaned forward, microphone poised, his expression a mix of curiosity and disbelief. "We have a very special guest tonight as we are streaming live with the man who has set America and the world on fire with bombshell revelations of corruption within our government and society as a whole. A potential future President of the United States of America, James Machiavelli."

Machiavelli nodded, his presence commanding yet relaxed. "Thank you, Joe, for having me on. And you can call me James, no need for formalities."

Joe grinned. "Same here, just call me Joe."

Joe exhaled sharply, shaking his head as he gathered his thoughts. "Before I ask you anything, I need to recap what happened last week at the RNC. I'm still trying to wrap my head around it. We're all just trying to catch up."

He took a deep breath before launching into the now-legendary events: the silencing of Plump's microphone, the damning recordings, the revelation of Machiavelli's supposed assassination, and the unmasking of a web of corruption stretching from the highest offices of power down to the media itself. By the time he finished, the weight of the moment was palpable.

Joe leaned back, rubbing his temple. "Bro... just hearing that again gives me chills. What was going through your mind when you walked into that room, knowing you were about to drop the biggest political nuke in history?"

Machiavelli smiled faintly. "Joe, the truth is, I wasn't nervous. Because I wasn't alone. That moment wasn't just about me. It was about every American who has been betrayed, lied to, and left behind. I was just the vessel. The people who made this possible, who gathered the information, who risked their lives—this wasn't a solo act. This was millions of Americans working together for eighteen months to burst on the scene at that moment. This was a movement stepping into the light."

Joe nodded, impressed. "Alright, let's break this down. The first recording—the one where Plump orders the assassination of you and your family. How did you get it?"

Machiavelli chuckled. "I can't give away all our secrets, but let's just say not everyone in the government is loyal to the people in charge. Some still believe in the Constitution."

Joe leaned forward. "But why you? I mean, sure, you exposed corruption, but what made you such a threat that they wanted you dead?"

Machiavelli's expression darkened. "Because I presented solutions. Corruption thrives on two things: secrecy and apathy. People get overwhelmed, they get distracted, and they believe change isn't possible. My thesis, The People's Awakening, shattered that illusion. It laid out a clear, achievable path to dismantling their power structure without bloodshed. And that scared the hell out of them."

Joe's eyebrows shot up. "So, you're saying they weren't just afraid of you exposing them, they were afraid of you giving people hope?"

"Exactly," Machiavelli said. "They can manage scandals. They survive by weathering storms and waiting for the next distraction. But an actual blueprint for change? That's their nightmare."

Joe ran a hand over his head. "Damn. Okay, let's talk about what happened after the RNC. You started dropping dirt, one scandal every hour. A sitting senator orchestrating a murder and framing an innocent man? A far-right congresswoman hiding her own gender transition while attacking LGBTQ rights? And the biggest of all, the revelation that the top news networks were literally conspiring with political leaders to control information. How deep does this go?"

Machiavelli's expression was unreadable. "Joe, what we've released so far is just the surface. We have enough material to expose decades of corruption across both parties, corporate elites, and the media. But releasing it all at once? That would cause chaos. The goal isn't to burn everything down. It's to rebuild."

Joe smirks, shaking his head in disbelief. "Man, I just can't wrap my head around you coming out of nowhere like that. I must've replayed that video at least twenty times in the last week."

Machiavelli chuckles, leaning back in his chair. "I felt like 'The Undertaker' rising from the dead, appearing out of parts unknown."

Joe bursts out laughing, slapping the table. "Dude, you were in all black too! Full-on WWE entrance vibes."

Machiavelli grins. "Oh, Joe, that was entirely intentional. We wanted that dramatic, wrestling-style entrance, shock factor and all. I've been a wrestling fan for as long as I can remember. The first Undertaker vs. Shawn Michaels match at WrestleMania? Absolute masterpiece. But if we're talking about personal favorites, I'd have to go with one of the early Money in the Bank matches. You know, the one where Jeff Hardy climbed that ridiculously high ladder and just, BOOM, leg dropped Edge, snapping him and the ladder in half."

Joe's eyes light up. "Oh, hell yes! But nothing, nothing, beats the Undertaker throwing Mankind off the top of Hell in a Cell."

Machiavelli shakes his head with a laugh. "Damn, man, that's an all-timer. Nobody forgets that. Mick Foley didn't just take a bump; he got straight-up sacrificed. Honestly, if you want, we can spend the rest of this podcast talking about wrestling."

Joe laughs, shaking his head. "You kill me, dude. You just dropped the biggest political bomb of all time, and you want to talk about wrestling? And you don't even look like a politician right now. Black Deadpool T-shirt, black cargo shorts, skater shoes. Let me see what's on that shirt."

Machiavelli tugs at the front of his shirt, making the text visible.

Joe reads aloud, laughing. "I am the kind of man that when my feet hit the floor each morning, the devil says, 'OH CRAP. HE'S UP.'" He leans back, shaking his head. "Man, I love it. I don't know about the devil, but Ronald Plump sure as hell knows you're up."

Machiavelli smirks. "With his dementia, you never know. That coward-ass motherfucker is probably shitting the bed for an entirely different reason."

Joe grins. "Oh, we're still talking wrestling, huh? Because that was a No Holds Barred comment."

Machiavelli leans forward, grinning. "I bet he's listening

right now, tweeting furiously. Did you ever notice that for a guy with such tiny hands, he has fat fingers? His whole life of anger probably started when his dad told him he couldn't be a proctologist. And you know Plump; he probably thought it was because of his fat fingers, but in reality? It was because he's a fucking moron."

Joe whistles. "Damn. Be real with me. Have you done stand-up comedy?"

Machiavelli shakes his head. "God, no. I wouldn't disrespect the craft. The time, the effort comedians put into refining their material? That's something I could never do. I'm just riffing here, but doing this on stage, night after night? Nah."

Joe nods, still grinning. "Alright, but let's be real, these people don't just roll over. Have you had any threats since stepping back into the public eye?"

Machiavelli smirks. "Of course. But here's the thing: they already tried their worst. I was declared dead. My family was nearly wiped out. Now? Every move they make is being watched by millions. Their old playbook doesn't work anymore."

Joe crosses his arms. "And yet, the media coverage is all over the place. Fox News and OAN are obsessed with this Democratic senator scandal, but they've barely mentioned Plump trying to have you assassinated. Meanwhile, CNN and MSNBC are laser-focused on Plump and that crazy Congresswoman Lime's story, but they won't touch the Democratic scandal. And yet, the biggest story of all, the one that implicates both sides, the conspiracy between the CEOs of Fox and CNN to manipulate information, suppress truth, and profit off division? That's getting buried completely."

Machiavelli nods. "Exactly. And that's why we did it this way. We knew they'd focus on the fires we set, and in doing so, they'd expose their own bias. The more they try to manipulate the narrative, the more proof we release. They can't outrun the truth."

Joe leans forward. "But hold on, how is the media manipulation scandal bigger than the President of the United States ordering an assassination?"

Machiavelli's expression hardens. "Because, Joe, as insane as that is, it directly affects a handful of people. A crime? Yes. Shocking? Of course. But the impact? Limited. Now, the Fox-CNN conspiracy? That's decades of deception affecting hundreds of millions of people, shaping their views, bending reality, and controlling what they believe to be true. The media has been the architect of our division. They manufacture outrage, tell people who to hate, who to trust, and all of it serves their bottom line. They make you think you're being informed, but you're actually being manipulated."

Joe exhales, nodding slowly. "When you put it that way... damn. It's crazy to think about how different our thoughts and opinions might be if we'd actually been told the truth."

Machiavelli leans back. "That's the point. And trust me,

we're only scratching the surface. There's so much more corruption to expose, and this time, they won't be able to bury it."

Joe tilts his head. "Honestly, I'm surprised more politicians haven't come after you directly. I mean, other than Plump throwing his usual tantrum on Twitter, most of them seem either paralyzed or scrambling for damage control. It's not a Mike Tyson first-round knockout, but they're definitely struggling to get off the mat. Their knees are wobbly."

Machiavelli smirks. "What are they gonna say? I've got dirt on every single one of these motherfuckers, and it's worse than anything I've ever done. They can scream louder, repeat their lies, but now people know their communication outlets are compromised. Even Plump is quieter than usual. You know why? His handlers have finally managed to put a muzzle on him. He has no self-control, the ultimate nepo baby. Hell, I wouldn't be surprised if his parents were twin siblings. That's rich-people incest at its finest."

Joe chuckles. "Jesus."

Machiavelli shrugs. "But for real? I'm gonna love every second of torturing him with the truth. And trust me, the story about him trying to have me killed? That's not even close to the most damaging dirt we have on him. Just wait. Give it a few weeks."

Joe raises an eyebrow. "When you drop it, let me know. I'll release it on my platforms. What's it gonna cost me?"

Machiavelli grins. "Nothing. The truth is free."

Joe nods. "Alright, damn. But let's get back to this. You're running for President. What's your strategy?"

Machiavelli leaned forward. "First, we expose the system for what it is. Second, we educate the people. Third, we implement direct structural changes that return power to the majority. We eliminate partisan primaries, enforce term limits, establish transparent governance through public accountability logs, and restructure the judicial system so that judges are no longer political appointees."

Joe sat back. "Dude, you're talking about reshaping America from the ground up."

"Because it needs to happen," Machiavelli said firmly. "The country isn't broken. It's rigged. And the people rigging it have had free rein for too long."

Joe exhaled. "Alright, let's switch gears for a second. We've talked about politics, corruption, revolution... but let's talk about you. Who is James Machiavelli?"

Machiavelli chuckled. "A guy who grew up believing in the American Dream and then realized it was a lie, but one that could be turned into reality if we fought for it."

Joe smirked, leaning back in his chair. "Come on, man. Give me something real."

Machiavelli exhaled sharply, his expression shifting. He leaned forward, elbows on his knees. "Alright, you want real? I had a fucked-up childhood—chaotic, unstable. And if I've ever had one goal in life, it's been to do right by the people who depend on me. I want to make sure kids growing up in situations like mine have genuine opportunities, genuine hope, that if they work hard, life can get better." He paused, his voice steady but firm. "The elites and the corrupt will paint me as someone who hates rich people. I don't. Most wealthy people earned their success honestly, and I respect that. But there's a small, rotten group, the ones who rig the system for their own personal gain and their friends' benefit. That's not ambition. That's greed. That's laziness."

Joe, who had been gently bobbing his head, now sat up straighter. His smirk was gone. "Damn," he said, voice quieter than before. "That's not the answer I was expecting." He studied Machiavelli for a beat. "Can we go deeper into your background?"

Machiavelli offered a small smile but shook his head. "Not today, Joe. But soon. Let's set up another interview in a month."

Joe pointed at him. "I'm holding you to that." Then, sensing the shift in mood, he grinned. "Alright, let's lighten things up a bit. What's your vice? You a whiskey guy? Got a favorite band?"

Machiavelli chuckled. "I don't drink much, but when I do? Whiskey, for sure." He rubbed his chin, thinking. "Music? Man, my taste is all over the place. Classic rock, grunge, metal, rap, house, old-school hip-hop." His grin widened. "But if I had to pick one band that's basically the soundtrack to my campaign? Rage Against the Machine."

Joe let out a short laugh. "Yeah, that checks out." Joe

grinned. "Alright. Now the real test… aliens. You think the government's hiding something?"

Machiavelli leaned in. "Joe, after everything you just heard tonight, do you really think they'd tell us the truth about that?"

The studio erupted in laughter, but beneath the humor, the weight of the conversation lingered. The night's discussion wasn't just another podcast episode. It was a declaration that the game had changed.

Joe's expression turned serious again. "James, if there's one thing you want people to take away from this conversation, what is it?"

Machiavelli's gaze hardened. "That the power has always belonged to the people. They just need to remember it."

The screen faded to black, but the revolution was just beginning.

16

THE ART OF EXPOSURE
PRESENT DAY
AUGUST 2028 — 7:00 P.M.

Harrisburg, PA.

The night was electric at the New Holland Arena in Harrisburg, Pennsylvania. Supporters packed the venue, waving their flags and donning red hats as they eagerly awaited their leader's arrival. When Ronald Plump finally took the stage, the crowd erupted in deafening cheers. The former president basked in the adoration, launching into his speech about how successful he was at deporting illegal immigrants, how America was better off under his leadership, and how he alone had fixed the country's problems.

But just as Plump was hitting his stride, the microphone cut out. A confused murmur spread through the crowd. Then, the massive screen behind him flickered and changed.

Instead of Plump's usual campaign imagery, a live stream appeared, showing a man walking confidently toward the arena's entrance.

James Machiavelli.

A hush fell over the crowd as they watched the screen, recognizing the man who had been making waves across the country with his blunt rhetoric and relentless pursuit of truth. The feed continued to play as Machiavelli, flanked by his security team, entered the venue. At the same time, a series of damning revelations about Plump's business dealings began rolling across the screen.

Video evidence surfaced, exposing Plump's decades-long hypocrisy on immigration. Footage showed his businesses hiring undocumented workers, many still employed today, while he publicly denounced illegal immigration. There were testimonies from former employees, explaining how they were discarded for illegal immigrants whenever they became inconvenient or demanded fair wages. Another clip revealed Plump's close associates benefiting from cheap, undocumented labor while secretly ensuring those workers were deported before they could speak out or claim their rightful pay.

Then, the most shocking piece of evidence appeared: an authenticated email exchange between Plump and billionaire tech mogul Felon Musk. In the emails, Musk laid out a plan to falsely classify jobs lost to artificial intelligence as "newly created" positions to manipulate employment statistics. He also suggested that corporations submit phony salary figures on their tax forms, allowing CEOs to hoard more money while paying less in taxes. Plump's response? "Great idea. Go ahead. Just make sure these CEOs kick some of that money back into my campaign."

Gasps rippled through the audience. Some stared in disbelief. Others looked at Plump, waiting for an explanation. But before he could speak, Machiavelli and his security team had nearly reached the stage. A wall of Secret Service agents formed between them and Plump.

Machiavelli, unfazed, raised a hand, signaling his team to halt. He addressed the Secret Service with respect. "These men and women are Americans doing their jobs. We keep this peaceful."

Then, he turned his attention back to the stage. "Turn Plump's mic back on. Let's debate these issues right here, right now. But let's be real, tiny dick on stage is going to do his best Dementia Dump impression. He'll threaten me, call me names, avoid accountability, blame everyone but himself, and rant incoherently to distract from his corruption. He's a fuckin' moron."

Plump's face turned a deep shade of red. As predicted, he launched into an unhinged tirade. His voice, even without the microphone, was shrill and desperate. He flailed his arms, calling Machiavelli part of the deep-state, screeching that the video evidence was a hoax, that it was all rigged against him. The more he ranted, the more erratic he became, until his team had to intervene. His aides rushed onto the stage, struggling to contain him as he continued to shout conspiracies.

"This is election interference! It's all fake! FAKE!" he bellowed as his staffers physically dragged him off stage, his legs kicking at nothing.

Machiavelli smirked, watching the scene unfold. Then, with the calm of a man who had just checkmated his opponent, he spoke into the microphone. "The truth isn't election interference, Donnie. You just can't outrun your lies anymore."

The audience sat in stunned silence. Some of Plump's most loyal supporters looked conflicted, while others shifted uncomfortably, processing what they had just seen.

Machiavelli turned to them, his tone shifting from confrontational to reflective. "Notice how he only started acting tough after my team and I stopped moving? After we made it clear we wanted to keep this peaceful? But wait, let's roll back the footage from a few minutes ago."

On cue, the screen replayed a video taken from another angle, Plump's face as Machiavelli's team approached. The color drained from his skin. His lips trembled. His eyes darted around, searching for a way out. Then, as soon as he saw his Secret Service agents stepping in, his fear vanished, replaced by faux bravado.

"Damn," Machiavelli laughed. "Look at him. Scared. Looks like he's about to cry and shit his pants. Hell, he probably did shit his pants, and his little tantrum was just an excuse to get off stage fast. That right there is a coward-ass motherfuckin' bitch who will never have the balls to debate me one-on-one."

A ripple of laughter spread through the audience. Some clapped. Others nodded, finally seeing the man they had followed for years in a new light.

Machiavelli's voice grew more serious. "I know for a long time, many of you have fiercely supported him. You believed in him. You wanted him to be one of us. But I'm here to show you the truth. He never was, and he never wanted to be. He doesn't care about us. He never did."

He let the words hang in the air before continuing. "We need more of *you*, not billionaires, not elites, but working-class Americans, fighting for us. We need you in Congress, in our justice system, and in our education system. We have to do this ourselves. For too long, we've relied on elite motherfuckers like him, thinking they'd help us make this country great. They won't. They never will. The power belongs to us, but only if we take it."

A smattering of boos rippled through the crowd, but they were met with an equal measure of hesitant cheers. Some of Plump's staunchest supporters clenched their fists, faces red with anger, unwilling to accept Machiavelli's words. Others shifted uncomfortably, doubt creeping into their expressions. A few in the crowd nodded, whispering amongst themselves.

A sparsely scattered chant started in the crowd. "We have to do it ourselves! We have to do it ourselves!"

Machiavelli nodded, satisfied. "That's right. And this

fight isn't just for tonight. Plump doesn't get to run away from the truth. Starting now, I'm holding impromptu town hall meetings before every one of his rallies. Three hours before he takes the stage, I'll be in the same city, answering your unfiltered questions. No bullshit, no lies, no handlers whispering in my ear. Tomorrow, we'll be in Charlotte. And we'll keep doing this at every stop until Plump faces the truth."

The reaction was mixed. A chorus of boos erupted, but it was no longer the overwhelming, unified jeering that would have drowned him out earlier in the night. Some in the audience exchanged glances, nodding slightly, considering his words. Others remained steadfast, arms crossed, eyes narrowed in defiance.

Then, a small but growing section of the crowd broke into cheers. The sound spread, hesitant at first, then swelling. Some still clung to their loyalty to Plump, but the cracks in his foundation had begun to show. People who had once believed in him without question were now questioning for the first time.

Machiavelli was piercing Plump's base. The movement had begun.

As Machiavelli exited the arena floor, he could feel the momentum shifting. Plump had been exposed, his lies laid bare. But this was only the beginning.

Tomorrow, they would do it again.

And this time, even more people would be watching.

17
NO SCRIPT, JUST US
PRESENT DAY
AUGUST 2028 — 6:00 P.M.

Charlotte, NC.

Machiavelli sat backstage, sipping a Dr. Pepper as he scrolled through the morning news. The headline on nearly every major outlet blared the same message:

PLUMP FILES LAWSUIT AND RESTRAINING ORDER AGAINST MACHAVELLI FOR SLANDER.

He exhaled, setting his phone face down on the table. "Right on schedule," he muttered. His team had seen this coming. They had mapped out every possible move Plump could make, and this one had been inevitable. But tonight wasn't about Plump. It was about the people in this town, many of whom had only heard of him a week ago and were still figuring out if they even liked him.

A member of his small inner circle, a group of ten sharp minds who met before every event, stuck their head in. "Crowd's filling up. You ready?"

Machiavelli nodded. "Let's go meet 'em."

The town hall was packed, but the energy wasn't raucous. It was cautious. People had shown up not as fans, but as skeptics. They weren't here to cheer; they were here to listen. That was fine with Machiavelli. He wasn't here to put on a show. He was here to talk.

He stepped onto the stage and immediately grabbed the podium, moving it off to the side. He preferred space. He was a pacer. Hands in his pockets, he took a moment to scan the room. No teleprompter. No script. Just him, the microphone, and a few hundred people who weren't sure what to make of him yet.

"Evening," he said simply. "I appreciate you being here. I know most of you don't know me. That's fair. I'm not a politician. I hate politics. But this is the role I play in something much bigger than myself. So, let's just talk."

There was no eruption of applause, no rally-style energy, just a serene curiosity settling over the room.

Machiavelli sat on the edge of the stage, casually taking a sip of his Dr. Pepper before smirking slightly. "By the way, before we get into it, let's address the elephant in the room. Plump and his lawsuit."

A few chuckles rippled through the crowd.

"Look, we knew this was coming. My team? They're sharp. They had mapped it out weeks ago and knew exactly how it would play out. And they were *ready*." He gestured toward the back of the room. "So, full credit to them. Because I don't do this alone. Never have, never will."

He pulled his phone from his pocket and scrolled to a screenshot of a whiteboard covered in strategic outlines. He held it up for the crowd to see.

"This? This was three months ago. We wrote every move he might make. Lawsuit was second on the list."

The audience murmured, intrigued.

"That being said, I do have to admit I'm a little disappointed. I expected something *more creative* from him."

The audience chuckled, some nodding. The tension eased slightly.

The first question came from a woman in her sixties, dressed in a simple cardigan and jeans. "How can the elderly population trust that you respect us and have our best interests at heart, especially with how you treat Plump?"

Machiavelli nodded, giving the question its due respect. "That's a fair question. But here's my honest answer: you should never fully trust me, or any person in a position of influence. Trust has to be earned, and that takes time."

He leaned forward. "Personally, I have nothing but

respect for our retirees. Some of the most important people in my life were elders. My great-grandfather, Nonno, gave me advice I still use today. My grandfather was a firefighter, working extra shifts in sheet metal to provide for his family. I trusted them because they were real with me. No nonsense. Just honesty."

He gestured to the crowd. "That's how I operate. And that's why our network is already working on programs to keep grandparents involved in their grandkids' lives, to provide seniors with self-driving cars, and most importantly, to implement a healthcare initiative that provides free healthcare to our oldest and youngest. We'll get there, step by step."

Then he leaned forward slightly. "But let me turn it back on you. What do you think we're missing?"

The woman hesitated, then smiled. "Well, besides better healthcare benefits, I really like your idea of free healthcare for seniors and children. But what about 100% pension coverage and financial security for older adults, like they have in Norway?"

Machiavelli nodded thoughtfully. "That's an excellent point. Would you be open to collaborating with us on that, helping shape what that could look like here?"

The crowd murmured with interest as she nodded. "Absolutely. We need to make sure no senior ever has to choose between food and medication."

"Agreed," Machiavelli said. "We'll follow up on that."

The next question came from a white man in his early

forties. "You've claimed you're going to *redistribute wealth* in this country. How are you actually goin' to do that?"

Machiavelli didn't hesitate. "First, let's talk about *campaigning*. It's a *billion-dollar* business designed to do nothing but manipulate *you*. We need to dismantle that system so that *all* citizens have a say, no more rigged primaries or party-controlled candidate selections."

The man interjected, "So, it's about cutting money out of politics?"

Machiavelli nodded. "Exactly. And here's the kicker. We're going to make the people who built this corrupt system fund its undoing. Political parties, lobbyists, wealthy donors, they'll be forced to reinvest in the communities they've neglected. That means funding *real* education, *real* small business support, *real* military family assistance, and *real* senior programs."

The man leaned forward, skeptical. "You're talking about a total overhaul of the system. Do you really think that's possible? These people have too much power, too many connections. You think you can take them down?"

Machiavelli met his gaze, unwavering. "The system is rigged, and that's exactly why it has to change. But it's not just about taking them down. It's about building something better from the ground up. It won't be easy, but change is possible when the people demand it."

The man chuckled, shaking his head. "You make it sound so simple, like it's just a matter of will. What makes you think the people are ready for something like this?"

Machiavelli's voice grew more impassioned, though his body remained composed. He moved with silent purpose, pacing a short distance before stopping; not out of nerves, but as if assembling thoughts mid-stride. Hands loosely clasped behind his back, he turned toward the audience, his expression calm, but his eyes burning with conviction.

"Because the people are already suffering. They're tired of being told that the system is broken, but no one will fix it. They're tired of being sold out by politicians who only care about maintaining the status quo. When enough people stand up and say 'enough,' that's when actual change happens. And I'm ready to lead that fight."

The man took a moment, then nodded slowly. "Alright, let's say you get this far. How do you plan to actually redistribute the wealth once you've torn down the system? What's your plan for that?"

Machiavelli smiled, taking a deep breath. "It's not just about tearing down the old system. It's about building a new one where everyone has access to opportunity. We'll create equitable tax systems, eliminate corporate loopholes, invest heavily in public services, and provide incentives for companies that choose to contribute to the well-being of their communities. Wealth will be redistributed through policies that prioritize the collective good over individual profit."

The man seemed to soften, just a little. "Sounds ambitious. But if you really want to do this, you're going to need more than just the people. You'll need the power of legislation, the support of politicians. How are you going to convince them to join your cause?"

Machiavelli chuckled, his tone confident. "Here's where the real strength of this plan comes in. We're not just going to convince them. We're going to hold them accountable. I'm not asking you to take my word for it, because I'm not a politician. I'm going to prove it to you before you even cast your vote. Next week, we'll be on the Harold Stern Show, and that's where we'll reveal our next step in this strategy. No empty promises, just real action."

A teacher in her early fifties stood up next. "What's your plan to help educators?"

Machiavelli's tone shifted. "The most valuable asset of any nation is its *people*. And yet, we under-invest in our educators just like we under-invest in our soldiers. That doesn't work."

She leaned forward. "But *how* are you going to change that?"

Machiavelli didn't miss a beat. "Teachers should be middle class, at minimum. They should have top-tier resources. And we need to hold the profession to a *high ethical standard*. No more underpaying and overloading teachers while expecting them to fix every societal problem on their own."

She pushed back. "We hear that every election cycle. What makes you different?"

Machiavelli smirked. "I don't make promises. I make *plans*. First step: a teacher grant program funded by corporate wealth tax. Second step: free advanced education for teachers. Third step: a National Educators Advisory Board that reports directly to the public."

She raised an eyebrow. "That's... actually structured."

"That's the point," Machiavelli said. "We don't need more words. We need action."

The teacher looked thoughtful, but her expression remained skeptical. "Okay, but it's not just about the money and support. It's also about the conditions teachers are working under. Class sizes are bigger than ever, and teachers are stretched thin. How do you plan to tackle that?"

Machiavelli's eyes lit up. He took a slow step forward, then dropped into a low crouch—calculated, deliberate, bringing himself closer to the audience's eye level, as if inviting them into a shared thought. His voice remained calm, but sharp with conviction. "Glad you brought that up. My plan includes reducing class sizes to no more than eight and no less than five students per teacher. That's right, eight at most. When you're teaching a class of thirty, it's impossible to give each student the attention they deserve. Smaller classes mean better individual attention, more effective teaching, and a higher quality education for all students."

She raised an eyebrow. "Reducing class sizes to only eight? That's a huge shift. How do you plan to make that happen?"

Machiavelli leaned in, his tone resolute. "It starts by prioritizing education funding. We'll reallocate resources from bloated administrative costs and unnecessary expenditures. Schools will be given the support to hire more teachers, and the government will provide incentives to encourage teaching careers. It won't happen overnight, but it's the kind of investment that will pay off for generations. We're moving to a year-round schedule with three quarters and five weeks off between each one. This structure no longer means long summer breaks where kids forget what they've learned, and it gives families the flexibility to plan around breaks that work for them. Teachers will get a break in April, August, and the end of November, plus all of December off. This way, they can recharge and return to the classroom ready to teach."

The teacher seemed intrigued but cautious. "Year-round school is a big change. How will families feel about it?"

Machiavelli held up a finger. "We'll involve families in the process. The schedule will be flexible enough to accommodate different family needs, but the key is that it will create a more balanced, consistent learning environment. No more burnout from long breaks or the pressure of cramming everything into a few short months. I'm also advocating for a national ban on homework. It's an outdated practice that just adds unnecessary stress for students and their families. The best learning happens in the classroom, where teachers can actively engage with their students. Homework is not the solution. It just creates more work for everyone."

She looked at him, impressed. "A national ban on homework? That's something I've never heard before. But I'm curious, how will students get the practice they need without it?"

Machiavelli nodded. "Excellent question. Instead of busywork, we'll focus on in-class activities and projects that promote deeper learning. Teachers will have the time and resources to provide more personalized, hands-on learning experiences. The idea is to make every minute of the school day count so that students aren't leaving school with piles of work to do at home."

The teacher was silent for a moment, digesting the information. "You're really pushing for a full overhaul. But do you think teachers, families, and even students are ready for this kind of change?"

Machiavelli's eyes sparkled with determination. "Change is hard, but it's necessary. The current system isn't working, and people know it. When we show teachers that their work matters and that they'll have the resources they need, they'll be ready. When families see their kids thrive in a balanced, stress-free environment, they'll be on board. And the students? They'll be the first to tell you they want a system that respects their time and their future."

The teacher smiled, with a glimmer of hope in her eyes. "You're right. If we don't make a change, nothing's going to improve. But it's going to take all of us to make it happen."

Machiavelli nodded, his voice calm but resolute. "And that's why I'm asking for your support. This isn't just about politics; it's about building a future where every student, every teacher, and every family has a chance to thrive."

A few people clapped, but most just absorbed what he was saying.

Machiavelli raised his hand, signaling his final statement. "Listen, I'm not here to sell you anything. I'm just one guy in a much *larger* network of people who are tired of watching this country rot from the inside. This isn't about me. It's about all of us. So, take your time. Get to know me. You don't have to like me today. But if what I'm saying makes sense, then let's keep the conversation going."

The audience sat in thoughtful silence for a beat before the first person started clapping. Then another. Then a few more.

It wasn't an explosion of cheers. It was something even better.

It was the sound of people starting to *believe*.

James straightened his posture, his eyes scanning the room with a calm but commanding presence. "I want to make one thing clear. I am but one part of a much larger, diverse network of Americans, people from every walk of life, from every background, and from every corner of this country. But together, we are united in a singular mission: to create a better America for everyone. I am not a politician, and I never will be. I represent the collective will of the people."

He paused, allowing his words to sink in. "Now, let's talk about how decisions are made. Every law, every policy we put forward will be crafted with one principle in mind: it must benefit at least 80% of the population. Not 51%, not a narrow minority, 80%. That's the threshold. And let me be upfront with you: this doesn't always mean the same 80% each time."

A murmur rippled through the crowd. James raised a hand to quiet them, his voice steady. "There will be moments, difficult moments, when a law or decision doesn't directly benefit you personally, but it will benefit at least 80% of Americans. And when that happens, we make that choice. True leadership is not about appeasing everyone; it's about doing what's right for the majority."

He leaned forward slightly, emphasizing his point. "The ultimate goal is simple: four out of every five decisions we make will positively impact every citizen of this country, no matter their background, no matter their circumstance. We can no longer afford a system that benefits the few at the expense of the many. That's what we've been doing for too long, and it's time for a change."

James straightened up, his voice firm and resolute. "And now, I'm heading over to Plump's rally. But not to engage in petty politics. No. I'm there to focus on what truly matters, redistributing wealth and restoring accountability. It's time for real change. Real responsibility. The kind that creates a society where the wealth and power of this nation serve everyone, not just the privileged few. I am basically heading over there to fuck shit up."

The crowd broke out in laughter, with many standing and clapping. The energy shifted as they realized this wasn't just rhetoric. It was a promise of action.

18

THE SPIN ROOM
PRESENT DAY
AUGUST 2028 — 5:00 P.M.

Charlotte, NC.

The Bojangles Coliseum in Charlotte, North Carolina, had always been a venue of high energy, a place where crowds gathered in fervor for performances, speeches, and, in this case, a political rally featuring none other than Ronald J. Plump. The coliseum had been buzzing all day with Plump supporters, decked out in their red MAGA hats, waving banners, and chanting slogans in unison.

Backstage, the atmosphere was far less jubilant. Plump paced angrily, barking orders at his team. "I want extra security. No interruptions tonight. Machiavelli and his people, keep them out of my rally!" He glared at his security detail and IT personnel. "We vetted all of you, right? No leaks? No sabotage?"

His campaign manager nodded, his face a mask of forced confidence. "Yes, sir. We've locked everything down. No one from Machiavelli's camp is getting inside."

For weeks, Machiavelli, an enigmatic and relentless political disruptor, had been a thorn in Plump's side. His unconventional tactics, his ability to shift public opinion through sheer audacity, had rattled even the most seasoned political operatives. And tonight, Plump was determined to have his moment, uninterrupted.

But as he prepared to step on stage, something was off. The once-deafening roar of the crowd had diminished to a mere murmur. Plump's instincts, honed by years in the public eye, told him something was wrong.

His campaign manager's phone buzzed, and he paled as he read the update. "Sir, we have a situation."

"What situation?" Plump snapped.

"People are leaving. East Independence Boulevard is packed. Machiavelli and his team set up a massive cookout just outside the venue. Midwood Smokehouse is catering. They have tents, TV screens broadcasting your rally, and a huge crowd. They got a permit weeks ago to do this."

Plump's jaw tightened. "What the hell do you mean by cookout? A tailgate party?"

"Not just a tailgate, sir. It's a full-blown event. Free barbecue, drinks, and live entertainment. People are walking out to join them. The arena's nearly empty."

Plump clenched his fists. "Unbelievable. This guy thinks he can steal my crowd? I'm Ronald Plump!"

His communications team scrambled. They needed to control the optics. A near-empty rally? The media would have a field day. Quickly, they informed the remaining audience that Plump was feeling under the weather and wouldn't be speaking.

Unbeknownst to them, a cameraman had his feed live, capturing every moment of Plump's backstage meltdown. The footage played on the massive screens outside, where thousands of people were enjoying plates of pulled pork and brisket, sipping on beers, and laughing at the unfolding drama.

Then, the feed cut to a live broadcast from Machiavelli. He was grinning, standing in the middle of the packed street party, microphone in hand.

"Hey, Donny! Do you see this? This is what real support looks like. What's wrong, huh? I speak at town halls with fewer people than you have inside your arena right now. What? Are you too elite to speak to your own people? The same people who paid a lot of money to see you?"

The crowd outside laughed, some raising their beers in mock salute.

Machiavelli smirked. "Dude, you ain't nothing but a fuckin' pussy. A coward-ass motherfucker. If you want to speak in front of a huge crowd, why don't you come out and debate me? Come on, put on a strap-on so you can pretend you have real balls for once in your life."

The eruption of laughter was deafening. People were doubling over, smacking tables, wiping tears from their eyes. It was a roast, a spectacle unlike anything ever seen in modern politics.

Backstage, Plump was seething, his face beet red. He pointed at the screen, shaking with rage. "Shut it off! Cut the damn feed!"

Machiavelli noticed the abrupt cut. He grinned wider.

"Oh, hey dumbass, the microphone isn't on. We can't hear you. So why don't you get Felon Musk's dick out of your mouth, stop whining and come out here and debate? Our mics work just fine."

Plump's fury knew no bounds. He stormed off, surrounded by his team, who struggled to keep up with his frantic pace. He had been outmaneuvered, humiliated, and no damage control could undo the optics of this disaster.

Machiavelli turned back to the crowd, raising his drink. "Great! I'm glad he's gone. This is a cookout. Let's enjoy ourselves! No politics tonight, I fuckin' hate politics!"

As he spoke, the opening chords of Rage Against the Machine's "Killing in the Name" blasted from the speakers, shaking the street with raw energy. The bass thumped through the pavement as the crowd erupted once more, fists pumping in rhythm to the defiant anthem. People danced, laughed, and sang along, reveling in the moment. More drinks were poured, more plates were filled, and the night carried on in celebration, not of a candidate, not of an agenda, but of a movement that had turned the tables on the most dominant figure in American politics.

19

THE BRIEFING

PRESENT DAY

AUGUST 2028 — 7:00 P.M.

Washington D.C.

The atmosphere in the White House communications office was tense. They planned the upcoming press conference as a simple announcement: President Plump would step back from campaign duties to focus on running the country. The communications team had spent days fine-tuning every word, ensuring the message was clear, controlled, and free from controversy. But despite their meticulous preparations, an undercurrent of unease ran through the room. They knew that any deviation from the script, any unexpected question, could send them spiraling into chaos. Every staff member sat at their desks, fingers poised over keyboards, awaiting the moment they'd have to push out official statements or counter any narratives that threatened to emerge.

"Alright, everyone, let's go over this one last time," Media Director Caroline Hughes said, pacing in front of her team. "The President has decided that he will not be holding any campaign rallies until further notice. He hates disappointing his supporters, but continuing to Make America Great Again is his top priority. That's why they voted for him, and that's why they'll vote for him again."

She stopped and locked eyes with each person in the room. "Sandra, you'll start by announcing the campaign pause. Then you'll pivot to our message about national security and stability. Keep it simple. No distractions, no unnecessary detours."

Press Secretary Sandra Woodley nodded, adjusting the stack of notes in front of her. "Got it."

An aide suddenly rushed in and leaned close to Hughes, whispering urgently. Her face remained composed, but something in her eyes darkened.

"The NSA has confirmed that the assassination records Machiavelli released at the RNC are authentic."

Hughes's grip tightened around the papers in her hand. She whispered back, "What are you saying?"

The aide repeated the statement louder, as if to force the reality of it upon her.

Woodley gasped. "What? He really did that?"

The tension in the room was suffocating. The media director clenched her jaw and gestured for the aide to step outside. As the door closed behind them, muffled voices filled the hallway.

Woodley watched through the glass panel. Caroline was angry, furious, even. Her gestures were sharp, commanding, and whatever she was saying was not open for debate. When she finally returned, she straightened her blazer and took a deep breath before addressing the room.

"We have received word from the NSA that the recordings were AI-generated," Hughes announced, her voice devoid of hesitation.

Woodley's face twisted in disbelief. "That is not what he said. We all heard him. The recordings are real. Mr. Plump ordered the assassination of an American family. How can you ignore that?"

The entire room fell silent. A few aides exchanged nervous glances, sensing that things were about to escalate.

Hughes stepped closer, her voice dropping to a low, icy tone. "If you want to keep your job, you will go out there and tell the American people the truth, that the recordings are a fake. For the rest of you, if one word is said otherwise, you are fired and could be prosecuted for treason."

A heavy silence hung in the air.

"Ms. Woodley, do we have a problem?" Hughes asked, her eyes locked onto Woodley's.

The Press Secretary hesitated, then swallowed hard. "No, we don't."

"Good." Hughes took a step back. "Well, get out there, then. The American people are waiting for the truth."

Woodley stepped up to the podium in the White House Press Briefing Room, scanning the crowd of reporters. Cameras flashed. The murmurs in the room quieted as she raised her hand.

"I ask that all questions be held until after I make a few announcements."

She took a steady breath before beginning. "President Plump has decided to temporarily step back from campaign duties to focus entirely on running the country. He understands his supporters may be disappointed, but his commitment remains the same, ensuring the safety, prosperity, and greatness of this nation. At this time, he will not be holding campaign rallies until further notice."

She paused, letting the message sink in before transitioning.

"We have also received an update from the NSA about the inflammatory recordings heard at the RNC, accusing the President of an unconscionable plot."

A hush fell over the room. Everyone was waiting for the official denial, for the carefully constructed statement that would attempt to sweep the controversy away.

Woodley exhaled sharply. Then, before she could stop herself, she spoke.

"The NSA confirmed they are real, and I won't work for anybody that would do that."

Gasps filled the room. Reporters bolted from their seats, whispering and scrambling to take notes. Cameras clicked rapidly. Woodley reached up, unfastened her press credentials, and placed them firmly on the podium.

"I quit."

Without another word, she turned and walked away. The room erupted. Journalists shouted questions, voices overlapping in chaos. Some rushed out to follow her, desperate for a statement. Others sprinted toward their news vans, ready to break the biggest story of the year.

Caroline Hughes stormed out from behind the curtain, barely concealing her rage as she stepped up to the podium.

"Ladies and gentlemen, what you just witnessed was the latest attempt by the deep state to undermine our fine president," she declared, her voice sharp with feigned authority. "Ms. Woodley was already informed that she was being let go at the end of the month due to internal performance issues. She chose to lash out on her way out the door. Her statement holds no truth whatsoever."

But it was too late. Nobody was listening. The room had mostly emptied, journalists already outside reporting the bombshell revelation.

Hughes gritted her teeth, gripping the edges of the podium. This was not how today was supposed to go.

In the halls of the White House, Press Secretary Sandra Woodley walked briskly toward the exit, her phone buzzing with incoming calls. She ignored them all.

Outside, a swarm of reporters waited for her, microphones and cameras pointed in her direction.

She stopped, looked at them, and finally spoke.

"For too long, I convinced myself that manipulating the truth, even outright lying, was for the greater good of the country. But I see now that a lie is still a lie, no matter the justification. I won't do it anymore. If they need someone to deceive the American people, they'll have to find someone else."

And with that, she walked into history.

20

ECHO CHAMBER

PRESENT DAY

AUGUST 2028 — 8:00 P.M.

Washington D.C.

The moment Sandra Woodley stepped away from the podium, the media machine roared to life. Every major network interrupted its programming to broadcast the shocking resignation in real time. The political world, already fractured and on edge, erupted into chaos.

Cable News Networks

On Fox News, Sean Hannity appeared visibly agitated as he rushed to defend President Plump. "This is just another witch hunt orchestrated by the radical left. The Deep State clearly compromised Sandra Woodley. We don't know who got to her, but mark my words, this is all about power. Machiavelli is nothing but a thug trying to destroy our way of life."

Jesse Watters took a different angle, speculating, "What if this is a calculated ploy to sway voters? The media loves a dramatic defection story, but let's not kid ourselves; this looks like a coordinated attack. I wouldn't be surprised if Machiavelli is using his web of lies to pressure Ms. Woodley into making this statement."

Over on MSNBC, Rachel Maddow's voice was heavy with urgency. "If this recording is real, if what Sandra Woodley just admitted is true, then we are looking at an unprecedented abuse of power—one that demands immediate accountability." CNN played the resignation clip on loop, with anchors openly speculating about potential legal consequences for the administration.

Late Night Talk Shows

Stephen Colbert played the clip of Woodley's resignation three times before dramatically mimicking her. "I quit! That's it! America's Press Secretary just rage-quit live on air!" Jimmy Kimmel joked, "This is the political version of storming out of a terrible date, except the date is democracy, and the guy across from you is Ronald Plump." Trevor Noah analyzed the moment with a more serious tone, emphasizing how rare it was for an insider to turn on a sitting president in such a public way.

. . .

Plump's Allies and Opponents

Within the Republican Party, reactions were mixed. House Speaker Mike Johnson called the resignation "unfortunate," and insisted, "This administration remains committed to the American people." Meanwhile, Senator Josh Hawley warned, "We need to be very careful about jumping to conclusions. The media is using this to push their own narrative. The good people of America won't be manipulated."

Democratic leaders wasted no time demanding action. Alexandria Ocasio-Cortez tweeted, "The GOP has defended Plump at every turn. Will they still defend him now? Or will they finally put country over party?" Senator Bernie Sanders called for a full congressional investigation, stating, "I will be contacting several people in the intelligence community to see if they have truly concluded that the recordings are real and authentic. If so, they are beyond impeachable."

World Leaders React

Across the globe, foreign governments reacted swiftly. The United Kingdom's Prime Minister issued a carefully worded statement: "These are serious allegations, and we trust in the American people's commitment to democracy and the rule of law." China's state-run media mocked the

U.S., calling it "a government in disarray." Russia's Vladimir Poutine took a more subdued approach, merely stating, "America's internal affairs are its own. We will continue to observe the situation."

Social Media and Podcasts

Twitter and Reddit exploded within minutes. The hashtags `#PlumpResign`, `#WoodleySpeaks`, and `#CoupAt-TheWhiteHouse` trended worldwide. Conservative influencers scrambled to discredit Woodley, questioning her motives and suggesting she had been "turned" by Democratic operatives. Liberal commentators hailed her as a whistleblower, with one viral tweet calling her "the new Deep Throat."

Podcasts across the spectrum dedicated entire episodes to dissecting the bombshell revelation. *The Joe Brogan Experience* hosted a panel of experts debating the implications, with Brogan himself visibly shaken. "Look, this is insane. Sandra Woodley just confirmed it. President Plump ordered the assassination of an American family. You don't walk away from a job like that unless something serious is going down. We literally had Machiavelli on the show last week, and I'll be honest, I liked the guy. But after this? Screw Plump. Machiavelli is going to win this election, and I'm all in."

Pod Save America released an emergency episode, with former Obama staffers sounding the alarm. "This is Watergate-level corruption, and anyone who refuses to see it is willfully blind. Those of us in politics and media need to take responsibility for the divided reaction among the American people. For decades, we've shaped and controlled narratives to serve our own interests. And now, we're facing the ultimate consequence, an American president ordering the assassination of a U.S. citizen, while half the media scrambles to deny it, spin it, or discredit the truth."

Hollywood and Celebrity Reactions

George Clooney tweeted, "Sandra Woodley is a hero. She saw evil and refused to be part of it." Taylor Swift posted an Instagram story encouraging her fans to "stay engaged and demand accountability." In contrast, Kid Rock dismissed the news, writing, "Fake news media at it again. Plump 2028, baby!"

Comedians and influencers on TikTok reenacted the moment, with some satirizing Plump's reaction. "Can you imagine? 'Sir, your press secretary just quit on live TV.' Plump: 'Was she hot?'" one viral video quipped.

21

ON AIR

PRESENT DAY

AUGUST 2028 — 7:00 P.M.

New York City, NY.

The anticipation was electric. As James Machiavelli prepared to step into the studio of *The Harold Stern Show*, he knew this was no ordinary interview. Stern had a way of cutting through the bullshit, stripping guests down to their rawest, unfiltered selves. He was irreverent, unpredictable, and ruthless, but also capable of drawing out the kind of authenticity no political debate or campaign rally ever could.

Machiavelli had spoken at rallies, engaged in town halls, and survived assassination attempts, but this was something different. He wasn't walking into a staged, polished interview; he was stepping into the lion's den of American media. Harold Stern wasn't going to hold back, and neither was he.

The intro music blared, Rob Zombie's *Dragula*, as Harold's unmistakable voice cut through the airwaves.

"All right, everybody, hold on to your asses, because today we have the man of the moment. The most wanted man in politics. The guy who went from 'who the hell is this?' to 'holy shit, this guy is taking over the country.' We're talking about James Machiavelli. The man is either a revolutionary genius or a lunatic with a death wish. And today, we find out which."

Fred played a soundbite of a bomb exploding, followed by a Plump impersonation shouting, "This guy's a total loser!" The studio erupted in laughter.

Harold's voice then turned serious. "Before we dive in, let's recap the insanity of the past week. The NSA has confirmed that the leaked recordings of Plump ordering the assassination of James Machiavelli and his family are authentic. This is unprecedented. A sitting U.S. President caught red-handed, and instead of denying it, his base is just… shrugging it off? I mean, what the hell?"

Machiavelli smirked, leaning into the mic. "Glad to be here, Harold. I was hoping to talk about my love life and embarrassing bodily functions before we get to the political assassination attempts."

Harold laughed but leaned in. "Let's cut the bullshit. What the hell happened in that year and a half you were in hiding?"

Machiavelli's expression hardened. "Working. Once we got over the initial shock and realized nothing would ever be the same, my wife and I got to work. Our network of millions of Americans worked every single day building simulations, testing policies, gathering intelligence, and setting legal strategies. We organized, we prepared, and we built a coalition that is looking out for the American people's best interests."

Harold blinked. "So, millions of people knew you were alive?"

"No, only about forty people knew. But in one way or another, we've worked with tens of millions of Americans over the last year and a half to create this movement. Crashing the RNC, Plump's Harrisburg rally, holding that block party in Charlotte, none of that happens without millions of dedicated people."

Harold sat back, impressed. "I have to say, I find your willingness to praise the people who work for you—"

Machiavelli interrupted. "Harold, nobody works *for* me. They work *with* me. This isn't a dictatorship, and I'm not a king. There are people much smarter than me who have expanded my little thesis into something I could have never dreamed of."

Harold nodded. "Well, who else is responsible?"

Machiavelli smirked. "I believe we all are, but if you want a name, my wife, Paola."

Harold grinned. "Tell us more about her. Is she joining the campaign?"

Machiavelli's face softened. "Yes, she's joining next week. Right now, she and our boys are spending time with her family. After everything we've been through, they needed a break. Honestly, without her strength and intelligence, none of this would have been possible. She's been my rock. She was a full-time mother, a full-time employee, managing our finances while I authored my thesis. I was a broke single dad before she came into my life. She took my son in as her own, and when we almost died because of my work, she didn't hesitate. She said, 'If this is our new reality, let's make it count.' I wouldn't be here without her."

Harold looked stunned. "Wow. That was a real answer. No political spin. Just honesty."

Machiavelli shrugged. "I'm not a politician."

Harold nodded and then shifted gears. "Serious question: there are people who say what you're doing is dangerous, that it could destabilize the country. Are you worried about that?"

Machiavelli's expression grew serious. "What's dangerous is pretending that the country isn't already destabilized. What's dangerous is allowing corruption to continue unchecked while people suffer. The system isn't just broken; it's been hijacked. If exposing that truth shakes things up, then so be it. But I'll tell you what's truly dangerous, letting things stay the way they are and hoping for the best."

Harold nodded. "That's a hell of an answer." Then he grinned. "All right, let's have some fun. What's the weirdest thing you've read about yourself online since this all started?"

Machiavelli laughed. "Oh man, where do I start? Someone actually wrote a theory that I'm not real, that I'm some kind of deep-fake AI created by a rogue faction in the government. Apparently, I don't 'blink enough' in interviews."

Harold burst out laughing. "Oh my God, you're a government cyborg! That's hilarious."

Machiavelli smirked. "Yep, just a well-programmed deep-fake trying to save democracy."

Harold chuckled. "You're too good. Okay, let's get back to business. My producer just told me we have a very special caller."

Machiavelli smirked. "Well, if they're special, we know it's not Plump."

Harold cackled. "No, it's not Plump, we'd hang up on Plump. Please introduce yourself, special guest."

A familiar voice came through the speakers. "What's up, James? This is Eminem."

Machiavelli's eyes widened. "Oh shit. Are you serious?"

Eminem laughed. "Yeah, man. I just wanted to say that what you're doing is giving a lot of people hope. You're opening a lot of eyes, and I want to work with someone like that. My team will reach out. There's something special brewing, and I want to be a part of it. Keep it up. We believe in you. Peace out!"

Eminem hung up, leaving Machiavelli stunned. He turned to Harold, gleeful. "Dude, that was Eminem."

Harold leaned back, shaking his head. "I've been in this business for over forty years, and it's hard to surprise me. This? This surprised me."

Machiavelli exhaled, shaking his head. "Damn. Okay. Let's get to the big announcement."

Harold nodded, leaning forward as if the weight of Machiavelli's words had suddenly drawn him in. "Now that everyone knows you're not bluffing about the dirt you've got, what's next?"

Machiavelli sat up straighter, his presence commanding the room like a general preparing for war. His voice sharpened, deliberate and unwavering. "If Congress doesn't pass a yearly budget that greatly benefits the American people by September 1st, less than three weeks from now, we will start releasing damning evidence on at least twenty members of Congress every single day, starting September 2nd. We're talking about corruption, bribery, offshore accounts, backdoor deals, everything they thought they buried so deeply that no one could ever dig it up. I have it all. The public will know exactly who has been selling them out."

A heavy silence blanketed the studio. Even the camera crew, normally desensitized to political drama, seemed frozen in place. Harold's fingers drummed against his desk, his mind racing.

Machiavelli continued, his tone darkening, each word deliberate and cutting. "And let me be perfectly clear, if

Congress passes the budget, but Plump refuses to sign it into law by 8 p.m. Eastern on September 2nd, he will have sealed his fate. And let me add one more condition: he doesn't get to take credit for the deal. He must publicly acknowledge the work of Congress, praise everyone involved except himself." He let the weight of his words settle, his pause calculated, before delivering the final blow. "If he fails to comply, then we start dropping the receipts. And I'm not talking about petty scandals or political missteps; I mean personal scandals so devastating, so undeniable, that they will make Watergate look like a clerical error."

Harold exhaled sharply. He ran a hand through his hair, then leaned back in his chair, blinking as if he needed a second to process the gravity of what had just been said. Then, with a low whistle, he muttered, "Well, holy shit."

Machiavelli smirked, but there was no humor in it, just the cold certainty of a man who knew exactly what he was doing. "Indeed."

Harold shook his head in disbelief before turning back to the audience. "Folks, I don't know where this is headed, but I know one thing: this is the wildest political movement I've ever seen. Give it up for him!"

The audience erupted in thunderous applause, cheers filling the studio like the opening shots of a revolution. Some clapped enthusiastically; others hesitated, as if unsure whether they were witnessing history or a catastrophe in the making.

22

CONGRESS CORNERED

PRESENT DAY

AUGUST 2028 — 1:00 P.M.

Washington D.C.

T he headlines in the following day's papers were stark.

POLITICAL EARTHQUAKE: Machiavelli Puts Congress on Notice

   —The New York Times

A New Kind of Warfare: Machiavelli's Blackmail or Revolution?
—*The Washington Post*

James Machiavelli Declares War on Washington
—*The Wall Street Journal*

Networks scrambled to line up experts, former politicians, and legal analysts to assess what this meant for the nation.

CNN opened its Primetime slot with Anderson Cooper's deadpan delivery.

"Tonight, we have breaking news that shakes the very foundation of American governance. James Machiavelli, the independent insurgent presidential candidate, has given Congress a three-week ultimatum: pass a budget that benefits the people or face daily revelations of high-level corruption. The implications are staggering. We'll discuss what this means with former Senator Mark Ellison, political strategist Jessica Lane, and journalist Robert Kane."

The camera panned to a semicircle of guests seated under the same cold studio lights. Three chairs, three seasoned voices, each one carefully chosen for what they brought to the unfolding political quake.

Mark Ellison, the former senator, sat upright with the posture of a man trained by decades in Washington decorum. His hands rested calmly on his knees; one ankle crossed neatly over the other. His eyes were sharp but not theatrical, measured, and calculating.

"Senator Ellison," Anderson began, turning toward him with a slight tilt of his head, "let's start with you. How unprecedented is this?"

"Anderson, this is beyond unprecedented," Ellison said, his voice carrying the weight of institutional memory. "We are looking at an ultimatum that fundamentally challenges how power operates in Washington. If Machiavelli follows through, this could trigger mass resignations, criminal investigations, and even a constitutional crisis. It's a complete paradigm shift."

Jessica Lane, seated beside him, leaned in slightly, one leg elegantly crossed, her hands steepled in front of her. Her expression was intense but composed, like someone who'd run a hundred war-room simulations and still wasn't sure which direction this one would go.

"Jessica Lane," Anderson said, pivoting slightly toward her, "as a political strategist, what's your take? Is this a genius move or reckless political suicide?"

"It's both, Anderson," she said smoothly, the words falling from her lips with practiced certainty. "Machiavelli is forcing a level of accountability that voters have craved for decades. But he's also making enemies in every corner of the establishment. There's no way of predicting the long-term fallout. Will he be seen as a reformer or a villain? That depends on what he has and whether he delivers."

Across from them, Robert Kane leaned forward in his chair, elbows on the table, fingers loosely clasped as if bracing for impact. His thin glasses caught a glint of light as he turned his gaze toward Anderson.

"Robert Kane," Anderson asked, "you've covered political scandals for years. How does this compare?"

"This makes Watergate look like a parking violation," Kane said flatly. "If Machiavelli releases daily bombshells exposing deep-rooted corruption, we could see a level of public outrage that forces radical government overhaul. The real question is: will Congress try to fight back? Or will they cave?"

Anderson looked back at Ellison, the moment hanging in the air.

"Senator Ellison, do you think Machiavelli has the evidence he claims?"

"If he weren't serious, this would be political suicide," Ellison answered, shifting slightly in his seat. "But let's be real, his network is remarkably sophisticated. Just weeks ago, Machiavelli's evidence led to Senator Shift facing a criminal indictment and intense pressure to resign. Meanwhile, Congresswoman Lime, or should I say Congressman Lime, has been completely sidelined and has already conceded her reelection. If he's bluffing, he's risking everything on his credibility. But I don't think he's bluffing."

Jessica sat with her arms now loosely crossed, her eyes scanning some invisible point just past the camera lens.

"Jessica," Anderson said, "what does this do to the Democratic National Convention next week?"

She sighed, brushing a strand of hair behind her ear before answering.

"It's a nightmare for the DNC. They were hoping to rally support, unify behind their nominee, and now they're forced to respond to a crisis that takes center stage. With every speech, this ticking time bomb will overshadow every headline."

Anderson turned to Kane again.

"Robert, let's talk about the Republican response. How does Plump's camp react?"

Kane didn't hesitate. "Plump is going to attack Machiavelli relentlessly. He's already labeled him a fraud and a deep-state puppet. But behind the scenes, his team is in full panic mode. Nothing Plump has done has slowed Machiavelli's surging support, and now he's even peeling away Plump's own base. Just imagine what else Machiavelli might have on him."

Silence again, charged and electric.

"Senator Ellison," Anderson continued, "if Congress does nothing, and Machiavelli starts leaking evidence, what happens?"

"Total chaos," Ellison said, his voice lower now, more grave. "You could see members of Congress resigning overnight, criminal charges filed, stock markets reacting violently. We are standing on the edge of a political earthquake."

Anderson turned again to Jessica, who now sat with her hands clasped in front of her, expression serious, posture rigid.

"Jessica, how should Congress handle this? Call his bluff or meet his demands?"

She didn't answer immediately. She was calculating. Measuring. Then she spoke quietly but clearly.

"It's a no-win situation. If they comply, they look weak. If they refuse, and the leaks are real, they'll be exposed. They need to act fast and negotiate something that satisfies the public without completely surrendering to Machiavelli."

Anderson leaned back just a touch, exhaling almost imperceptibly as he drew the final question.

"Final question. Does Machiavelli come out of this as a hero or a villain? Robert?"

Kane gave a slow shake of the head, his hands folding together once more.

"Too early to tell. If he cleans house and forces reform, he'll be a legend. If this spirals into instability, history will judge him differently."

"Senator Ellison?"

"If he truly exposes corruption and forces accountability," Ellison said, eyes narrowing, "it could be the most important political event of the century."

"Jessica?"

She didn't flinch. Her voice was low, measured. "One thing is certain; Machiavelli has already changed the game forever."

Over at Fox News, the framing was different.

23
A FRACTURED GOP
PRESENT DAY
AUGUST 2028 — 7:00 P.M.

Washington D.C.

Behind closed doors, the Republican elite were in full-blown crisis mode. The GOP was already battling the chaos of Plump's leaked assassination attempt, and now James Machiavelli had turned their political nightmare into a full-scale disaster.

An emergency leadership call had been convened, secure, encrypted, and off the official books. In a private Capitol Hill conference room, Senate Majority Leader Dick Scot stood at the head of the table, face flushed, fingers gripping the edge of the polished oak like a man holding back a dam on the verge of collapse.

Phones buzzed. Tablets flickered. Voices clicked in and out from across the country. Some appeared on large screens mounted along the wall. Others were audio-only, calling in from undisclosed locations or undisclosed levels of panic.

"This is unacceptable," Scot snapped, voice echoing slightly off the glass and paneling. "We cannot let this radical dictate terms to the United States Congress. We need to push back."

Across from him, Senator Joe Hawkton leaned forward in a stiff-backed chair, sleeves rolled up, his brow furrowed like a man halfway through defusing a bomb.

"Push back how?" Hawkton asked. "We don't even know what he has. If he actually has the receipts, we're screwed."

Congresswoman Kim Young, seated two chairs away, never looked up from her tablet. Her stylus tapped in sharp, staccato bursts, her focus absolute.

"We need to find out where this information is coming from and who his sources are," she said. "If we can discredit him before the first leak, we win."

Congresswoman Laura Robert, arms crossed, sat farther down the table, staring at the ceiling like it might offer divine intervention. She finally spoke with the weight of someone who had seen too many disasters from too close.

"And if we can't discredit him?" she asked. "If he drops irrefutable proof, we could see resignations by the dozens, maybe worse. We can't afford another scandal after the Plump debacle."

Scot turned sharply.

"So, what do you suggest?" he shot back. "Surrender? Roll over and let this man blackmail the government?"

Hawkton's hands opened in a slight gesture of caution. "I'm saying we need a strategy beyond just fighting back. We have to prepare for damage control."

"No." Kim looked up now, eyes cold and resolute. "We have to destroy him before he destroys us."

Robert leaned forward, elbows on the table. "Destroying him might not be an option. He's built a movement. If we go after him publicly, it only feeds the narrative that we're corrupt and afraid of him. Right now, half of the country is listening to him. If we make him a martyr, that number grows."

Scot turned away, his voice low and rumbling as he stared out a narrow window.

"So what?" he said. "Do we do nothing? That's political suicide. If we let him win, we lose control of Congress, the White House, hell, even our donors are going to panic."

"We need intel," Hawkton said. "We have no idea what he has. The worst thing we can do right now is make a move that backfires."

"We don't have the luxury of waiting," Kim snapped. "Every second we hesitate; he's controlling the narrative. If we act now, we can at least muddy the waters."

Senator Cindi Smith had been silent until now. She folded her hands in her lap and looked around the room.

"And how exactly do you propose we do that?"

"Leak something on him," Kim replied without hesitation. "Find something. Make something. If we create enough doubt around him before September 2nd, we can make this look like a stunt instead of a crisis."

Robert's eyes narrowed. "That's a dangerous game. If we fabricate something and he has proof of the real corruption, we'll be buried even deeper."

Scot slammed his hand onto the back of a chair. "What about the courts? Can we get an injunction? National security? Something?"

Hawkton shook his head deliberately. "Do you think a judge is going to issue an order stopping a man from exposing corruption? The second we try that, it confirms everything he's saying about us."

Kim set down her tablet, her voice growing harder. "Then we go with Plan B. Divide and conquer. We know there are people in Congress who are vulnerable. We need to find out who he's targeting first and turn them against him."

"You want us to throw some of our own under the bus?" Cindi asked incredulously.

"If that's what it takes to protect the party, yes," Kim said.

"This is insane," Scot muttered, pacing again. "If we sacrifice some of our own, we look like we're just scrambling to save ourselves. It gives him credibility. What we need is leverage over him. Something that forces him to back down."

"And what if he doesn't?" Hawkton asked. "What if we

threaten him and he doubles down? Do we have a plan for that?"

Kim's eyes glinted. "We have people looking into his past. If we can find something."

Cindi scoffed. "Do you think no one's tried that already? The man's been underground for over a year, and his support has only grown. If there was dirt, it would have surfaced by now."

Robert looked at the clock, her voice somber. "We might be out of time. If Congress doesn't act soon, the first leaks are coming. The question is: do we let that happen and react, or do we try to control the damage before it starts?"

"We need a contingency plan for both scenarios," Scot said, collecting himself. "Step one: We quietly reach out to moderate Democrats to see if there's any way to control the narrative on the budget. If we get ahead of it, we can claim partial credit and reduce the damage. Step two: We identify the most at-risk members of Congress and prepare responses for potential leaks. Step three: If Machiavelli refuses to back down, we go after him with everything we've got."

Hawkton folded his arms, voice steady but grave. "And if none of that works?"

Kim's words landed like a blade. "Then we do what we've always done. Adapt, survive, and make sure he doesn't win in November."

.   .   .

The Republican Public Response

Washington, D.C.–Today, the Republican leadership addressed the recent claims made by the Independent Presidential Candidate James Machiavelli, who has threatened to release damaging information about members of Congress unless certain budgetary demands are met.

We reject this attempt to subvert the democratic process through coercion and blackmail.

Standing behind a podium in front of a wall of flags and stern-faced aides, Senate Majority Leader Dick Scot read from a statement prepared in haste but designed for maximum control.

First and foremost, let us be clear: Congress is an institution founded on the principles of democracy, transparency, and the will of the American people. While political disagreements exist, we will not allow an anonymous figure, operating outside the bounds of accountability, to dictate policy under the threat of blackmail. This is not how a free nation operates.

His words were direct, forceful, and rehearsed. Cameras clicked. Reporters typed rapidly. Scot's expression remained unreadable.

The Republican Party has always stood for law and order. If Machiavelli possesses legitimate evidence of wrongdoing, we encourage him to follow the proper legal channels. The Department of Justice, the FBI, and various congressional ethics committees exist to investigate and address corruption. However, making vague, unsubstantiated threats in an effort to pressure lawmakers is not a pursuit of justice; it is an attack on the integrity of our democratic system.

His tone sharpened as he leaned against the podium.

Furthermore, we question the motives behind this campaign. Who is Machiavelli? Who is funding and supporting this effort? Is this an independent actor, or is this part of a broader attempt to undermine conservative leadership and disrupt the functioning of Congress? Given the politically charged nature of this threat, we urge the public to remain skeptical of sensationalist claims that serve only to sow division.

Scot's eyes locked on the cameras, driving home the core message:

It is no secret that the American people are frustrated with Washington. We understand those frustrations and share the desire for more transparency and accountability. That is why Republican leaders continue to push for reforms that reduce government overreach, cut unnecessary spending, and ensure taxpayer dollars are used responsibly. However, those reforms must come through open debate, not through fear and intimidation.

He paused for effect before continuing:

At the same time, we will not be distracted from our legislative priorities. The Republican Party remains committed to securing our borders, strengthening the economy, reducing inflation, and protecting American values. These are the issues that matter to hardworking citizens, and we refuse to let a political stunt distract us from serving the people who elected us.

And finally, the warning:

We also caution the media and the American public against taking any forthcoming "leaks" at face value. In today's digital world, misinformation is rampant, and foreign adversaries frequently attempt to manipulate political discourse. We will work diligently to assess any claims that arise, but we will not allow our legislative work to be dictated by anonymous actors who seek chaos rather than solutions.

He concluded with a tone of finality, an attempt at authority, but laced with the faintest thread of dread:

In closing, we reaffirm our commitment to serving the American people with integrity. If wrongdoing is discovered among any elected officials, Republican or Democrat, it should be handled through proper legal and ethical processes—not through coercion and blackmail. We will not be bullied into submission, nor will we allow distractions to hinder our mission of building a stronger, more prosperous America.

No questions were taken. The room cleared in silence.

But the storm hadn't passed. It hadn't even arrived.

24
INFIGHTING
PRESENT DAY
AUGUST 2028 — 7:00 P.M.

Washington D.C.

On the Democratic side, reactions were no less chaotic. The timing of Machiavelli's ultimatum could not have been worse. The Democratic National Convention was slated to begin the following week. A culmination of months of planning, coordination, and a carefully crafted message of party unity. Now, the message was in danger of being completely overshadowed by legislative panic.

In a private war room inside DNC headquarters, the top brass had gathered. The room was cold, clinical—fluorescent lights humming softly above polished steel chairs and a long walnut table cluttered with phones, briefing folders, and untouched coffee. The tension hung thick in the air.

DNC Chairman Ted Martin stood at the head of the table, fists planted firmly on its surface, jaw clenched. His voice cracked through the silence.

"This is deliberate. He knows exactly what he's doing. He's forcing us off our platform and into crisis mode."

House Minority Leader Joakin Jefferies sat across from him, leaning back slightly in his chair, arms crossed tightly over his chest. His eyes were sharp; his tone sharper.

"It's beyond deliberate. He's hijacking our moment and making it all about himself. He's not just an insurgent candidate; he's a wrecking ball with no concern for collateral damage."

Senate Minority Leader Beth Warren was pacing slowly near the windows, her heels tapping against the marble floor in a steady rhythm. She stopped, turned, and threw her hands up in frustration.

"And the worst part? We can't even ignore him. The media is eating this up, and now we're being forced to respond instead of controlling our own narrative. We've worked months, years, to craft this convention, and now it's all going up in flames."

Ted Martin's voice dropped into a growl as he pulled out a chair but remained standing. "He's an egotistical maniac playing a dangerous game. If we give in, we're admitting that this kind of political blackmail works."

Joakin leaned forward, placing his forearms on the table. "And if we don't, we're painted as corrupt. He's cornered us, and he knows it."

Beth stopped pacing and leaned her palms on the table. "So, what's the plan? How do we neutralize him before he derails everything?"

From the far end of the room, DNC Communications Director Patricia Hill, younger, composed but visibly rattled, clicked her pen and began scribbling notes on a yellow legal pad. She didn't look up as she spoke.

"We need to go on the offensive. Paint him as reckless, unhinged, and make the public question whether they really want a leader who governs by threat."

Ted Martin slowly lowered himself into his chair, sighing through his nose. "That's not enough. He's already convinced millions that he's some kind of messiah. We need something that shakes his credibility."

Joakin's eyes narrowed. "What if we force Congress into a counterattack? Call his bluff. If we make a strong public stand and dare him to release something, we might create doubt. What if he doesn't have as much as he claims?"

Beth's arms were now crossed, her weight shifted to one hip. "That's a hell of a gamble. If he really does have evidence about sitting members of Congress and drops it, we're dead in the water."

Patricia looked up, flipping a page. "Then we need an alternative attack. Something that questions his integrity. Who funds him? Who are his allies? If we can tie him to anything remotely suspicious, we shift the conversation from 'is Congress corrupt?' to 'who is really pulling Machiavelli's strings?'"

Ted nodded slowly. "That's our best bet. We dig into his past, his associates, and we hit back hard."

Joakin gestured toward a chart on the wall outlining convention week speakers and media hits. "And what about our budget negotiations? Do we try to appease him?"

Beth's voice was like ice. "Absolutely not. If we cave now, we set a precedent. What's next? Any outsider with a laptop and a grudge can hold Congress hostage? No. We stand firm. We make it clear that governance by extortion is unacceptable."

Patricia's voice cut in again, quieter, but focused. "We need to prepare for his next move. If he releases something, how do we respond?"

Ted leaned back, fingers steepled. "We discredit the source. We attack the timing. We frame it as a desperate stunt. We make it about him, not the people he's targeting."

Joakin shook his head. "The problem is, if what he releases is real, people won't care about our framing. They'll see it as truth versus deception."

Beth leaned in, her voice low but firm. "Then we make him the villain. We shift the story from corruption to instability. We say he's destabilizing the country, that his actions will have dire consequences. If we can make the public fear what comes next, we might turn this tide."

Patricia tapped her pen against the pad. "So, we paint him as a reckless demagogue who is threatening the foundation of democracy?"

Ted Martin gave a slow, grim nod. "Exactly. If we can't disprove his evidence, we make sure the country fears what happens if he gets what he wants."

Joakin sighed. "And what if that doesn't work?"

Beth stared out the window at the Capitol dome glowing under a stormy sky. "Then we pray that Machiavelli overplays his hand. If we wait long enough, he might make a mistake, and when he does, we'll be ready."

Democrats' Public Response

Washington, D.C.—The Democratic Party put out a statement that read:

The DNC unequivocally condemns the reckless and dangerous actions of the self-proclaimed Independent Presidential Candidate James Machiavelli. His blatant attempt to blackmail Congress, derail the democratic process, and hijack the national agenda is an affront to everything we stand for as a nation.

The timing of this ultimatum, mere days before the Democratic National Convention, makes his intentions clear. This is not about truth. This is not about justice. This is a calculated attack on democracy itself, designed to create chaos, manipulate public perception, and force lawmakers into submission. We refuse to allow our government to be held hostage by a single individual's threats.

. . .

Governance by Coercion is Not Democracy

Throughout American history, we have faced political challenges, controversies, and crises, but we have never bowed to blackmail. Today, we reaffirm our commitment to governing through integrity, debate, and the will of the people, not through extortion and fear. If Machiavelli truly possesses credible evidence of wrongdoing, we urge him to follow proper legal channels, as any responsible whistle-blower would. Instead, he has chosen the path of an insurgent, leveraging threats over transparency, coercion over accountability.

A Coordinated Effort to Destabilize Our Institutions

Let's be clear: This is not just about one man. It is part of a broader effort to undermine our institutions, weaken public trust, and throw the country into political turmoil. The timing, the strategy, and the tactics all point to a deliberate operation to disrupt the government at a critical moment. The American people deserve to know: Who is backing Machiavelli? What are his true motives? And what does he stand to gain from this reckless power play?

We Will Not Be Intimidated

Democrats remain steadfast in our commitment to the American people. We will not negotiate with blackmailers, nor will we allow legislative decisions to be dictated by anonymous threats. While we acknowledge the public's right to transparency in government, that transparency must come through due process, not through reckless leaks that could compromise national security, public trust, and the stability of our democracy.

Our Path Forward

- We Stand United—Despite this attempt to fracture our party and derail our convention, we will move forward with our platform, our policies, and our vision for a stronger, more just America.
- We Hold the Line—We reject any attempt to legislate under duress. No policy, no budget, and no decision will be made under the shadow of blackmail.
- We Investigate the Source—The American people deserve to know the full truth, not just about alleged corruption, but about Machiavelli himself. His background, his funding, and his real agenda must be scrutinized.

At a time when America faces real challenges like economic recovery, climate change, voting rights, and global security, we will not be distracted by political theatrics.

Machiavelli seeks to make himself the center of this story. We refuse to let him.

This is not just about Democrats or Republicans. This is about defending the integrity of our democracy. And in that fight, we will not waver.

25
DISINFORMATION WAR
PRESENT DAY
AUGUST 2028 — 3:00 P.M.

Palm Beach, FL.

Down in Florida, Ronald Plump was in a state of pure rage. The leaked tapes of him ordering Machiavelli's assassination had already weakened him. Now, Machiavelli's ultimatum threatened to finish the job.

He stormed through the gold-trimmed halls of his estate, red-faced and muttering under his breath, his fist clamped around his phone. Staffers pressed against the walls as he passed. Once he reached his lounge, he collapsed into a leather armchair and began pounding out messages on Truth Social, his fury splashing across the screen in block caps and exclamation points.

"Machiavelli is a total fraud!
A liar! A LOSER! He has
NOTHING! Just another Deep
State PUPPET! SAD!!!"

In the adjacent war room, a crisis meeting was already underway. Stephen Pabst, Nickolas Greene, and Hope Candles sat beneath the soft glow of recessed lights, the air thick with cigar smoke and dread. A television on the wall replayed Machiavelli's ultimatum on a loop.

Tension crackled. No one leaned back. Everyone perched forward, arms crossed or tapping nervously against the table, watching Plump's political power threaten to unravel.

Pabst broke the silence. "We hit him back hard. Discredit him, call him a foreign plant, whatever it takes. If we don't crush him now, he'll control the narrative by morning."

Greene shook his head. "That's suicide. If we overreact and he's holding more tapes, we look guilty. We go too far, we lose the middle."

Before he could continue, the door burst open.

Plump stormed in, his phone still in hand. "Lose the middle?" he barked. "You think I care about the middle? The base loves me. The people know the truth. Machiavelli's a clown, a fraud, a nobody!"

"Sir," Greene began carefully, "the recordings—"

"I don't care about recordings!" Plump snapped, pacing in tight circles. "I'm the victim here! Everyone knows it!"

Hope Candles rose from her seat, tablet in hand. "With respect, sir, the numbers don't agree. Machiavelli's driving the news cycle. Every network's running his ultimatum on loop. We need to change the story before—"

"I am the story!" Plump roared, pointing at the TV. "Look at the likes! Look at the engagement! They're all talking about me!"

No one answered. The silence was louder than his shouting.

Pabst finally spoke. "The base isn't enough anymore. Independents are tuning in. The NSA's confirmed the tapes are real. And those reports about your labor practices."

Plump froze. His jaw tightened.

"Fake news," he muttered, though quieter this time.

Greene echoed the warning. They needed a strategy. If they struck too early and Machiavelli had something real, the entire operation could implode.

Plump nodded approvingly. "That's the spirit," he said. "Now get it done."

As his team dispersed to carry out the assault, Plump leaned back in his chair once more, seething.

Machiavelli had dared to challenge him.

That was a mistake.

A mistake Plump intended to make him regret.

Plump's Public Reaction

"Machiavelli is a TOTAL FRAUD!
A Deep State puppet! FAKE NEWS
is pushing his lies because
they're DESPERATE!!! They know
I'm winning!!!"

"Another WITCH HUNT! First
Russia, then Ukraine, then the
rigged election, now this!
They NEVER stop because they
FEAR ME!!! But the American
people KNOW THE TRUTH!!!"

"Where's Hunter? Where's the
Epstein list? The real
criminals walk free while they
try to smear me! This is
election interference!!!"

26

COLLATERAL HEARTS

PRESENT DAY

AUGUST 2028 — 11:00 A.M.

Manhattan, NY.

[Scene opens with the hosts of *The View* seated at their table, the audience buzzing with anticipation. Paola Machiavelli, elegantly dressed but with a somber expression, sits across from them.]

The show's moderator, Ana Navarro, leans in, her voice both empathetic and inquisitive. "Paola, thank you so much for being here today, especially with everything your family has been through. We all saw your husband's interview with Harold Stern just a few days ago, and now, here you are. How are you holding up?"

Paola takes a deep breath, her gaze steady. "Thank you, Ana. It's been... a lot, to say the least. But I'm here because people deserve to know the truth about what happened to us."

Sunny Hostin, never one to shy away from hard questions, chimes in. "And we want to hear the truth. Can you walk us through what happened the day you and your children were taken into protective custody?"

Paola nods, her voice composed as she begins her story. "Of course. That morning started like any other. I was driving my eldest son to work, and my youngest to school. We were just talking about the day ahead. My youngest was worried about a test. My eldest was making plans with friends for the weekend. Nothing seemed out of the ordinary."

She pauses, a slight tremor in her voice. "Then, as I pulled into the shopping mall where my eldest works, a black SUV cut me off. I was startled, of course. At first, I thought it was some reckless driver or maybe security. But then, a man stepped out, walking toward my car with a sense of purpose. There was an intensity in his eyes, but he wasn't aggressive. He knocked on my window and asked me to step out."

Ana, visibly alarmed, gasps. "Did he identify himself right away?"

Paola responds with a shake of her head, her eyes narrowing as she recalls the fear that surged through her. "Not immediately. That's the part that scared me. My first instinct was to lock the doors and drive away, but something told me to hear him out. That's when he finally pulled out his NSA badge and said, 'Mrs. Machiavelli, you don't have to come with us, but you and your family are in immediate danger. I've been given orders to get you to safety.'"

Sunny, her tone heavy with concern, says, "That had to be terrifying. What was going through your mind at that moment?"

Paola's face softens with a mixture of regret and resolve. "Everything in me was screaming not to trust him. I mean, as a mother, your first instinct is to protect your kids, and running seemed like the safest option. But the way he spoke, he wasn't forceful. He was patient. He could tell I was skeptical, and he understood. That was what convinced me this wasn't some kind of kidnapping."

But within her mind, the truth is closer, rawer. *My heart hammered so loudly I thought the children could hear it. Every instinct screamed to fight, to run, to protect.*

"So, after a few moments, I told my kids to get out of the car, and we went with them. I had no idea what was happening, only that it was serious."

Ana, trying to absorb the gravity of the situation, asks, "And they took you to a safe house?"

Paola responds, her voice thickening with emotion. "Yes. It was only after we arrived that they told me the unthinkable. President Plump had ordered the assassination of my entire family."

The audience gasps in disbelief, and the hosts exchange shocked glances. The tension in the air is palpable.

Sunny, her eyes wide with disbelief, says, "When you heard that… what was your initial reaction?"

Paola's hands grip the edge of the table as she answers, her voice trembling. "Disbelief. Complete and utter disbelief. I thought it had to be some kind of mistake or a cruel joke. I even dismissed it when they played the first recording. But I played along because I needed time to process it all."

Ana leans forward, her eyes searching for understanding. "What changed? What finally made you believe it?"

Paola closes her eyes for a moment, as if reliving the haunting realization. "It wasn't until nearly two weeks later, after they had staged our deaths for our own protection, that I heard the second recording. That's when it hit me. This was real. This wasn't paranoia or political games. Someone had tried to erase my family from existence."

Inside, the memory is a storm. *Erase us. I remember the rage that boiled in me that night, the kind of fury that doesn't fade. The thought that if I could get my hands on the man who signed off on this, if I could look him in the eyes, there would be nothing civilized about what I'd want to do. I'd cut off his balls and stuff them down his throat, make him choke on the pieces of himself the way he tried to make my family choke on fear.*

And then the thought grows darker, colder. *No… even that would be too quick. Too merciful. What he deserves isn't a sudden end; it's to feel every ounce of dread, every suffocating second of helplessness that he forced on us. A slow unraveling. Pain measured out carefully, the way he measured out our destruction. Not an execution. A lesson.*

Sunny, her voice barely above a whisper, asks, "And during this time, you were completely cut off from James?"

Paola nods solemnly. "Yes. We weren't allowed to communicate with him for security reasons. It wasn't until three days after I heard the second recording that we were finally reunited. That was one of the hardest parts—not knowing if he was safe or even alive."

Ana, her voice filled with empathy, responds, "That must have been incredibly difficult. But you've also mentioned that despite everything, you were well taken care of?"

Paola nods again, her gaze softening. "Yes. Oddly enough, we were living better than we ever had in our little two-bedroom apartment. They made sure we had every-thing we needed. It never felt like we were prisoners. It just felt necessary. Temporary, but necessary."

Sunny, still trying to absorb the depth of Paola's experi-ence, replies, "I can't even imagine. And now, here you are, alive, speaking out, just as your husband has. What do you want the American people to take away from your story?"

Paola's expression hardens with determination as she looks directly into the camera. "That the truth matters. That corruption at the highest levels of government is real. And that if *my* family could be targeted, anyone can. But we are not afraid. We survived, and we are here to make sure this never happens again, to anyone."

Ana, moved by Paola's courage, says, "Paola, thank you

for your bravery and for sharing your story with us today. We hope you and your family continue to stay safe."

Paola's eyes flicker with gratitude as she responds, "Thank you for giving me this platform to speak. The truth has to come out."

As the commercial break comes, Ana Navarro turns to Paola with a reassuring smile. "Paola, thank you again for sharing your incredible story. We're going to bring in the rest of the hosts now, and they'll have some questions for you as well."

She gestures towards the other hosts, who are preparing to join the conversation. "We'll be right back with more from Paola Machiavelli."

The camera cuts to a quick teaser of the upcoming discussion, heightening anticipation for what's to come, before smoothly transitioning back to the stage.

The View returned from commercial break, the studio audience buzzing with energy as Sara Haines turned to the guest seated across from her. "Paola, that is just such an incredible story," she said, her voice tinged with admiration.

Alyssa Farah Griffin, never one to miss an opportunity for a sharp remark, quipped, "I mean, I've heard of political enemies, but Plump trying to assassinate Machiavelli? That's a new one. Someone's been reading too much history and taking all the wrong lessons."

The audience chuckled at her wit, but Ana Navarro, ever the force of focus, leaned in. "Okay, let's move on. You and your husband came out of nowhere, and in a month's time, you have the entire political community panicking. Honestly, we know very little about you and your husband. Let's get to know you. Tell us what your lives were like before the assassination attempt."

Paola smiled, but there was a weight behind her expression. "Honestly, we are the same people we were before. It's just that our circumstances have changed. My husband is very quiet, soft-spoken, and a deep thinker."

Sunny Hostin raised a skeptical brow. "Really? He hasn't been very quiet as of lately."

Paola laughed. "Well, he can't be now. What everybody should know is that my husband is not a politician. He hates politics because he hates the fact that our lives, the everyday American people's lives, are just a game to be won by these people."

The room grew still as the weight of her words settled in. This wasn't just another political family with an agenda. There was something different about them. Something raw.

"My husband is a process improver," Paola continued, her voice steady. "And then he likes to continually improve that process so that it is the best for as many people as possible. He can't be quiet because it is his job not to be. And he has always been a great worker. These politicians may say that he can't lead, or that he doesn't know what he is doing because he hasn't done it before. They couldn't be further from the truth. He will do it better than any of them because he isn't concerned with getting the credit. He isn't concerned with perception. And he definitely doesn't care what people think of him. He only cares about getting the best result, regardless of how it happens."

She took a breath, her hands resting calmly on the table, though her energy was anything but calm. "That is why we were saved from being assassinated by that bitch Plump, because there was already a network of over ten million Americans building on top of my husband's ideas, which laid the foundation. They asked him to lead this movement because of who he is as a person."

The silence that followed was not one of discomfort, but of understanding. The weight of truth had been laid bare, and the world was finally paying attention.

To understand the significance of this moment, one must first understand who James Machiavelli truly was. Before the attempt on their lives, before their names became a rallying cry across the nation, James and Paola Machiavelli were an unassuming couple leading an ordinary life, or so it seemed.

James was not a man of theatrics. He never sought the limelight, nor did he hunger for power. If anything, he had spent his life avoiding it. A man of intellect and discipline, he found satisfaction in structure, in the refinement of efficiency, in the relentless pursuit of improvement. He had no interest in the game of politics. To him, governance should be about results, not rhetoric. And yet, in a cruel twist of fate, the very system he despised had forced him into the arena.

Paola had always been his balance. Where James was

introspective, she was expressive. Where he analyzed, she felt. Together, they had built a life that revolved around progress, not for personal gain, but for the betterment of those around them.

Their journey into the public eye had not been voluntary. It had been thrust upon them the moment the assassination order had been uncovered. The revelation that President Ronald J. Plump had orchestrated an attempt on their lives sent shockwaves through the nation. The NSA's confirmation of the authenticity of the records only solidified the gravity of the situation.

Why had they been targeted? Because James Machiavelli, a man with no political aspirations, had inadvertently become the most dangerous man in America. His ideas, practical, unshackled by the constraints of party lines, focused solely on what worked—had gained traction in ways no one had anticipated. His disdain for the inefficiency and corruption of government resonated with millions who were tired of being pawns in a game they never agreed to play.

The movement had started small, a ripple in the ocean of political discourse. But ripples, when aligned with the tides of history, could become tsunamis. And the movement that started with James Machiavelli's thesis had become a tidal force, not by choice, but by necessity.

As the commercial break ended, the audience settled back into their seats, eagerly anticipating the final segment of "The View" featuring Paola Machiavelli. The camera panned across the hosts, each of them visibly excited and intrigued by their guest's candid and often unpredictable nature.

Alyssa Farah Griffin leaned forward with a warm smile. "So, Paola, tell us how you and your husband met."

Paola chuckled, shaking her head slightly as she reminisced. "We met in EMT class. He had actually let his certification lapse, so he had to take the course again, and I was taking it for the first time."

Sunny Hostin tilted her head curiously. "So, did you hit it off right away?"

Paola let out a small laugh. "Yes, and no. We got along fantastically from the get-go, but he's a very shy and reserved person. We actually didn't start dating until after the class had ended, even though we had a marvelous time in that class."

She paused, shaking her head as if recalling a particularly ridiculous memory. "I remember we were practicing assisting a patient going through childbirth, and the dummy that was used only provided the bottom half of a woman— stomach, legs, and vagina. We had this young kid in our group who was kind of a talker and decided to go first. So, he walks right up to the dummy's vagina and starts speaking to it like he was talking to the patient."

Ana Navarro gasped, already laughing before Paola could finish.

Paola grinned. "James, my husband, looks at this kid and goes, 'What the fuck are you doing, officer? Why don't you ask her for her license and registration?' Then he takes out his own driver's license and sticks it right through the dummy's vagina, like the vagina was handing the license to the kid."

The studio erupted into laughter, the hosts nearly falling out of their chairs.

Sara Haines, wiping tears from her eyes, managed to ask, "What was your reaction?"

"I was laughing so hard because I was wondering, 'What the fuck is going on?'" Paola said with fun sass, making the audience roar even louder.

Ana, still catching her breath, said, "Okay, so you start dating your husband, and at the time, he is a single father with a five-year-old."

Paola interjected, "First, I had to ask him out. And second, he had a son who was in the process of being diagnosed with autism. Furthermore, his son's mother was living her worst life with an abusive husband, that she ditched her son for."

Sunny's eyes widened. "Oh man, that situation would have sent me straight for the hills."

Paola nodded. "Seriously, it crossed my mind. But James was very kind and annoyingly honest. Plus, the first time I met our son, Luciano, we hit it off. I'm not sure why. My only guess is because he reacted to the calm his father had around me. But the first time we met, he reached for my hand to hold. James looked at me, stunned, and was like, 'He has never done that before.' Then we took him out for ice cream, and as we were leaving, Luciano was holding my hand while James walked behind us. James said something inappropriate, per usual, so I swung my arm back to playfully smack him in the stomach, but I accidentally hit him square in the balls."

The hosts gasped and then burst out laughing again.

Paola smirked. "Luciano just lost it with laughter as James doubled over in pain, and I had my hands covering my mouth, trying not to laugh. To his credit, James just smirked because he knew it was worth the pain for his son to have another meaningful connection with somebody. From that point on, we never looked back."

Alyssa smiled. "Wow, that is incredible."

As the audience clapped, Ana turned back to the camera. "Our final segment with Paola Machiavelli after this break."

As the show resumed, Ana Navarro leaned in, her tone shifting slightly. "Now, Paola, we have to ask about your husband's ultimatum. There's a lot of talk about what he plans to do if Congress and President Plump don't take action."

Paola tilted her head, a knowing smirk on her lips. "Well, let's be honest. He doesn't believe Congress and Plump can get it done. So, he already has fifty scandals ready to release on day one."

The studio went silent for a beat before the hosts erupted into questions.

Sunny's eyes widened. "Wait, I thought he said only twenty scandals would be released on day one?"

Paola nodded. "You're right, twenty Congress members. The other thirty? Mega donors from both parties, Republican and Democratic committee members, and some high-profile media members and CEOs."

Sara sat back in shock. "Did he just forget to mention that a few days ago?"

Paola chuckled. "Nope. This has been part of our overall strategy. We planned for me to release these facts on this show, my first national interview. And we wanted it to end with a bang."

The audience gasped as the realization hit. Ana leaned back, shaking her head. "Well, Paola, you certainly didn't disappoint. This will definitely be making headlines."

Paola shrugged with a smirk. "That was the plan."

Alyssa, still processing, leaned forward. "Do you think this level of exposure will backfire? Surely, some very powerful people won't take kindly to this."

Paola's expression remained unbothered. "Oh, they're already scrambling. We've been tracking their moves for weeks. They thought they had more time, but we don't operate on their schedule."

Sunny let out a low whistle. "Damn. This is going to be a political earthquake."

Ana nodded. "And on that note, we're out of time. Paola Machiavelli, thank you for joining us today. This was one unforgettable interview."

As the audience applauded, the screen faded to black, but the buzz in the studio was just beginning.

27
UPRISING
PRESENT DAY
AUGUST 2028 — 10:00 A.M.

Washington D.C.

After Paola Machiavelli's stunning amendment to her husband's threat, the impact was immediate and seismic.

Members of Congress who had planned to extend their vacations rushed back to Washington, abandoning their leisurely summers in the Hamptons, Martha's Vineyard, and Aspen. The corridors of the Capitol became a war zone of frantic negotiations, whispered side deals, and desperate calls to lawyers and PR teams. Some members even took private meetings with Machiavelli's representatives, hoping to find a way to mitigate their risk.

There was no escape.

The American people, long accustomed to congressional

inaction, watched in awe as their elected officials, who had historically taken months, if not years, to pass meaningful legislation, suddenly worked at a breakneck pace. With their reputations, careers, and perhaps even freedom on the line, lawmakers did the unthinkable: they put aside their differences and got to work.

Over the next two weeks, the impossible happened.

Education funding, which had been neglected for decades, received a significant boost, ensuring better teacher salaries, improved school infrastructure, and more resources for students in underprivileged areas. The budget also expanded funding for senior citizens, increasing Social Security benefits and ensuring better healthcare coverage for retirees. Military personnel, often used as political pawns, finally saw real benefits, higher wages, better housing options, and improved access to mental health services.

The American people rejoiced. For the first time in years, a budget had been passed that actually prioritized their needs rather than corporate interests or party agendas. But as September 1st approached, one crucial hurdle remained: President Plump.

The bill landed on Plump's desk late in the afternoon on September 1st. His aides were divided. Some urged him to resist or risk looking weak, while others, particularly those with deep ties to the mega-donors now at risk of exposure, pushed him to sign. Machiavelli's threat had sent shockwaves beyond Congress, striking fear into the billionaire class, media conglomerates, and powerful CEOs who had long operated with impunity. They leaned on Plump, reminding him that if he didn't give in, their secrets might soon be next.

Plump, notorious for never wanting to appear weak, initially dug in his heels. He saw signing the bill as an admission of defeat, a move that would shatter his carefully cultivated image of dominance. But then, the pressure mounted. The mega-donors, the same people who had funded his campaigns and propped up his political machine, issued an ultimatum of their own: Sign the bill, or they would pull their financial support. The threat was too great to ignore. Even Plump, the self-styled political fighter, could not afford to alienate his wealthiest backers.

The President, never one to bow to pressure without making a spectacle of it, remained silent for most of September 2nd. The deadline loomed. The press speculated wildly. Social media exploded with theories. Would he sign? Would Machiavelli make good on his promise? Would the American people finally see what happened behind closed doors?

At 7:45 p.m. Eastern, mere minutes before the deadline, Plump finally stepped before the cameras. With a smirk and a dramatic flourish, he signed the bill into law, stating, "I always planned to sign this. Believe me, folks, it's the best budget. A tremendous budget."

The nation exhaled. The revelations were avoided for now.

The moment was historic, but the ramifications would

be felt for years to come. The American people had witnessed the impossible: a government that had worked for them under the threat of exposure. The Machiavelli's had forced Congress and the President's hand, proving that when politicians were held accountable, real change could happen.

Some members of Congress, especially those who had fought against the bill, seethed with rage. They knew they had been backed into a corner, and many would seek retribution. But for the everyday American, the message was clear. Power could be wrestled from the elite if wielded correctly.

28

BROGAN LIVE

PRESENT DAY

SEPTEMBER 2, 2028 — 3:00 P.M.

San Antonio, TX.

Joe Brogan sat in his usual spot, leaning back in his chair with a mix of curiosity and amusement as he addressed the man sitting across from him. "Well, they passed the budget, and Plump signed it fifteen minutes before the deadline," Brogan said, shaking his head. "Although he really didn't give credit to anybody."

Machiavelli nodded slowly. "He also didn't really take credit himself. He also didn't lie. It is the best budget we've had in decades. For a man who just signed a budget that greatly benefits the American people, this is probably the least we've ever heard him speak."

Eminem, leaning forward with an intense expression, interjected, "It's because you exposed those motherfuckers for the frauds that they are. We just proved that with the proper motivation, real change can be achieved, and it doesn't need Congress to take years to get it done."

Machiavelli, always measured, replied, "But first, we need to give credit where credit is due. Behind the scenes were millions of people within our network who built this budget and worked with Congress to shape it. None of this would have happened without them. They are the real heroes of the American people. You have to give credit to all the Congress members and President Plump for passing this budget."

Joe was stunned. "Wow, I wasn't expecting to genuinely give credit to Congress members and President Plump for passing this budget."

Eminem smirked. "Joe, this man's only focus is providing the best possible government for the American people. He doesn't care about credit. He treats everybody as his equal, or better, and he will only wield power for the good of the American collective, never for himself. That's what I hope people learn about Don."

Joe squinted, confused. "Don?"

Eminem's smirk widened. "Don Machiavelli. He made those motherfuckers an offer they couldn't refuse."

Joe laughed so hard he nearly fell out of his seat, while Machiavelli offered only a slight smile, clearly embarrassed by the attention.

Eminem leaned forward, pointing at Machiavelli. "This dude just punked Congress and that bitch Plump, and he shies away from any compliment. I'll tell you, Joe, the more I learn about this man, the more I believe this is different. He's becoming a ghetto superstar, and still, he wants to defer all the praise and accolades onto others because he knows they deserve it. That's why people love working with him. He is just another cog in the wheel, and he will do his job to the best of his ability because he doesn't want to let you down. That is a leader."

Machiavelli, shaking his head, replied, "You like me so much because you know that I am not stupid enough to rap one of your songs like these dumb fucks who think they are cool. They are too self-centered to realize that they shouldn't be doing it."

Eminem groaned. "Like that dumb fuck Vivek. Fuck, don't remind me."

Machiavelli chuckled. "That dumb fuck should lose himself where nobody can find him ever again."

Joe, still chuckling, shifted gears. "So, Eminem, what are your thoughts on Machiavelli?"

Eminem leaned back, rubbing his chin. "I had a conversation with someone in Machiavelli's network the same day he made that threat on Harold Stern. What I learned was wild. They knew the Republicans, the Democrats, and Plump would respond with defiance. Machiavelli wanted them to. That was always the plan—to have Paola Machiavelli drop the amended threat after they made their first move. She's brilliant. She's cerebral. She wanted to expose them as the true puppets they are."

Joe raised an eyebrow. "Wait, so they knew exactly how everyone would react? That's some 4D chess shit."

Eminem nodded. "Exactly. They played right into it. They thought they were standing their ground, but really, they were just walking into a trap."

Machiavelli smirked. "People in power get predictable when they think they're untouchable."

Joe shook his head in disbelief. "That's crazy. So, you're telling me this whole thing was premeditated? The initial threat, their reaction, Paola's response—it was all planned?"

Eminem leaned forward. "100%. They set themselves up. And once they exposed their true priorities, it became easy to show the American people who they really serve."

Machiavelli shrugged. "Politics is just another form of strategy. The only difference is I'm not playing for power; I'm playing for the people."

Joe, still digesting this, pulled up the latest poll numbers. "So, get this. In just six weeks, Machiavelli has skyrocketed to 20%. Gavin Newtsum, the Democratic nominee, is at 35%, Plump at 37%, and 8% are undecided."

Eminem buried his face in his hands. "Come on, Joe."

Joe, confused, shrugged. "What?"

Eminem shook his head and sighed. "You really don't see the problem with that?"

Joe frowned. "It's a poll. What am I missing?"

Eminem looked over at Machiavelli. "Hey James, you want to take this one?"

Machiavelli nodded. "Sure thing. So, this poll got 2,107

responses. Yet the headline reads that 'most Americans believe Plump is the best candidate.' Let's break it down: 843 people out of 2,107 is 38%. Last time I checked, America has about 350 million citizens, and more than 270 million are of voting age. How the hell is 843 people 'most Americans'?"

Joe leaned forward. "Okay, but isn't that just how polling works? They take a sample and try to make it representative?"

Eminem scoffed. "That's the illusion, Joe. They make you think it's representative, but in reality, it's manipulated. Who were these 2,107 people? What states are they from? Are they mostly older conservatives? Are they from rural areas? Are they college-educated? Are they voters who actually show up to the polls? The way they select these people determines the outcome of the poll before it's even taken."

Machiavelli added, "And let's not forget the phrasing of the questions. That's another way they rig the results. If you ask, 'Do you think Plump has done a good job on the economy?' and give people a 'yes or no' answer, that's going to be different from asking, 'Do you think Plump's policies have personally benefited you?' One sounds like an approval question; the other forces people to think about their own situation. Polls are as much about psychology as they are about numbers."

Joe sat back, absorbing it. "So, you're saying the media uses these polls to shape public perception rather than reflect it?"

Eminem snapped his fingers. "Bingo! That's exactly it. They don't report on what people think. They tell people what to think by making it seem like 'most Americans' already believe something. It creates peer pressure. If you see a poll saying, 'most Americans think Plump is the best candidate,' then people who are undecided might start thinking, 'Well, maybe he is the best choice.' It's social conditioning."

Joe whistled. "That's some manipulative shit."

Machiavelli nodded. "It's not just about manipulation. It's about control. If they can control the narrative, they can control how people vote, how they think, how they react. That's why independent media and real discussions like this are so important. Because we can actually challenge the bullshit."

Joe exhaled heavily, running a hand through his hair. "Damn. That's a fair point. I never really thought about it like that."

Joe scrolled through more notes. "Speaking of media, Fox News and CNN viewership are still declining. There are even rumors they've reached out to you for interviews."

Machiavelli smirked. "The rumors are true, but we've declined."

Joe raised an eyebrow. "You don't think it'd be worth going on, even just to call them out on their bullshit live?"

Machiavelli shook his head. "Not on their terms. They control the narrative in those settings, and I'm not about to play their game."

Eminem's eyes lit up. "You know what? That gives me an idea. You should agree, but only if it's a joint broadcast. Make it like a podcast format. Hell, we can have Joe and Harold Stern on to keep it real. One host from each network joins, but Joe and Harold livestream in case Fox or CNN try to pull the plug mid-show."

Joe leaned forward. "Oh, shit. That would be insane. They'd never go for it, though."

Machiavelli perked up. "That's the point. If they say no, it proves they don't actually want the truth. And if they say yes, we control the discussion. Either way, we win."

Eminem laughed. "Now we're thinking like gangsters. Force their hand, give them no way out."

Joe grinned. "Damn, man. You really operate on another level. And what if Plump dodges the debate again?"

Machiavelli leaned back, arms crossed. "Then I give him until the start of the show to commit to a debate on October 8th, or I release more dirt on him. Gavin Nutcum has already accepted the debate."

Joe burst out laughing again. "Gavin Nutcum? Jesus, man."

Eminem shook his head, grinning. "This is what I mean. This guy doesn't give a fuck about playing by their rules. He plays by the people's rules."

Machiavelli shrugged. "That's the only way change happens."

Joe chuckled. "Man, I hope this actually happens. The internet would explode."

Eminem leaned in. "Oh, it's happening. And if it doesn't, we make sure everyone knows why."

The studio fell into silence for a moment. Then, Brogan leaned in. "So, what's next?"

Machiavelli's eyes darkened with focus. "We keep exposing the game. We keep fighting. And we make sure the American people win."

Eminem nodded. "And if they don't listen?"

Machiavelli smirked. "Then we make them listen."

Joe raised an eyebrow. "What's on your schedule next?"

Machiavelli answered, "We're still following the same schedule, town halls in all the cities Plump was supposed to rally in. Meanwhile, he's hiding in Washington, only holding small events for the American Oligarch class."

Eminem chimed in, grinning. "I can't believe how you're able to reach the people so efficiently and do it while only spending a fraction of the cost that the Republicans and Democrats are spending. I have never heard a campaign tell people to keep their money 'don't donate, we have enough money to complete this campaign.' That's crazy. I mean, it's honestly impressive. I can't wait until Plump finally decides to stop hiding from you and gets back out on the campaign trail, so you can continue to punk his bitch ass at his rallies."

Joe smirked. "You're still going to confront him at every one of his rallies?"

Machiavelli leaned forward. "Hell yeah, I am. It's about showing up, not just talking. He's all about the spectacle, the drama. Well, we can do that too, but with real issues on the line. It's not about playing to the rich and powerful; it's about connecting with the everyday person. I want people to feel like they actually matter, not just spectators."

Eminem nodded, his expression serious now. "I like that. It's different from what anyone's done before. It's not just politics; it's personal. You're in it for the long haul."

Joe chuckled. "Sounds like you've made up your mind, Machiavelli. So, when do you hit the road again?"

Machiavelli stood up, his smile widening. "Tomorrow. We have work to do."

Joe gave him a firm handshake. "Good luck, man. You're not just running a campaign; you're starting a movement."

Machiavelli's eyes glinted with resolve. "It's not about luck. It's about making it happen."

The conversation came to an end, but the sense of urgency and purpose in the room lingered. The interview had been a glimpse into something larger than politics. There was little doubt that the road ahead was going to be tough, but Machiavelli wasn't the type to back down.

The Joe Brogan Experience had never felt more like history in the making.

29
BOOT CAMP
17 MONTHS AGO
FEBRUARY 2027 — 6:00 P.M.

Undisclosed Location

J ames Machiavelli sat by the fireplace, the glow of the flames casting long shadows across the richly furnished living room of the secure compound. His oldest son, Luciano, sat on the couch, pretending to read but clearly too restless for the words to sink in. Every so often, his eyes darted toward the window, as if expecting danger to materialize at any moment. Angelo, only twelve, shuffled a deck of cards on the coffee table, his movements quick and fidgety. James's heart tightened. His boy should be carefree, laughing, not trapped in a cage of fear and secrets. He could hear the rhythmic breathing of his wife, Paola, sitting beside him, her hands wrapped around a cup of tea, its steam curling into the air. Weeks had passed since the assassination attempt ordered by the President of the United States, and though they were technically safe here, James could feel the vulnerability pressing down on them all like a vice. A gilded prison was still a prison.

The soft knock at the door broke the silence. It was the former Chief of Staff. His background as a military officer was evident in his measured movements and the way his sharp eyes scanned the room, assessing every detail. He carried the aura of a man who had seen war, who had faced danger head-on and lived to tell the tale.

His gaze flicked toward the boys, then back to James and Paola. "Take a walk with me. We need to talk."

James felt Paola's eyes on him. A silent question. A silent fear. He gave her the faintest nod before turning to Luciano. "Watch your brother, okay? We won't be long."

Luciano closed the book and set it aside, his expression firm, his voice steady. "Got it." There was no trace of the boy he once was—only a young man shouldering responsibility, determined to be more than just the son protected in the shadows. James saw it, and the mixture of pride and sorrow twisted inside him like a blade.

James let out a heavy sigh before stepping outside. The chilly night air wrapped around him as the past unfolded before his eyes once more.

They walked alongside him in silence for a moment before speaking. "You both know the security teams will do everything in their power to protect you. But let's be realistic; if someone wants you dead badly enough, they'll find a way. You need to be ready for that."

James exhaled heavily. "We understand the risks. But we're not soldiers. We don't have your training. What do you expect us to do, become warriors overnight?"

The former Chief of Staff met his gaze with an unwavering stare. "I expect you to survive. And for that, you need training. Real training."

He handed James a leather folder. Inside there were four names and photographs.

"David Boone, former Marine Recon. Ruth Vega, Marine Recon. Marcus Caldwell, Army Ranger. Nathan Carter, Navy SEAL." Hayes pointed to each name as he spoke. "These are the best in their units. And they are the best trainers. They've all agreed to work with you to make sure you both learn the fundamentals of combat, survival, and strategy."

Paola set down her tea. "What kind of training are we talking about?"

"Intensive," he replied. "Four hours of basic boot camp activities each day, strength training, endurance, weapons handling. Two hours of strategy and reconnaissance, so you can think like an operative. And two hours of policy simulations, because knowledge is just as important as firepower."

James exchanged a look with Paola. He saw the doubt flicker in her eyes, but also the fire. She was no stranger to struggle; he'd always admired that stable resilience. It was daunting, but necessary. He clenched his jaw and nodded once. "When do we start?"

The first morning came brutally early. The sky was still painted in darkness when Boone and Vega stormed in to wake them. Boone's voice was gravel and authority, barking orders like a whip-crack, while Vega's sharp-eyed gaze cut through them with surgical precision. "On your feet!" Boone ordered. "Outside, now!"

James and Paola scrambled out of bed, throwing on their training gear and stepping into the cold morning air. The crisp mountain air was a stark contrast to the warmth of the cabin, shocking their senses awake.

"Drop down. Push-ups. Now!" Boone commanded.

James hesitated for a split second too long, and Vega was on him. "Move it, Machiavelli! You think an assassin's going to wait for you to get comfortable?"

Shame flushed through him, and he hit the dirt. His palms pressed into the cold earth, each push-up a reminder of how soft he'd grown. Paola dropped beside him, her movements fueled by subdued fury. At the world... at their situation... at the men who had forced their family into hiding. She would not be broken.

By the time they moved onto sprints, James's lungs were on fire. He wanted to stop, but every glance at Paola's determined face pushed him forward. She would not quit—and he refused to fail beside her. Boone and Vega were relentless shadows, barking, pushing, breaking them down.

After what felt like an eternity, Boone called a halt.

"Good start," he said gruffly. "But you've got a long way to go."

Back at the clearing, Caldwell and Carter were waiting. Caldwell, the former Army Ranger, was stocky with a no-nonsense demeanor, while Carter, the SEAL, carried himself with a sober confidence that spoke of experience in the most dangerous missions.

"Now the real work begins," Caldwell announced. "Weapons training."

James and Paola were handed firearms, and Carter stepped forward. "First, you learn safety. Then, you learn accuracy. Then, you learn how to use it under pressure."

The next two hours were a crash course in marksmanship. Paola took to it quickly; her steady hands and keen focus allowed her to hit her targets with impressive precision. James, on the other hand, struggled at first, his shots inconsistent. Caldwell stepped in, correcting his grip and stance, making minute adjustments that gradually improved his aim.

The morning continued in a grueling cycle of physical and mental exertion. They practiced hand-to-hand combat, learning how to disarm an opponent, how to break free from holds, and how to use their surroundings as weapons.

By the time the first session ended, James and Paola were exhausted but resolute. They returned to their room in the compound for a brief respite before the next phase began.

Vega and Caldwell led strategy and reconnaissance

training. Maps were spread across the table as they discussed tactics, surveillance, and counter-surveillance.

"Knowing how to fight is one thing," Vega said, "but knowing when to fight is another. More importantly, knowing when to avoid a fight altogether."

They were taught how to scan an environment, how to spot potential threats before they materialized, and how to think several steps ahead of an adversary. Caldwell ran them through scenario after scenario, forcing them to think critically under pressure.

The final two hours of the day were dedicated to policy simulations, a test of their ability to navigate the political landscape even under duress. The former Chief of Staff himself led these sessions, presenting them with real-world crises and challenging them to find solutions while under constant scrutiny.

"It's not just about surviving," he told them. "It's about maintaining control. Your enemies don't just want you dead, they want you discredited, broken. You must be unshakable."

By the end of the first day, James and Paola collapsed onto their bed, every muscle screaming in protest. But beneath the exhaustion was a fire. They were no longer just victims of an attack; they were preparing to take control of their own fate.

30
REACHING OUT
PRESENT DAY
SEPTEMBER 2028 — 11:00 P.M.

Manhattan, NY.

[Stephen Colbert steps onto the stage, his usual grin widening as the audience erupts in applause. He waits a beat, soaking it in before raising his hand to soothe the crowd.]

"Ladies and gentlemen, welcome to *The Late Show*! We have a rare show for you tonight. We're shaking things up with a different format because, well, we have some extraordinary guests. Joining us tonight are the Independent Presidential Candidate James Machiavelli, his wife Paola, his brother Giovanni, and his sister-in-law Rachele."

The audience claps again, their excitement palpable.

"Now, James Machiavelli has been making waves. The guy is rising in the polls at an unprecedented rate, especially after successfully, and let's be honest, brilliantly extorting Congress and President Plump into signing what is being called the best yearly budget for the American people in recent memory. And it doesn't stop there. Eminem, a huge supporter and member of the Machiavelli campaign, just dropped a remix of *The Real Slim Shady* called *The Real Slim Velli*, which has gone viral. I even caught my staff singing it in the hallways today. Business leaders like Mark Cuban, Bill Gates, and Steve Ballmer are rallying behind him. Military leaders, veterans, senior citizen advocates, education groups, and this independent candidate is pulling support from everywhere!"

The applause is deafening as Stephen gestures toward the entrance. "Let's bring them out!"

James, Paola, Giovanni, and Rachele step onto the stage, waving at the audience. They take their seats as Stephen shakes hands with each of them.

As they settle in, Stephen leans forward. "Before we even get into things, I have to say, security was intense tonight. I felt like I was being screened for the CIA."

Giovanni smirks. "Hell yeah, it is. We've pissed off some very powerful and very corrupt people."

He leans slightly to the right, looking over to their head of security, Nathan Carter, raising his voice just enough so he could hear. "What were you telling me earlier? That you've identified one-hundred-thirty-seven potential threats in the past month and neutralized thirteen actual attempts?"

Nathan, standing at attention near the edge of the stage,

corrects him. "Fourteen neutralized attempts. We had one just fifteen minutes ago."

Stephen blinks in shock. "Wait, what happened?"

Nathan remains composed. "A young man, posing as an aide attempted to infiltrate the dressing room area with a 3D-printed gun. New York's finest have taken him into custody, and our network is already tracing who may have sent him."

Giovanni chuckles. "I stand corrected... fourteen attempts neutralized."

Stephen shakes his head. "That is insane."

Paola leans in with a wry smile. "Don't be so shocked, Stephen. The President isn't the only one trying to kill us."

Rachele adds, "Yeah, providing truth and reality to the masses is dangerous. The people who control the narrative aren't thrilled with us right now."

Stephen exhales dramatically, then claps his hands together. "Okay, let's lighten the mood before I have a full-blown panic attack right here at my desk. Speaking of shaking things up, Eminem's remix, *The Real Slim Velli*... Hilarious! I have already listened to it like ten times. It's brilliant."

Giovanni grins. "Hey Stephen, let's have your audience watch the music video."

Stephen looks puzzled. "What music video?"

Rachele chimes in, "Oh yeah, Eminem wanted to premiere the parody music video right here on your show. Someone just handed it to your producers."

Stephen turns toward his producer, who gives him a thumbs-up. "If we're good, play it. I need to see this."

The studio darkens as the music starts. The familiar beat of *The Real Slim Shady* kicks in, but with a twist. The audience erupted into cheers as the lyrics began.

"May I have your attention, please? May I have your attention, please? Will the real Slim Velli please stand up? I repeat, will the real Slim Velli please stand up? We're gonna have a problem here!"

The crowd roars as clips flash across the screen, Eminem dressed in a colonial wig, rapping from a mock Oval Office, then cutaways to him dodging cartoonishly exaggerated political attacks.

Stephen is already laughing, pointing at the screen. "Oh my God, he's actually dressed like Machiavelli!"

The video continues:

"Obama don't gotta cuss in his speeches to win elections. Well, Velli does, so fuck him and fuck you too. You think he gives a damn about an election? Half of you critics can't even stomach him, let alone stand him. But Velli, what if you win, wouldn't it be weird? Why, so you guys could just lie to get him here? So, you can sit him here next to Senator Spears? Shit, President Plump better switch me chairs. So, he can sit next to Vlad Poutine and Felon Musk and hear 'em argue over who Plump gave head to first. Little bitch put me on blast on OAN."

The audience cheers as Eminem in the video throws stacks of fake money into a flaming trash can labeled "Congressional Budget."

By the end of the song, Stephen is wiping tears from his

eyes, barely able to catch his breath from laughing so hard. The audience is in hysterics, clapping and cheering wildly.

Paola smirks. "That Eminem is a true genius."

Stephen, still chuckling, shakes his head. "James, we're nearly a third of the way into this show, and you haven't said a thing."

Giovanni pats his brother on the shoulder. "This is how my brother usually is. He's a deep thinker and a superb listener. He doesn't care about being the center of attention. Right now, he's just thinking, 'Hey, you're all having a great time; I don't need to add anything. Why ruin the flow?'"

Stephen chuckles. "Okay, but I do need your thoughts on many in the business community supporting your campaign."

James finally spoke, his voice calm yet powerful. "First, Stephen, I have to say this is all very humbling. It's overwhelming in the best way. The efficiency of this network is beautiful to watch. None of this would have happened without everyone working together, from Eminem, to my wife, my children, my brother, my sister-in-law, our legal team, most of whom are working pro bono, our security, strategists, policy writers, IT teams, simulation teams, media teams, content creators, ground teams spreading our message, and their families who support them. What they've built is extraordinary, and America will be better because of their hard work. I hope the American people are forever grateful because I know I am."

The audience erupted in applause. James let the

moment breathe, his words sinking into the collective consciousness of those gathered. He knew that politics was a performance, but he was determined to make his message real. This wasn't about optics. It was about the future of a country teetering on the edge of change.

Stephen leaned in, his journalistic instincts honing in on the moment. "And what about business leaders? Why are so many backing you?"

James nodded, his expression serious. "Most business leaders would rather invest in their personnel than in a political party. They're tired of having to play the game, donating just to get a fair shot, lobbying to remove unnecessary barriers, or in some cases, just to be able to run a business in this country. They know I'm not here to milk them for kickbacks. I care about making sure the American people have jobs, better wages, and better benefits. Some business leaders like the system the way it is because it keeps them at the top. But I'm here to spread the wealth. That makes me hard to control. Because I'm not selfish. And that, Stephen, is why they hate me. That's why they fear this movement."

A murmur of agreement rippled through the audience. James had seen firsthand how the political system had been rigged for those at the top. He had spoken with business owners, both small and large, who were frustrated with the status quo. The honest ones wanted change. The corrupt ones wanted him silenced.

One such business leader, seated in the front row, gave a

knowing nod. He had been part of corporate America for decades and had seen how the system rewarded the few at the expense of the many. He had chosen to back James, not because it was safe, but because it was right.

James continued, his passion intensifying. "I want to make something very clear. A strong economy isn't just about stock prices or GDP growth. It's about people, workers, families, communities. A company thrives when its employees thrive. Yet for too long, our system has prioritized shareholders over workers. We've seen wages stagnate while executive bonuses skyrocket. We've seen jobs shipped overseas for cheaper labor, leaving American families struggling. That's not capitalism; that's exploitation."

The applause grew louder. James took a breath, glancing at the crowd. He saw the faces of hardworking Americans. Teachers, nurses, factory workers, entrepreneurs. They were the backbone of the country, and they deserved better.

"So why are business leaders supporting me? Because I'm offering them a better deal. A system that rewards innovation, hard work, and ethical leadership. I'm not here to punish success; I'm here to ensure success is shared. The best businesses understand that when workers have fair wages and decent benefits, productivity goes up, loyalty goes up, and communities flourish. The old way of doing things isn't just unethical… it's unsustainable."

Stephen leaned forward, intrigued. "James, you talk about spreading the wealth. But let's be real, some people hear that and immediately think 'socialism.' What do you say to that?"

James smiled, unfazed. "I say that's a lazy argument. What I'm talking about isn't socialism; it's economic fairness. It's making sure workers get a fair return for their labor. It's making sure small businesses have a chance to compete. It's making sure corporations pay their fair share. The irony is, the same people who cry 'socialism' when we talk about helping working-class Americans have no problem with corporate welfare, tax loopholes, and billion-dollar bailouts. They've been redistributing wealth upwards for decades, and no one called that socialism. I'm just trying to level the playing field."

The crowd roared in approval. James was cutting through the noise, exposing the hypocrisy that had plagued politics for too long.

A woman in the audience stood up, a small business owner who had struggled to keep her company afloat during economic downturns. "James, what do you say to small business owners like me who feel squeezed between big corporations and rising costs?"

James met her gaze. "I say you deserve a government that works for you, not just for the giants. Small businesses are the lifeblood of this country, yet they face higher tax burdens, predatory lending, and monopolistic practices that make competition nearly impossible. Our administration will push for policies that level the playing field, tax breaks for small businesses, stricter regulations on monopolies, and accessible capital for entrepreneurs. You're the job creators too, and you deserve support."

She nodded, hope lighting up her face. She wasn't alone in her struggle, and James had given her something too many politicians had failed to deliver, acknowledgment.

Stephen wrapped up the conversation. "James, you've given us a lot to think about. Any final words for the American people?"

James straightened, his voice steady. "Yes. We have a choice. We can keep playing by the old rules, where power is hoarded and opportunity is rationed. Or we can build something better. An economy that works for all of us. I believe in the American people. I believe in our ability to rise, to innovate, to come together. This movement isn't just about me; it's about us. And together, we will change this country for the better."

The standing ovation that followed wasn't just applause. It was a statement.

"By the way, congratulations," Stephen said, leaning forward again. "It was announced today that a judge had dismissed the Plump campaign slander lawsuit against you."

Paola smirked. "That lawsuit never stood a chance. When is the truth slander?"

The audience roared in agreement. Colbert chuckled and shook his head. "A piece of gossip coming out of the courtroom was that Plump's attorneys argued you couldn't remark about the size of his penis without providing proof."

Rachele, sitting comfortably beside Paola, interjected

smoothly, "To wit, our attorney said, 'Just because we haven't provided the proof doesn't mean we won't.'"

Stephen's jaw dropped in mock shock. "So that really happened?"

Rachele nodded solemnly, then leaned into the microphone. "Yes, micropenis really had his lawyers argue this in court. What's worse is that the money they're spending on his legal fees is coming directly from the Republican National Committee's financial resources. He's using money from benefactors to dispute penis size in court."

The crowd exploded again. Stephen's eyebrows shot up as he let the sheer absurdity of the statement settle in. Before he could react, Rachele continued with a mischievous glint in her eyes. "The truth is, it's up to Plump when we reveal this information. If he wants the world to see the proof, all he has to do is not agree to the October 8th debate. We are not Russian to prove this information." She paused dramatically and gave the audience a huge wink and smile.

Stephen covered his face with his hands, laughing uncontrollably. "Oh my God," he said between chuckles. "You're saying…"

Giovanni leaned in, his voice cutting through the din. "Plump will never agree to a debate where he has to stand on the same stage as my brother, with my brother much closer to him than his security team."

Stephen, still recovering from laughter, managed to ask, "Why is that?"

Giovanni didn't hesitate. "Because he's a fake tough guy.

His whole life, he's had other people do his dirty work. At heart, he is a fuckin' pussy. Just look at what happened at the Harrisburg Rally. You can play the footage."

On cue, the studio screen lit up with a clip from the Harrisburg rally. The audience quieted slightly as the video played. Plump's face was the focal point, his expression shifting rapidly as Machiavelli's team approached. The color drained from his skin. His lips trembled. His eyes darted around, searching for a way out. Then, as soon as he saw the Secret Service stepping in, his fear vanished, replaced by faux bravado.

Stephen watched the footage intently before turning back to the panel. "Wow. That's... something."

The studio erupted in a mixture of laughter and murmurs. Giovanni shrugged. "It's who he's always been. Without security, he's a coward. That's why he won't debate. That's why he hides behind lawsuits. He needs a system to shield him because he's not built for an actual fight."

Paola chimed in, "And the best part? He knows we're telling the truth. He wouldn't be panicking otherwise."

Stephen shook his head in disbelief. "So, let me get this straight. Plump's campaign donors are paying for a lawsuit about his... let's say, inadequacies. And now, you're saying he has a chance of preventing this 'proof' from coming out by debating?"

Rachele grinned. "That's right."

Stephen exhaled dramatically, running a hand through

his hair. "That might be the single most insane political strategy I've ever heard."

Giovanni crossed his arms. "It's not insane if it works."

The crowd burst into laughter again as Stephen pointed at him. "Fair point." He turned back to the camera. "Ladies and gentlemen, I don't know what's going to happen on October 8th, but I know one thing: we are all about to witness the most hilarious political game of chicken in history."

As the segment wrapped, the energy in the studio remained electric. Whether Plump would take the bait was uncertain, but one thing was clear: this was a moment that would not be forgotten anytime soon.

31

THEY WILL NOT WIN

PRESENT DAY

SEPTEMBER 2028 — 6:00 P.M.

Savannah, GA.

The Mercer Theatre was alive with energy, the kind that sent shivers down spines and left hearts pounding in anticipation. Every seat was filled, the aisles brimming with eager attendees who had come to witness history in the making. The air buzzed with conversation, speculation, and an undercurrent of sheer excitement as the crowd awaited the arrival of James and Paola Machiavelli. Their names had become synonymous with defiance, justice, and, most importantly, results.

When the couple finally emerged onto the stage, the response was immediate and deafening. The thunderous applause was not just admiration; it was gratitude. It was the sound of a people who, for the first time in decades, felt seen, heard, and truly represented.

James and Paola paused at center stage, letting the over-whelming appreciation wash over them. Paola, poised yet radiant, acknowledged the crowd with a warm smile before taking her seat beside her husband. James, ever the composed leader, raised a hand, and gradually, the applause softened to a murmur.

The evening's format was simple: an open forum, unfil-tered questions, unvarnished answers. No dodging, no scripted responses, just the truth.

The first question came from an elderly gentleman in the front row. He stood with a slight wobble, adjusting his glasses before clearing his throat. "First, I just want to say thank you. For years, we've watched politicians promise the world and deliver nothing. But you two... you made them do their jobs. My question is: How long do you think you'll be able to extort Congress into doing what they were elected to do?"

The room burst into laughter, the man's bluntness hitting a chord with the audience. Even James let out a chuckle before responding. "My goal isn't to always extort Congress. Blackmail only goes so far. Believe it or not, there are members who are tired of being extorted by their polit-ical parties and mega-donors. These members of Congress are realizing that there is a better way, especially if our network is successful in this election."

The audience murmured in agreement, heads nodding, eyes glinting with understanding.

James continued, his tone unwavering. "For those who benefit from the system as it is now, well, I have no problem making them fall in line out of fear. We've already exposed the corruption of Senator Shift, Congresswoman Lime, President Plump, and senior leaders from Fox News and CNN. Eventually, we will weed out these career politicians and replace them with real Americans, people who care about something more than their own power."

A new round of applause thundered through the theatre. The audience wasn't just supportive; they were emboldened. The Machiavelli's hadn't just changed policy; they had changed the people's expectations of government.

Another question came from a middle-aged woman in the back. "Paola, you have been instrumental in reshaping how political negotiations work in Washington. What do you think was the most important shift that made this budget possible?"

Paola leaned forward, her eyes sharp with intellect and passion. "It was a combination of pressure and transparency. Washington has operated in the shadows for too long. Politicians make backroom deals, cushioned by the assumption that the public either won't notice or won't care. We shattered that illusion. Every deal, every vote, every meeting was put under scrutiny, and we forced those in power to make choices they could no longer hide. The people held them accountable. That pressure made the difference."

The crowd erupted in applause once more.

The next question came from a woman standing in the front row. "It's been almost two months since you announced your VP choice, Newt Ork, but no one has seen or met him. What's going on?"

Paola leaned forward to answer. "Unfortunately, with all the security concerns, we need a succession plan in case my husband is assassinated before the election."

A hush fell over the room at her words.

"I pray that never happens, but from a security stand-point, it is much easier to protect one candidate rather than two at this stage. That's also why you haven't seen our sons on the campaign trail. We've already survived one assassination attempt from the President, and our enemies have only grown since then. We must be cautious, but make no mistake, we are prepared."

There was a solemn silence, followed by a murmur of agreement. The people knew that what Paola was saying was not paranoia. It was reality.

A man in the back, his voice filled with concern, stood up. "If you're expecting that level of danger, how can we protect you? How can we make sure this movement doesn't die if something happens to you?"

James nodded solemnly. "That's the right question. This movement was never meant to be about me or Paola alone. It's about all of us. If something happens to me, you stand by Paola. If something happens to Paola, you stand by Newt Ork. And if something happens to all of us, you stand by the truth we've built together. The power of this movement isn't in a single leader; it's in the will of the people."

The theatre erupted in a mix of applause and steely resolve. They understood now more than ever that this was bigger than one election, bigger than one budget.

The third question came from a young man in his twenties, his voice carrying an earnest curiosity. "You've talked a lot about fixing our government, but how do you plan on changing the election process?"

Paola took the microphone again, her expression thoughtful but determined. "Right now, politicians spend more time campaigning than they do governing," she said. "Every decision is filtered through how it plays in the next election cycle instead of what's best for the people. We need a structured campaign season with strict limitations on election activities outside that period. Other democracies already do this—and they do it well. In the United Kingdom, national campaigns typically last only a few weeks between the dissolution of Parliament and election day. In Canada, federal campaigns are legally capped at a few dozen days. Japan limits political advertising and requires equal media access for all candidates. These systems keep leaders focused on governing between elections instead of running perpetual campaigns. We can learn from that discipline."

She paced slightly, her voice gaining momentum. "What

those examples show is that a healthy democracy doesn't need endless fundraising and nonstop election coverage to function. It needs clarity, structure, and accountability. A set campaign window would level the playing field, reduce the influence of money, and force candidates to make their case directly to voters instead of relying on years of donor-driven advertising. There's no reason we can't adopt a similar model—one that restores focus to governing rather than politicking. But that's just the beginning."

She paused, scanning the room to ensure she had everyone's attention. "We also need government analytics to measure the impact of our elected officials, something like baseball's WAR statistic, but for legislation. Citizens need tools to evaluate their representatives effectively, to hold them accountable. Alongside that, we need an educational platform that empowers the public to understand these metrics and apply them in future elections."

The crowd murmured, captivated by the idea of a more informed electorate.

"Moreover," Paola continued, "the current system discourages quality candidates from running due to astronomical campaign costs and the overwhelming dominance of political parties. We must overhaul the candidate selection process to create an environment that elevates the best candidates, regardless of their background or affiliation. Every American should have a voice in choosing candidates, not just party elites."

The audience nodded in agreement, their murmurs growing louder. The notion of reforming elections was daunting, but Paola's words painted a vision that made the task feel not only possible but essential.

The final question came from a man in military uniform, his posture rigid and his tone respectful. "How do you plan on improving the lives of military families?"

James stood and walked to the edge of the stage, his gaze sweeping over the crowd before locking onto the soldier. "Restoring trust between the government and its citizens starts with taking care of those who risk their lives to defend this country."

He paused, his voice steady yet filled with conviction. "We need to increase financial compensation for service members, expand educational opportunities, and enhance career prospects for both active-duty and retired personnel. Post-service benefits must be improved, and we must ensure that military families have a better work-life balance. It's unacceptable that the people who sacrifice the most often receive the least in return."

The soldier nodded, his expression softening, and the audience responded with a round of applause, acknowledging the gravity of James's words.

With the final question answered, James and Paola stood side by side at the center of the stage. James looked out at the crowd, his face a mask of determination. "We are not here to make empty promises. We are here to fight for you, for your families, and for the future of this nation. This is only the beginning. With your help, we will reclaim our government and return it to the people."

The crowd erupted in cheers, its collective energy surging through the theater. Security began ushering James and Paola off the stage, navigating them through the dense crowd of supporters. Hands reached out, some shaking theirs, others offering words of gratitude and support.

Then, in an instant, the atmosphere shifted.

A man emerged from the crowd, his movements swift and deliberate. Clutched in his hand was a switchblade; his eyes locked onto James Machiavelli's back. The security team, caught off guard, was too slow to react. But Paola wasn't.

Her instincts, sharpened by months of training at the compound, kicked in. She saw the threat before anyone else. In a blur of motion, she intercepted the man's wrist, twisting it with a speed and precision that left no room for error. The weapon flew from his hand, and before he could recover, Paola leveraged her weight, driving him to the ground with a controlled force, pinning him beneath her knee.

The security team surged forward, securing the attacker in a matter of seconds. Gasps rippled through the crowd as they processed the danger that had just unfolded.

James turned to see his wife standing over the subdued assailant, her chest heaving but her demeanor unwavering. He rushed to her side, his eyes scanning her for any sign of injury. "Are you okay?" he asked, his voice taut with concern.

She nodded, her face betraying no sign of fear. "I'm fine."

Paola stood tall, facing the crowd with a calm yet fierce resolve. "This is exactly why we fight," she said, gesturing to the restrained attacker. "Because there are those who would rather silence us than see change." Her gaze hardened as she spoke, her voice unwavering. "But they will not win. We will not back down."

The audience erupted in applause once more, their admiration for Paola's quick thinking and courage fueling their resolve. The tension in the room had transformed into a renewed determination.

After the Machiavelli's were escorted out of the theater under heightened security, James turned to Nathan Carter, his head of security. There was an unmistakable heaviness in his voice as he spoke. "This was my fault. I wasn't paying enough attention to where I was in relation to Paola, and I inadvertently spread the team too thin. All of you, please forgive me. It was my mistake that put all of your lives, including mine, in danger. I owe my wife and the entire team my deepest thanks for keeping us safe."

Nathan Carter, clearly moved by James's remorse, embraced him with a firm hug. "James, it's because of who you are that everyone believes in you," he said quietly, his words laced with sincerity. "It's an honor to work with you. We're all in this together."

James nodded, a sense of gratitude and responsibility settling over him. "I won't make the same mistake twice. I'll do better. I owe it to all of you."

As they moved out, the weight of the evening's events hung heavily in the air. But in that moment, one thing was clear: the Machiavelli's were in this fight for the long haul, and they were ready to face whatever challenges came next.

32
THE MACHIAVELLI SURGE
PRESENT DAY
SEPTEMBER 2028 — 10:00 P.M.

Undisclosed Location

Machiavelli had surged over 5% in the national polls after his audacious maneuver to strong-arm Congress and the Plump administration into passing a budget that actually addressed the needs of everyday Americans. In contrast, Plump had slipped by 4%, falling behind Democratic nominee Gavin Newtsum. Internal polling within the Plump campaign painted an even grimmer picture. Machiavelli's numbers weren't just rising; they were accelerating. If the trend continued, he could very well overtake Plump before the election. The realization sent shockwaves through Plump's inner circle, throwing his already chaotic re-election campaign into a full-blown crisis.

· · ·

The Budget That Changed Everything

Machiavelli's budget was a populist masterstroke, a calculated gamble that had paid off spectacularly. Education, long neglected in favor of corporate tax cuts and military-industrial contracts, saw unprecedented funding increases. Now, teachers received livable salaries. Ending decades of being underpaid and overworked. School infrastructure projects were being fast-tracked, and for the first time in years, underprivileged students saw an actual change in their classrooms. Senior citizens, an often-overlooked demographic despite their electoral significance, received substantial increases in Social Security benefits and improved access to healthcare.

But Machiavelli hadn't ignored the military, a critical voting bloc. Unlike previous administrations that merely paid lip service to supporting the troops, his budget delivered real, tangible benefits: increased wages, better housing, and expanded mental health services. By appealing to both economic populists and disaffected conservatives, he had built an unstoppable coalition.

The result? Machiavelli's base was electrified, and his momentum seemed unstoppable.

Chaos Inside the Plump Campaign

Legal battles, internal discord, had already marred Plump's re-election bid and declining public trust. Now, with Machiavelli closing in, the pressure was at an all-time high.

Internal polling from within Plump's campaign revealed a disturbing truth. While national polls showed Machiavelli trailing by 14%, their private numbers suggested the gap was much narrower. Worse still, focus groups indicated that undecided voters, those crucial swing votes that had determined the last two elections, were overwhelmingly gravitating toward Machiavelli.

Inside Plump's war room, the mood was grim. "We need to go on the attack," Pabst insisted. "Machiavelli has weaknesses. He's a political outsider, sure, but he's also unpredictable. We hammer him on experience, make him seem reckless."

Plump wasn't convinced.

"People like reckless," he grumbled. "I was reckless. They voted for me."

"But he's making you look weak, sir," Hope Candles interjected carefully. "He's the one setting the terms. The budget fight? That was his win. Now he's the one challenging you to a debate, on his terms."

That more than anything, irritated Plump. He had always been the one in control of the narrative, but Machiavelli had flipped the script. Worse yet, the ultimatum over the October 8th debate put Plump in an impossible position. If he refused, Machiavelli's camp would release damning information. If he accepted, he would walk into a debate where he could no longer rely on the tactics that had worked in 2016, 2020, and 2024. Interrupting, deflecting, and overpowering his opponents with sheer bravado.

Adding to the pressure, Gavin Newtsum had already agreed to the October 8th debate with Machiavelli. Now, Plump was facing mounting demands from major donors to enter the debate as well. His base was shrinking, and every day he stayed out of the spotlight, he lost more ground. The Republican National Committee was in full panic mode, knowing that if Plump didn't step in soon, Machiavelli would continue to define the race uncontested.

The Rachele Bombshell

Rachele, James Machiavelli's sister-in-law, had dropped one of the most shocking accusations in modern political history. The video clip of Rachele on The Late Night with Stephen Colbert went viral, running nonstop.

"To wit, our attorney said, just because we haven't provided the proof doesn't mean we won't," she declared, smiling confidently as the studio audience gasped.

Colbert, ever the showman, leaned in. "So that really happened?"

"Yes," Rachele confirmed. "Micropenis really had his lawyers argue this in court. What's worse is that the money they're spending on his legal fees is coming straight from the Republican National Committee's campaign fund. He is using donor money to argue penis size in court."

The audience erupted. Social media exploded. Within hours, #Microgate was trending worldwide.

. . .

The Fallout

The revelation was devastating, not just because of its content, but because of the sheer absurdity. Plump had weathered dozens of scandals, from hush-money payments to allegations of foreign collusion, but this was different. It was humiliating. It was petty. And it was exactly the kind of scandal that stuck in the public consciousness.

Worse still, it put Plump in a bind. Machiavelli's camp had made it clear: if Plump refused to debate on October 8th, they would release proof. The nature of that proof remained unclear, but the implication was enough to send Plump's team into full damage control mode.

At 3:00 a.m., Plump took to Truth Social.

```
"Fake news trying to push a
debate that nobody wants!
Machiavelli is a FRAUD. He
forced a corrupt Congress to
pass a TERRIBLE budget.
America will see through this
scam!!!"
```

The post generated millions of interactions, but it did little to change the reality: Machiavelli was rising.

And the clock was ticking.

Meanwhile, another crisis was unfolding, one that threatened to turn Machiavelli into an untouchable political figure. Just hours earlier after his Savannah, Georgia, Town Hall at Mercer Center, an assassin had attempted to stab him from behind in the midst of a cheering crowd. His own wife had thwarted the attack in a dramatic and unexpected fashion.

The footage went viral instantly. Social media was flooded with images of Paola standing defiantly as security took control of the situation. The hashtags #IronFirst-Lady and #MachiavelliSurvives dominated the online discourse.

The assassination attempt only solidified Machiavelli's growing legend. The image of a man so feared by the establishment that someone had tried to take his life, only to be saved by his fearless wife, was more powerful than any campaign ad. His supporters rallied behind him like never before, his approval numbers skyrocketing in the aftermath.

Plump's camp, already struggling with #Microgate, found themselves drowning in an even greater nightmare. The optics were clear: Machiavelli was a fighter, literally and politically, while Plump looked weak and evasive.

Machiavelli wasn't just rising. He was becoming inevitable.

33
FULL DISCLOSURE
PRESENT DAY
SEPTEMBER 15, 2028 — 6:00 P.M

Los Angeles, CA.

An hour before the Fox News and CNN joint interview with James Machiavelli, the political world erupted. The Plump campaign made a bombshell announcement, officially agreeing to an October debate against Democratic nominee Gavin Newtsum and Independent candidate James Machiavelli. News stations scrambled to dissect the implications, but inside the venue, two journalists were dealing with a far more personal crisis.

In their individual dressing rooms, Fox News rookie reporter Kyndra Anderson and CNN rookie reporter Samantha Kale received unexpected manila envelopes. Each contained damning evidence, not just about their respective networks but about their own lives.

James Machiavelli exhaled sharply as he stepped into the dimly lit dressing room of Kyndra Anderson. The tension in the air was thick, laced with an impending sense of doom that neither of them had orchestrated but both were about to unravel. Kyndra, sitting in front of a mirror, turned at the sound of his entrance. Her face was pale, her fingers still clutching the manila envelope she had received moments ago.

"You read it?" Machiavelli asked, his voice even.

Kyndra nodded, her lips pressing into a thin line. "I... I don't understand. Why would they do this? Why now?" Her voice quivered as she looked down at the email thread once more. The correspondence between two senior executives at Fox News revealed a discussion about her termination. One executive questioned why she was being discredited when it was the other who had originally recruited her. The response was chilling:

"Our relationship has run its course. She's a liability now."

Kyndra's eyes widened as she hesitated before reaching for it. "What is it?"

His expression darkened. "A conversation. A recorded one. In a company men's restroom. A conversation that proves there wasn't a relationship. That you were coerced. That you were assaulted."

The words hung in the air, a suffocating truth that Kyndra wasn't ready to confront. Her body tensed as tears welled up in her eyes. "So, you're going to blackmail me too? How did you even get this?"

Machiavelli shook his head. "No. I'm giving this to you because what happened to you was vile. And you're part of the American people, people who've been played, manipulated, and silenced. It's time to take your power back. You can release it tonight during the interview. You can release it during his trial. Or you can choose never to let it see the light of day. That decision is yours."

Kyndra stared at the flash drive, her breath uneven. "Why are you doing this for me? I'm supposed to rip you apart in this interview."

A small, tired smile tugged at the corner of Machiavelli's lips. "Because it would be wrong. I don't play politics. I'm tired of people in power fucking us over and making us turn against each other."

A single tear slipped down Kyndra's cheek. She wiped it away quickly and gave him a small nod. "I understand."

Machiavelli turned, knowing his next stop was just as heavy, if not heavier. He excused himself politely and made his way to Samantha Kale's dressing room at CNN.

Samantha Kale was pacing when Machiavelli entered. Unlike Kyndra, she had already ripped open her envelope, the damning documents scattered across the table in front of her. Her eyes snapped up at him, and the grief in them was raw.

"Is this real?" she asked, her voice hollow.

Machiavelli simply nodded. "Yes."

The documents laid out before her were even worse than she had imagined. A legal and financial paper trail exposing how CNN had accepted bribes to bury an investigative report about Michael Redman, the CEO of a Green Cleaning Service. Redman's company claimed to produce 100% biodegradable, sustainable cleaning products. But in reality, leaked internal research proved that the chemicals never fully broke down in landfills and oceans. Worse, they had seeped into the drinking water of a New Jersey town, leading to a devastating health crisis. In the past five years, one in four residents had been diagnosed with severe health issues; one in three were either terminal or already deceased.

Samantha let out a breathless, bitter laugh. "My parents lived in that town. Both of them. And now they're both dead. And CNN... my own network buried the story?"

"They did. And they were paid handsomely for it." Machiavelli stepped closer and slid an envelope across the table to her. "I thought you should see this too."

With trembling hands, she picked it up and pulled out the contents. Her breath hitched as she read the letter from the law firm. "They're reopening the case? Pro bono?"

He nodded. "And that..." he pointed to the second document "is a copy of the arrest warrant for the judge who dismissed the first case after receiving a kickback from Redman."

Samantha's legs gave out, and she sank onto the couch,

covering her mouth with one hand. "How did you get all this? Why are you giving this to me?"

Machiavelli crouched down to meet her eye level. "Because you needed to see what the people you work for are capable of. And because you, your children, and your community deserve justice. I expect nothing from you. In thirty minutes, you can walk out there and do your job, tear me apart, smear me, whatever they've ordered you to do. I'll understand. But justice will happen regardless of how tonight plays out."

She wiped her eyes, a deep, shaky breath filling her lungs. "For fifteen years, Redman made an extra thirty million dollars annually, and it only cost him two million to escape accountability."

Machiavelli's jaw clenched. "That's the game. The one we were never meant to win. But it doesn't have to stay that way."

Samantha set the documents down carefully, as if they were sacred. When she looked up, her eyes were clear. "Your network... you really mean it, don't you? 'Doing the right thing because it's the right thing' that's not just a slogan to you."

Machiavelli smiled faintly. "It never was."

She exhaled and straightened her shoulders. "Well, I guess we'll see what happens out there."

He nodded, knowing that whatever happened next, the truth was finally in the right hands.

34
THE SIT DOWN
PRESENT DAY
SEPTEMBER 15, 2028 — 6:00 P.M

Manhattan, NY.

The studio buzzed with electric tension as the countdown began. The stage was set for what promised to be one of the most controversial and revealing interviews in recent history. James Machiavelli, a political disruptor known for his unapologetic approach and razor-sharp insights, sat confidently at the center of the roundtable. Flanking him were Fox News rookie reporter Kyndra Anderson, CNN rookie reporter Samantha Kale, and two broadcasting legends, Joe Brogan and Harold Stern. The world was watching, and Machiavelli knew it.

The cameras rolled, and the host's voice rang out. "Ladies and gentlemen, welcome to what will undoubtedly be an explosive discussion. Tonight, we have James Machiavelli, a man who has shaken the foundations of the political establishment. This interview is being broadcast and streamed live, so if any network cuts the feed, rest assured, the truth will still get out."

James Machiavelli adjusted his skater shoes beneath the table, his signature black cargo shorts hanging loose as he leaned forward in his chair. The bold orange shirt he wore, "Guns don't kill political careers, I kill political careers" stretched across his chest, a smirk playing at the corner of his lips as he took in the nervous energy from the two rookie reporters seated across from him. To his left, Joe Brogan sat with arms crossed, studying the situation with a mix of curiosity and amusement, while Harold Stern adjusted his microphone, ready for the spectacle to unfold.

"Before we start," Machiavelli said, looking directly into the camera, "I want to remind everyone watching that this interview is being streamed live on YouTube, Twitch, Facebook, Twitter, and Truth Social. Just in case Fox or CNN cuts the feed early, you won't miss a thing. That would be incredibly embarrassing for them, and also very costly." He winked, letting the statement hang in the air before Kyndra Anderson, the young Fox News reporter, took a breath and launched into the first question.

"Mr. Machiavelli, I just want to start by saying I'm glad you're safe. The assassination attempt on your life at the Savannah, Georgia, Town Hall rally just a few days ago shocked the nation. My question to you is, what have you learned since that attack?"

Machiavelli exhaled, shaking his head slightly before responding. "What I've learned is that corruption doesn't have a party, and power doesn't discriminate. A Democratic mega-donor working in tandem with a prominent Republican think tank orchestrated the attempt on my life. The money trail is clear, shadow accounts funneling funds through the think tank and straight to the assassin. But that's not even the most disturbing part." He paused, letting the tension build before continuing. "I also uncovered the kind of information they never wanted to see the light of day. Legal, financial, and medical documents detailing thirty years of abuse. This donor? He physically abused his wife, children, and grandchildren, and in one horrifying case, he killed his two-year-old granddaughter. That's not just a crime; that's a rot that has spread through our entire system. Senators, congress members, executives, local police, doctors… hell, even a Republican judge who now sits on the Supreme Court helped cover it up."

The weight of the revelation settled over the room like a thick fog. Kyndra Anderson blinked rapidly, as if trying to process the gravity of what had just been revealed. "That's… horrifying. I mean, that's beyond politics. That's…" she shook her head, struggling to find words. "Have you turned this evidence over to the authorities?"

Machiavelli nodded. "It's in the hands of independent investigative bodies now. But let's be real, justice won't come from the system that protected them. It's going to take the people demanding it."

Samantha Kale, normally composed, looked visibly shaken. "You're telling us that sitting members of our government have been actively covering for a child murderer?"

Machiavelli's eyes locked onto hers, his voice firm. "That's exactly what I'm telling you. And not just covering up; it's deeper than that. These people operate in the shadows, pulling strings, making sure the powerful stay powerful, no matter the cost. You think this is the only case like this? It's not. This is just the one that nearly cost me my life."

Joe Brogan leaned back in his chair, rubbing his jaw. "Man, this is some real-life House of Cards shit. If this all checks out, and it sure sounds like it does, this isn't just corruption. This is a criminal empire running underneath the surface of our government."

Harold Stern let out a slow whistle, shaking his head. "I've heard a lot of insane stuff in my time, but this? This is next-level evil. The Supreme Court? Congress? The cops? Who the hell are we supposed to trust?"

Machiavelli let a beat pass before answering. "That's the point. Right now? No one. But that's why we're here. That's why this campaign exists. We're not just running to win an election. We're running to take a sledgehammer to the entire corrupt system."

Kyndra took a deep breath, steadying herself. "So, what happens next? What's stopping these people from covering it up again?"

Machiavelli smirked, but there was no humor in it.

"They can try, but this time, they don't control the narrative. This evidence is already out. Distributed across multiple independent networks, safe houses, and investigative groups. If something happens to me, if they try to bury this again, the next wave of information drops. And trust me, it only gets worse for them."

Samantha crossed her arms. "So, it's not just about bringing them to justice. It's about making sure they can never do this again."

"Exactly," Machiavelli said. "We're not playing their game anymore. We're burning the whole damn rulebook."

Joe Brogan exhaled, shaking his head in disbelief. "Well… shit. If anyone doubted you before, they're definitely paying attention now."

Harold Stern leaned forward, his voice uncharacteristically serious. "So, Machiavelli, are you ready for the war that's coming your way?"

Machiavelli met his gaze head-on. "I have to be."

Samantha Kale, the rookie CNN reporter, leaned forward, visibly shaken. "That's going to shake the political landscape in ways we can't even predict. My next question is what's the one thing you want voters to know about you and your network?"

Machiavelli met her gaze directly. "What I want Americans to understand, whether or not they vote, is that this campaign is run by the people, for the people. We're not just another political movement; we're a network of individuals working toward a single goal: ensuring that everyday Americans thrive, not just survive."

He leaned back slightly, his voice steady. "Right now, 60% of Americans live paycheck to paycheck. In fact, if we account for American households, the number struggling financially jumps to 83%. And despite all the empty political promises, real inflation-adjusted wages have declined over the last fifty years. Meanwhile, the wealth gap between the top 1% and the rest of America has expanded exponentially. The richest have never had it so good, but the rest of the country is being strangled."

Joe Brogan whistled low, shaking his head. "Those are some brutal numbers, man."

Harold Stern snorted. "And yet, people act like this is normal. Like it's just the way things are."

Machiavelli nodded. "That's what we intend to change. Our goal is to flip those numbers. We're working toward a system where at least 83% of Americans can live financially comfortable lives. Ideally, we want fewer than 5% living paycheck to paycheck. Now, don't get me wrong, there will always be super-rich and super-poor in any society. Some of the wealthy have earned their success, and that's fine. What's not fine is allowing them to manipulate the government for their benefit at the expense of the other 99%."

Kyndra looked skeptical. "But how do you make sure these changes stick? Governments have promised reform before, but once they're in power, it's business as usual."

Machiavelli nodded. "That's where our network is different. We're not just about passing reforms; we're about safeguarding them. We're putting in place policies that prioritize at least 80%, ideally 93%-97%, of the American population. And we're implementing systems to track the real impact. If we see a law that was benefiting 83% of Americans start to slip and only benefit 70%, we fix it. We improve it. We replace it. The ultimate goal is continuous improvement, not just one-time fixes."

Samantha Kale exhaled. "That's ambitious."

Joe Brogan chuckled. "That's an understatement."

Harold Stern leaned in, eyes gleaming. "But the real question is, how much is the establishment going to fight you on this?"

Machiavelli's smirk returned. "They already are. They've tried assassination. They've tried smearing me in the press. They'll keep trying. But here's the thing... they can't stop an idea whose time has come. And they definitely can't stop a movement that belongs to the people."

The room was silent for a moment, each person digesting the weight of what had just been said.

Kyndra Anderson leaned in for the next question, her voice steady. "Mr. Machiavelli, if you had the power to make one major change to the executive branch, what would it be?"

Machiavelli didn't hesitate. "I would make the presidential cabinet elected positions. The President is the decision maker, but the best minds in their fields should make up the Cabinet. We will use multiple metrics to build a pool of potential candidates for the public to vote on. Furthermore, we plan to expand the Executive Branch."

Joe Brogan raised an eyebrow. "Elected Cabinet positions? That's a game-changer."

Samantha Kale nodded. "That would fundamentally alter how executive power is wielded."

Harold Stern smirked. "And probably piss off a lot of career politicians."

Machiavelli grinned. "Exactly. The people deserve experts making policy decisions, not political cronies. We're here to change the game."

Kyndra Anderson tapped her fingers against the table, considering the implications. "How would you determine the candidates eligible for these positions?"

Machiavelli leaned forward. "We would create a rigorous vetting process that evaluates candidates based on experience, expertise, and a demonstrated history of ethical leadership. This process would involve independent review panels composed of subject matter experts, non-partisan organizations, and citizen oversight groups. Once the candidates are selected, the public would vote on who fills each Cabinet role."

Samantha Kale crossed her arms. "That sounds like a radical shift from the current system. What about the potential for campaign-style elections influencing who gets in?"

Machiavelli nodded. "That's a valid concern. To prevent candidates from being swayed by special interest money, we would implement strict campaign finance laws. There would be publicly funded debates, transparent funding disclosures, and limits on corporate and lobbyist donations. The focus would be on policy solutions, not fundraising."

Joe Brogan chuckled. "So, instead of a president filling the Cabinet with their allies, we'd actually have a team of experts chosen by the people?"

"Exactly," Machiavelli said. "Imagine a Secretary of Energy who is a leading scientist in renewable energy, a Secretary of Education who has spent decades reforming schools, or a Secretary of Defense with real-world experience in strategic planning, not just political connections. That's the kind of government we should have."

Harold Stern shook his head, laughing. "You're taking all the fun out of backroom deals and political favors, huh?"

Machiavelli smirked. "Damn right. The American people deserve a government that works for them, not for the highest bidder."

The conversation had only just begun, but already it was clear Machiavelli wasn't playing by the old rules.

Samantha Kale then asked, "Machiavelli, has your network planned how to remove politics from our justice system?"

Machiavelli responded, "Yes. We will create a truly independent Justice Department by eliminating political officials from appointing Supreme Court Justices, judges, prosecutors, and other Justice Department officials. This will prevent the justice system from being manipulated by political parties, lobbyists, and elites. We will also establish a non-partisan Judicial Ethics Committee composed of legal experts, ethicists, and representatives from various sectors to oversee appointments and ensure judicial integrity."

Joe Brogan leaned forward. "So, no more politically motivated judicial appointments?"

"Exactly," Machiavelli confirmed. "The current system allows politicians to stack the courts in their favor, ensuring rulings that align with their agendas rather than true justice. Our plan dismantles that framework entirely. The Judicial Ethics Committee will evaluate candidates based on qualifications, experience, and adherence to principles of fairness, nothing else."

Samantha Kale furrowed her brows. "That's a massive overhaul. Who would choose the members of this Judicial Ethics Committee?"

Machiavelli nodded. "Great question. Members of the committee would be chosen through a transparent and merit-based process, independent of any political influence. They would be selected from diverse sectors, including legal academia, civil rights organizations, professional bar associations, and even retired judges with impeccable records. Their tenure would be staggered to prevent any one administration from dominating appointments, ensuring long-term integrity."

Harold Stern smirked. "That's going to scare a lot of powerful people."

Machiavelli grinned. "Good."

Kyndra Anderson tapped her pen on the table. "So, just

to clarify, how would Supreme Court Justices and other judges be selected under your plan?"

Machiavelli leaned forward. "Instead of political appointments, the Judicial Ethics Committee would review and recommend candidates based on merit, legal expertise, and commitment to impartiality. The final selection process would be put to a public referendum, ensuring that judges serve the interests of justice rather than political ideology."

Joe Brogan raised an eyebrow. "So, people would actually vote for Supreme Court Justices?"

"Yes, but only from a vetted pool of qualified candidates," Machiavelli explained. "We're not talking about turning it into a popularity contest. The public deserves a say, but only after thorough vetting by an independent, expert-led committee that ensures candidates are chosen based on merit, not political allegiance."

Samantha Kale crossed her arms. "How do you ensure those judges remain accountable once they're on the bench? Historically, lifetime appointments have led to judges acting without fear of consequences, making decisions with little regard for the public or the law."

Machiavelli nodded, his tone steady but firm. "You're absolutely right. Lifetime appointments create a dangerous environment where judges are immune to the kind of scrutiny that should be a fundamental part of any system of justice. That's why we'll overhaul the structure entirely. We'll introduce periodic performance reviews and rigorous evaluations conducted by an independent Judicial Ethics

Committee. This committee will not only assess the effectiveness and integrity of each judge but also ensure they remain committed to the principles of fairness and impartiality."

He leaned forward, his eyes locking onto the camera. "But that's not enough. We will implement full transparency for all judicial rulings, requiring judges to publicly disclose the reasoning behind their decisions, especially in cases that have significant societal impact. If a ruling is found to be biased or in violation of ethical standards, there will be oversight mechanisms in place to investigate and address those violations swiftly."

He paused for emphasis, his voice growing more resolute. "In addition to this, we'll introduce a system of accountability that includes potential recall votes. If a judge is found to be acting in bad faith, whether through corruption, partisanship, or gross misconduct, the public will have the power to remove them. And perhaps most importantly, we'll put an end to lifetime appointments entirely. No judge should have a job for life without the possibility of review. Instead, we'll set term limits, five-year terms, renewable once. That means no more untouchable judges making life-altering decisions without fear of consequences. Every judge will have to answer to the people they serve."

He paused, letting the weight of his words settle. "The system will no longer protect those who abuse their power. It will protect justice."

Harold Stern chuckled. "That's a death sentence for judicial corruption."

"Exactly," Machiavelli said. "Our justice system should serve the people, not political elites. The moment a judge serves special interests instead of upholding the law, they should face real consequences."

Kyndra Anderson sighed, shaking her head. "You're dismantling one of the most entrenched power structures in American history. Have you thought about how the legal establishment is going to respond?"

Machiavelli smirked. "Oh, they'll fight tooth and nail. But we're ready. The truth is, Americans have lost faith in the justice system. If we bring this plan directly to the people, bypassing political games, we'll have the power of public opinion on our side. And when the people demand change, no amount of backroom deals or corporate lobbying can stop it."

Joe Brogan chuckled. "You really are looking to burn the whole system down and rebuild it, huh?"

Machiavelli shrugged. "Only the parts that have been rigged for far too long. Justice should never be a tool for the powerful. It should be the shield that protects everyday Americans."

Nearing the end of the interview, Machiavelli thanks both reporters, Joe Brogan and Harold Stern, for providing an environment that gave the American people an honest, unfiltered discussion on real issues. He then leans forward, his expression darkening. "Before we wrap up, I have a couple of surprises for the American people," he announces.

The air in the studio grows tense as he continues. "Ronald Plump agreed to debate me. But let's be honest, he's a coward. He'll back out. So, since he lacks the spine to face me like a man, I'm going to release something that will make sure the American people see him for who he really is."

Machiavelli clicks a button, and the screen behind them flickers to life. "Ladies and gentlemen, this is what Poutine used to blackmail Plump before his first presidential run. Ronald Plump didn't just sell out America... he sold out America to save himself."

The screen now plays a twenty-three-minute video showing Plump receiving golden showers from Russian prostitutes. The room falls into stunned silence for a moment before the reactions begin.

Joe Brogan leans back, eyes wide in disbelief. "Holy shit. I can't believe we voted for this douche."

Harold Stern, ever the provocateur, squints at the screen before bursting into laughter. "Look at him on his knees, begging for more urine. That is some next-level depravity."

Kyndra Anderson covers her mouth, eyes flickering between horror and fascination. "Oh, my God. Is he... crying?" she asked as the screen showed a prostitute slapping Plump across the face, a single tear rolling down his cheek.

Samantha Kale, wide-eyed and visibly stunned, blurts

out, "OMG. It's tiny. Like a small Chapstick tube." She watches for another second before gasping. "Oh my God, the other prostitute is only using three fingers to stroke him."

The room erupts in a mixture of laughter, disgust, and stunned silence as the video continues to play in the background. But Machiavelli isn't finished. As the grotesque display continues, he mentions another set of files on the screen.

"This isn't just about the humiliation. This is about how Plump sold this country to the highest bidder to keep this video from seeing the light of day. Here's proof of direct communication between Plump's attorneys and Poutine's administration, outlining exactly what he had to do to keep this buried."

The screen now displays a series of documents, emails, and transcripts. Machiavelli reads aloud:

"1. Slap tariffs on China… Poutine feared China was becoming more dominant than Russia."

"2. Strong-arm Ukraine, threaten its military aid, and keep them weak."

"3. Dissolve or gut NATO, reduce its power so Russia could move unchecked."

"4. Share U.S. intelligence gathered on Russia and Russia's enemies."

The weight of the revelations hangs in the air. No one speaks for a moment. Then, Joe Brogan shakes his head.

"So, he literally sold-out America to keep people from seeing… this? This is beyond pathetic."

Harold Stern sighs, looking directly into the camera. "This is a man who was willing to destroy alliances, threaten democracy, and destabilize the world just to protect his ego. Think about that."

Kyndra Anderson shakes her head. "The worst part is… this is probably just the tip of the iceberg. If this is what's coming out now, imagine what else he's been hiding."

Samantha Kale, still visibly shaken, rubbed her temples. "I can't believe this is real. How did we let this man hold the nuclear codes?"

Machiavelli, ever the strategist, lets the moment breathe before delivering the final blow. "The American people deserve the truth, no matter how ugly. And now, they have it. So, Plump, if you're watching, go ahead and try to run from this. The people won't let you."

35

CRISIS POINT

PRESENT DAY

SEPTEMBER 2028 — 3:00 P.M.

Washington D.C.

The Plump Administration was in full damage control mode following Machiavelli's explosive interview. Within hours, new White House Press Secretary Leigh Wagner was at the podium, attempting to distance the administration from the allegations.

"The claims made by James Machiavelli are not only deeply misleading but are part of a continued smear campaign against President Plump. The President has always put America first, and any insinuation that he would work with foreign powers for personal gain is baseless and irresponsible," Wagner said in an impassioned defense.

Behind closed doors, President Plump himself was furious. He took to social media, as he often does, to voice his anger directly.

"What Machiavelli is doing is dangerous, folks. He's trying to tear down everything I've worked for... everything we've done for the American people. His lies are just that... LIES! There's no evidence. No facts. And it's just the deep state trying to push me out. This country will never be the same if we let him and his supporters win. We'll expose the real corruption."

Plump's rhetoric was particularly harsh on the claims of foreign influence and blackmail, dismissing them as nothing but conspiracy theories cooked up by the media and his political enemies.

However, beneath the surface, a growing number of Plump's base began to question the man they once considered a political savior. In the wake of Machiavelli's revelations, a rift formed.

As the revelations about the Plump administration, Poutine's blackmail, and the alleged manipulations of foreign powers continued to unfold, a deepening fracture was evident within the ranks of Plump's loyal base. What had once been a monolithic support base for the former president was now showing significant signs of division.

Supporters Questioning Their Allegiance

At a campaign function for Plump, once fervent followers of the former president could now be seen questioning their loyalty. At this function in Ohio, a group of voters who had once proudly worn "Make America Great Again" hats stood in small huddles, quietly discussing the fallout from Machiavelli's interview. Some shook their heads, while others exchanged concerns.

"I'm starting to think Machiavelli might have a point," said Bill Grant, a long-time Plump supporter and small business owner. *"I voted for Plump because I thought he was different, but the whole thing with Russia, blackmail, prostitutes? It feels like the man I voted for is just another part of the establishment. I'm wondering if we've been played all along."*

Meanwhile, Kara Smith, a former Plump voter from Florida, posted a heartfelt message on social media: *"I'm seriously struggling with this. It's not just the Russia stuff, it's everything. I wanted a president who would stand up to corruption, but now it feels like he is the problem. Maybe we need a fresh start with someone like Machiavelli."*

This sentiment was echoed across social media platforms, where Twitter, Facebook, and Instagram were ablaze with discussions about Machiavelli's candidacy.

The National Media's Response: Fox News and OAN Criticize Plump

For the first time since Plump's rise to power, even conservative media outlets were showing signs of dissent. Historically, networks like **Fox News** and **OAN** had been staunch defenders of the former president, often downplaying scandals and casting doubt on any accusations against him. But the shocking details unveiled in Machiavelli's interview, including the confirmation of blackmail and the disturbing video, caused cracks to appear in the media's unwavering support.

Laura Ingraham, one of Fox News' most influential commentators, was visibly shaken during an evening broadcast. *"What we've learned today is disturbing, to say the least. The allegations about President Plump and Russia are not something we can ignore. While we've always been strong supporters of the President, we must hold everyone accountable, even those we've supported in the past. If these revelations prove true, it's a betrayal of the trust Americans placed in him."*

Even Sean Hannity, known for his unflinching support of Plump, was forced to tread carefully. In an evening broadcast, he admitted: *"Look, I've been a supporter of President Plump, but if these allegations… especially the video, turn out to be true, this is something we all have to reckon with. It changes everything. We are at a crossroads. And we need to ask ourselves, is this the kind of leadership we want moving forward?"*

The shift in tone from Fox News was seismic, as the network had been a pillar of Plump's political base. But the uncomfortable truth was that more and more Plump supporters, particularly those in the moderate and suburban segments of the electorate, were demanding answers, and Fox News, realizing its potential loss of influence, had little choice but to respond.

OAN, which had long been a staunch ally of Plump,

faced similar criticism. Although its broadcasts remained pro-Plump, hosts like **Dan Ball** questioned whether continued loyalty to Plump was worth the growing public backlash.

Republican Political Figures Renouncing Their Parties

The impact extended beyond the grassroots level. In the wake of the Poutine revelations, a wave of current and former Republican lawmakers began considering their futures outside the party.

Senator Lisa Murkowski, long a moderate voice in the Republican Party, broke her silence in an impassioned speech on the Senate floor.

"The actions described in this interview are not the values we stand for as Republicans. I cannot in good conscience continue to support someone who has put our country in such a compromising position. I will be exploring the possibility of switching to an independent status, as the party I once belonged to no longer represents the America I believe in."

Governor Larry Hogan of Maryland echoed Murkowski's sentiments.

"I'm done. This is not what I signed up for when I joined the Republican Party. The events we've seen unfold in the past few days, coupled with the disturbing allegations, make it clear that my future lies

outside of the party. I believe it's time for a new political movement in America."

Murkowski and Hogan's statements were the beginning of a broader trend within the party. Many other moderate Republicans, frustrated with the erosion of their party's integrity, began privately considering similar moves. The growing number of defections signaled the collapse of Plump's political empire, even within his own party.

Democrat Political Figures Renouncing Their Parties

As the revelations continued to unfold and public sentiment shifted, some prominent Democratic figures began to publicly voice their discontent, joining the growing number of Republicans distancing themselves from Plump. The scandal surrounding Plump and Poutine's alleged blackmail created a ripple effect, with several Democratic figures making bold moves.

Senator Mark Kelly of Arizona, a former astronaut and a key figure in the Democratic Party, was one of the first to break rank. In a statement on the Senate floor, Kelly announced:

"It's clear to me now that both parties have become entrenched in a system that fails the American people. We're not representing the people anymore; we're catering to lobbyists, special interests, and power brokers. I can no longer support a party that refuses to acknowledge this. As of today, I am leaving the Democratic Party and will be serving as an independent."

Kelly's departure was a blow to the party, especially coming when they were struggling to respond to the growing tide of disillusionment. His move, which mirrored the larger sentiment of distrust in the political establishment, showed a deepening fracture in Washington.

Another shock came when **Senator Catherine Cortez Masto** of Nevada, a popular and influential Democrat, announced she too was stepping away from the party. In a heartfelt post on social media, she said:

"The system is broken. Both parties have been complicit in perpetuating it, and the American people are suffering as a result. I'm walking away from the party I've supported for years to pursue a new path, one focused on the real needs of the people, not corporate interests. I'll be working independently from now on."

Cortez Masto's departure reflected the growing dissatisfaction with the Democratic Party's inability to break free from its own power structures. Her defection added momentum to the growing movement of political realignment.

As both Mark Kelly and Catherine Cortez Masto renounced their parties, more voters, both Democrats and Republicans, began considering James Machiavelli as a viable alternative. His message of breaking the political gridlock and prioritizing the people over entrenched power resonated profoundly with Americans disillusioned by both major parties. Focus groups showed a rising tide of support for Machiavelli, especially as he positioned himself as the outsider who could finally enact meaningful change.

China's Response to the Revelations

China, which had been locked in a trade war with the U.S. during Plump's presidency, responded carefully to the revelations about Poutine's involvement in the tariff imposition and blackmail allegations.

In an official statement issued by the Chinese Ministry of Foreign Affairs, spokesperson Hua Chunying said:

"The revelations from Machiavelli paint a troubling picture of foreign interference in the internal affairs of sovereign nations. China has always been committed to fair trade and diplomacy, but if these claims are true, it would mark a grave betrayal of the trust between nations. China remains open to negotiation, but it will not be coerced into agreements that undermine its sovereignty or its economic interests."

Russia's Response: Confirmation and Denial

Russia, meanwhile, was quick to respond, but their response was one of mixed denial and reluctant confirmation. A senior Kremlin official, speaking on the condition of anonymity, confirmed the blackmail aspect but denied that Russia had orchestrated or forced the tariffs on China.

"Yes, there were efforts to influence the situation behind the scenes, but the claim that Russia somehow manipulated the U.S. government to impose tariffs on China is categorically false. The Plump administration made these decisions based on their own strategic calculations, not under the pressure of external forces," the official said.

However, the same source admitted, *"There was indeed an understanding between Poutine and Plump regarding certain economic strategies. These were mutual benefits, with a shared interest in undermining global institutions that did not align with both nations' geopolitical goals. But blackmail? That's a stretch."*

The Kremlin continued to push a narrative that cast Russia's involvement as essentially transactional, focusing on its own interests in destabilizing Western alliances rather than manipulating internal U.S. policies for the benefit of any single leader. Russia denied any direct influence on U.S. tariffs, but the mention of "mutual benefits" only fueled suspicions that Russia had been working behind the scenes in a way that was more politically advantageous for Plump than the public was led to believe.

Global Leaders' Responses

The international community, already on edge from the revelations surrounding Plump's administration, responded with a mix of disbelief, concern, and strategic caution. European leaders, who had long been wary of Plump's "America First" policies, were now faced with a deepening crisis of confidence.

German Chancellor Angela Merkel offered a rare public rebuke, stating:

"If these claims are true, the global order is in much greater jeopardy than we thought. If America's legal system and its executive branch have become so compromised by personal and political interests, it will be difficult to trust any agreements made with the U.S. going forward."

French President Emmanuel Macron echoed these concerns, stating:

"Europe must remain vigilant. We will continue to seek fair relations with the U.S., but it's clear that new leadership is needed to restore trust in international agreements. The future of our alliances will depend on the U.S. restoring its integrity."

Social Media Reaction: Growing Support for Machiavelli

On social media, the narrative was shifting quickly. #Machiavelli2028 began trending, with hundreds of thousands of Americans voicing their support for the new candidate. Influencers and former Plump supporters, frustrated by the corruption and blackmail allegations, turned their attention toward Machiavelli, with many blatantly stating that they saw him as the only alternative to a corrupt political establishment.

On Reddit's /r/Politics, a flood of posts praised Machiavelli's "honesty," with many posters claiming they were seriously considering voting for him. *"I've been a Plump supporter for years, but I can't support someone who is so clearly compromised. Machiavelli is the kind of change we need,"* one post read.

TikTok was flooded with videos of young voters declaring their support of Machiavelli. One popular video featured a group of young adults saying, *"We were all about Plump before, but now? We're for Machiavelli. He's not afraid to tell the truth."*

As more voters considered Machiavelli, the momentum for his candidacy snowballed. Polls showed a significant shift in favor of Machiavelli, particularly among suburban women, independent voters, and younger voters who had previously supported Plump.

A National Turning Point: Machiavelli Gaining Majority Support

What had once seemed like a long shot for Machiavelli was now a real possibility. His clear and powerful answers during the interview, his revelations about the entrenched corruption within both parties, and his unwavering stance on bringing real change resonated with an American electorate fed up with business-as-usual politics.

In key battleground states like Pennsylvania, Michigan, and Wisconsin, Machiavelli's numbers rose sharply in polling. His message of restoring integrity to the political system and placing power back in the hands of the people resonated with voters who had grown disillusioned by Plump's scandals and the political gridlock in Washington.

By the end of the week, political commentators were openly discussing the possibility of Machiavelli emerging as the true alternative to both Plump and the traditional establishment. His message was simple, but powerful: *"This is the people's country, and it's time we take it back from those who have sold us out for their own gain."*

36

CONTROL SHIFT

PRESENT DAY

SEPTEMBER 2028 — 8:00 P.M.

Los Angeles, CA.

T he lights of the *Real Time* studio dimmed as Bill Matter settled into his chair, his signature smirk barely concealing the excitement behind his eyes. Across from him sat Mark Cuban, the billionaire entrepreneur known for his sharp business acumen and outspoken opinions. This wasn't just any episode. This was the first major television appearance since the political earthquake that James Machiavelli had set off days prior.

Matter leaned forward, tapping his fingers against his desk. "Alright, folks, welcome to *Real Time*! Tonight, we have a man who knows business like few others, a guy who has been calling bullshit on the system for years, Mark Cuban! Mark, it's fantastic to have you."

Cuban, dressed in a casual blazer and open-collared shirt, nodded, offering a relaxed but confident smile. "Happy to be here, Bill."

Matter wasted no time getting to the point. "Alright, let's not waste time. We've got to talk about the elephant, or should I say, the soaked, humiliated, and compromised elephant in the room. James Machiavelli just nuked Ronald Plump's entire political career with the press of a button. That video… Jesus."

Cuban exhaled sharply, shaking his head. "Yeah, Bill. I think it's safe to say we just witnessed the most explosive moment in modern political history. People have speculated for years that Plump was compromised, that he was Poutine's lapdog, but no one expected *this*. And, more importantly, no one had proof until now."

The audience murmured in agreement, still reeling from the recent revelations. Just days ago, Machiavelli had unveiled a damning twenty-three-minute video showing Plump in a deeply compromising situation, one that Poutine had allegedly used to blackmail him before his first presidential run. The video itself was beyond salacious, but the true scandal lay in the political ramifications. The documents and communications that Machiavelli had presented along with it painted a chilling picture: a sitting U.S. President bending to the will of a foreign adversary to bury his shame.

Matter shook his head in disbelief. "I mean, it's beyond humiliating. It's not just the act itself, though, holy hell, that was something… it's what it *means*. Plump didn't just embarrass himself; he sold out the country to keep that tape buried. The documents Machiavelli presented. Tariffs, NATO, Ukraine, classified intelligence—it's all right there."

Cuban nodded, his expression serious. "And that's why I'm backing James Machiavelli. Bill, you know me. I don't do politics for the sake of politics. I hate the system. It's corrupt, bloated, and designed to keep the same people in power while screwing over the average American. Machiavelli is the first candidate I've seen who isn't just talking about change; he's *executing* it in real-time."

Matter leaned back, intrigued. "Alright, let's get into that. Because, full disclosure, I've been watching this campaign, and it's kind of a masterclass in how to break the system without playing by its rules. They're dominating the political conversation while spending, what... a fraction of what Plump and Newtsum are?"

Cuban chuckled, his admiration evident. "Exactly. That's what makes it brilliant. Plump is burning through cash on ads that no one trusts anymore. Newtsum is running the same tired Democratic playbook, shaking hands and smiling for the cameras. Meanwhile, Machiavelli is running a campaign built for the 21st century. It's lean, it's efficient, and it's *authentic*."

He paused, letting the thought sink in before continuing. "They're live-streaming everything. No hidden donors, no dark money groups. They flat-out told people, 'Keep your money. We have enough.' That alone sent shockwaves through the establishment. No one does that. But it worked.

It made them *trustworthy*. When have you ever seen a politician say, 'We don't need your money, keep it' and actually mean it?"

Matter raised an eyebrow. "Never. Because they're all on the take. So, tell me, how the hell did Machiavelli pull this off? How did he get a two-and-a-half-year head start without anyone realizing what was coming?"

Cuban leaned in, his voice steady. "That's the beauty of it. While Plump and Newtsum were setting up their Candyland boards, Machiavelli was playing chess. His team built a movement before they ever declared a campaign. They spent time in towns and cities, talking to real people, building trust, and, more importantly, listening. And because they didn't reveal themselves early, they never became a target. By the time they hit the Republican National Convention and shocked the world, it was too late to stop them."

Matter tapped his pen against his desk. "And now, the business world is getting behind him. Why? You and I both know corporate America has played ball with Plump and Biden. What's changed?"

Cuban smirked. "Simple. Business leaders are tired of being hostages to the political system. The corrupt ones love the status quo, but the real entrepreneurs, the ones who built things from the ground up, they're sick of playing the game. They want a system that rewards hard work, not backroom deals.

Machiavelli is giving them an alternative. He's not

promising favors. He's promising fairness. And that's a threat to the power brokers who've been running this country behind the scenes for decades."

Matter chuckled. "Yeah, but you know what's coming, right? They're gonna call him a socialist, a radical, a danger to capitalism."

Cuban shrugged. "And they're gonna look like idiots doing it. James isn't anti-business; he's pro-fair business. He's pro-worker. He's pro-American economy. The real radicals are the ones who've been hoarding wealth, rigging markets, and offshoring jobs while calling it 'capitalism.'

Machiavelli's message is simple: 'If you work hard, you should be able to afford a decent life. If you run a business, you should be able to compete without politicians squeezing you for donations. And if you're filthy rich, maybe pay your fair share instead of expecting taxpayers to bail you out.' That's not socialism, Bill. That's common sense."

Matter exhaled, shaking his head. "So, what happens next? Where does this go from here?"

Cuban leaned forward, his expression sharpening. "It's bigger than politics. The business world is watching Machiavelli because he's proving something they've long suspected: government doesn't have to be a pay-to-play scheme. He's breaking the cycle of dependency between politicians and billionaires. That's why so many business leaders—real business leaders—are backing him. Not because they want handouts, but because they're sick of a system that forces them to lobby just to get a fair shot.

Matter sat back slightly, his eyebrows raised in cautious curiosity as he studied Cuban.

Cuban gestured emphatically with one hand, the other resting on the arm of his chair.

Think about it, Bill. How many small businesses have been crushed by monopolies because Congress refuses to enforce antitrust laws? How many entrepreneurs have been shut out of markets because legacy corporations spend millions rigging regulations in their favor? We've reached a point where competition isn't about innovation or quality anymore; it's about who has the deepest pockets and the most lobbyists in Washington. Big corporations write the rules, and politicians just rubber-stamp them. If you want to open a new bank? Good luck. The financial giants have locked down regulations so tightly that unless you have billions in capital, you don't even get to compete. If you want to challenge Big Tech? Forget it. They'll buy out your startup or bury you in legal fees before you even get off the ground.

Cuban leaned back briefly, then sat upright again, his hands moving to punctuate each phrase.

Machiavelli is calling all of that out. And it's resonating not just with CEOs, but with *workers*. He's exposing the truth. When the system is fair, when people earn what they deserve, the economy thrives for everyone, not just the top 1%.

Matter gave a slow, almost imperceptible nod, his eyes narrowing with interest.

For decades, we've been sold the idea that the market will sort itself out, but that's bullshit when the market is rigged. When corporations can donate unlimited money to campaigns, they're not donating out of goodwill; they're buying influence. They're making sure no politician, Democrat or Republican, will ever truly challenge them. And while the government bails them out during every crisis, working Americans are told to just 'pull themselves up by their bootstraps.' That's why Machiavelli's message is so powerful. He's not saying businesses shouldn't succeed; he's saying they should succeed on merit, not manipulation. That's why people are listening."

Matter nodded, rubbing his chin. "And the American people? What does he mean to them?"

Cuban's voice softened somewhat, but his conviction remained strong. "He represents hope. Real, tangible hope. Not slogans, not empty promises, but a leader who is showing in real-time that he doesn't need corporate money to win. That he's not for sale. Americans have been let down over and over again by both parties. They see politicians getting richer while they struggle to pay rent. They see billionaires exploiting loopholes while they work two jobs just to get by.

When Machiavelli says he wants to level the playing field, it's not about punishing success; it's about making sure success isn't reserved for a handful of insiders. If you're a worker, it means higher wages, fair treatment, and real job security. If you're a small business owner, it means a fair shot at competing without being crushed by monopolies. If you're an entrepreneur, it means innovation can actually thrive again instead of being choked out by billion-dollar giants protecting their turf. This isn't radical. This is what capitalism was *supposed* to be before the system got hijacked.

James Machiavelli is proof that change is possible. That someone can take on the system and win. He's not talking about a revolution. He *is* the revolution. And the American people are waking up to that."

Matter turned to the camera, his expression more serious than usual. "Well, buckle up, folks. This is gonna be one hell of an election."

37
CHANGING SIDES
PRESENT DAY
SEPTEMBER 2028 — 9:00 A.M

Los Angeles, CA.

The bright lights of the Fox & Friends studio illuminated Nikki Haylie as she took her seat, her expression grim, her posture rigid. The air was thick with tension. The hosts, usually stalwart defenders of the Republican establishment, shifted uneasily in their chairs, aware of the bombshell revelations that had rocked the political landscape just days before.

"Nikki," Steve Doocy began hesitantly, "you've been a loyal conservative voice for years. But you've had some strong words about former President Plump after what James Machiavelli exposed. Where do you stand now?"

Haylie let out a slow breath, fortifying herself. "Steve, let's stop pretending. What we saw... what the entire world saw… wasn't just humiliating; it was catastrophic. That wasn't just a personal disgrace for Plump; it was a national disgrace. He wasn't just compromised; he sold this country out to protect himself."

Brian Kilmeade, usually quick to defend Plump, remained silent, his lips pressed together in a thin line. Ainsley Earhardt's brows furrowed, her discomfort evident.

"I should have spoken up sooner," Haylie admitted, shaking her head. "After I lost to him in the 2024 primary, I had a choice. I could have put country first and called him out for what he was, weak, reckless, and dangerous. But I stayed silent. And for that, I take responsibility. I failed to do what was right when it mattered most."

The hosts exchanged glances, sensing the seismic shift in Haylie's tone.

"And now?" Earhardt asked cautiously.

Haylie's expression hardened. "Now, I won't make that mistake again. America is weaker because of Ronald Plump. Our global standing is in tatters, our alliances have frayed, and we've emboldened our enemies. Plump gutted NATO, played into Poutine's hands, and put personal gain above national security. He didn't just make poor decisions; he actively betrayed this country. And now, we have the proof."

Kilmeade finally spoke, his voice quieter than usual. "You're saying he's unfit?"

"I'm saying he was never fit to begin with. Let's not sugarcoat this. He is a danger to our democracy, a national security risk, and a man who values his own ego over the well-being of the American people. He lacked the discipline, the knowledge, and the moral compass to lead this country. And now we know for certain, he was compromised from the start. We have the emails, the deals, the direct evidence of how he betrayed us to save his own skin. This isn't about partisanship anymore. This is about America."

Doocy nodded slowly. "So, what now? What does this mean for you politically?"

Haylie took a deep breath, her next words carrying the weight of finality. "It means I'm done with the Republican Party. I'm leaving it behind because the party I believed in no longer exists. It's been twisted beyond recognition, and Plump is the rot at its core. I have spent my entire career fighting for conservative principles, for strong national security, for a world where America leads. But I can't continue to stand under a banner that has become synonymous with corruption, cowardice, and betrayal. I refuse to be complicit any longer."

Doocy shifted in his chair. "You understand what this means, right? You're turning your back on the party that helped *make* you."

Haylie gave him a small, sad smile. "Steve, I'm not turning my back on the party. The party turned its back on America. It turned its back on integrity, on national security, and on the values it once stood for. The Republican Party isn't the party of Reagan anymore; it's the party of a man who let a dictator blackmail him and who sold out our allies. How can I stand by that?"

For the first time, Brian Kilmeade nodded in agreement. "I have to say, Nikki, you're not wrong. We defended him for years, but the facts are right there in front of us now. There's no spinning this. He's unfit."

Ainsley Earhardt hesitated before speaking. "I've always supported conservative values, but after what we've seen... how can we explain this away? How do we tell Americans this is okay?"

Haylie met their eyes, conviction burning in her gaze. "We don't. We stop lying to ourselves, to the voters. We tell the truth, no matter how painful it is. And we do what's necessary to put America back on the right path. That's why I'm endorsing James Machiavelli for President. He's the only one who is telling the truth, the only one with the backbone to expose what Plump did. And I'm not just endorsing him, I'm offering my experience, my knowledge, and my commitment to fixing the damage Plump has done to our standing in the world. America needs strong leadership in foreign policy again. If Machiavelli wins, I will work with him in whatever capacity necessary to repair our alliances, rebuild our credibility, and ensure that no president ever sells out this country again."

The silence in the studio was deafening. A rare moment on Fox & Friends where no one rushed to push back, no one scrambled to defend Plump. The shift was undeniable.

Ainsley Earhardt finally spoke, her voice softer than before. "That's... a big step."

"It is," Haylie agreed. "But it's the right one. America

needs to wake up. We cannot let this man anywhere near power again. We cannot let our country be held hostage by his ego any longer. And if that means leaving behind the party I've dedicated my life to, so be it. Because my loyalty is to America first, and at one time, I forgot that. I will not forget again."

Kilmeade exhaled sharply. "So, you're endorsing Machiavelli. Do you think others will follow?"

Haylie's eyes flickered with determination. "I know they will. The question is, will they have the courage to do it publicly before it's too late?"

Doocy furrowed his brow, his expression serious. "Plump is still the sitting president, and he's running for a third term. He's not the kind of man to go down quietly. What do you think his next move will be?"

Haylie didn't hesitate. "He will do everything in his power to hold on to control. He will attack, he will deflect, and he will try to paint himself as the victim. But more dangerously, I fear he will try to use the office of the presidency to silence dissent. We've already seen him abuse his authority time and time again. If he feels truly cornered, I wouldn't put it past him to undermine the election itself. That's why this moment is so critical. We have to be vigilant. We have to make sure democracy holds. And that starts with telling the truth, no matter the cost."

Kilmeade leaned forward, his voice hushed. "You're saying he could go further? What exactly do you think he's capable of?"

Haylie exhaled sharply, her eyes narrowing with intensity. "We already know what he's capable of. He tried to have Machiavelli and his family assassinated. That was a sitting President of the United States attempting to eliminate a political rival through sheer brute force. And do you know what's terrifying? He failed, and he learned from it. The next time, he'll be more careful, more strategic. He won't just send hired guns. He'll use the Department of Justice to fabricate charges, he'll turn intelligence agencies into his personal enforcers, and he'll leverage every government institution to intimidate and silence his enemies. We're talking about a man who has no limits, no moral restraint. If he thinks staying in power is his only option for survival, then he will do whatever it takes, no matter what destruction it causes."

Ainsley Earhardt swallowed hard, the movement visible even in the high-definition close-up. She shifted in her chair, fingers tightening around her coffee mug as though bracing herself. "So, you're saying... he could try to overturn the election? Even use force?"

Haylie nodded grimly. "I am saying exactly that. We've seen the warning signs already. The way he's purged his inner circle of anyone who questions him, the way he's cultivated loyalty not to the country, but to himself. He's surrounded by people who will follow orders without hesitation. And the worst part? He has a base of supporters that he has primed for violence. He will tell them that democracy itself is the enemy if it means staying in power. And if that doesn't work? He has the full weight of the federal government at his disposal. We are looking at the potential for martial law, the refusal to accept election results, and the destruction of our democratic institutions. If we do not take this threat seriously, we may not have a country left to save."

Brian Kilmeade raised an eyebrow, obviously alarmed. "Martial law? You think Plump could actually go that far?"

Haylie looked him in the eye, her voice unwavering. "Absolutely. Martial law is the ultimate tool for a president desperate to maintain control. If he can't win the election, he will do everything in his power to prevent it from happening. Martial law would allow him to suspend the election, shut down courts, and even dissolve Congress if necessary. It would give him unprecedented power to control the nation's streets, the media, and the narrative itself. He could deploy military forces in major cities under the guise of 'restoring order,' silencing protestors, and suppressing any form of opposition. The military could be used to enforce curfews, round up dissidents, and stop the free movement of Americans. Plump could effectively rule by decree, eliminating all checks and balances on his authority. In such a scenario, the American people would lose their fundamental freedoms. Democracy would be suspended, and we would be living under an authoritarian regime."

Ainsley's lips parted, but no sound came for a moment. She blinked rapidly, the weight of the scenario dawning on her. When she finally spoke, her voice trembled on the edge of disbelief. "But you said he's lost some of his base, right?"

Haylie nodded. "Yes, he has. Plump has already lost a significant portion of his base. His die-hard followers are still out there, but they are a shrinking minority. More and more Republicans are waking up to the truth. They are seeing what his presidency has done to this country, and they no longer want to follow a man who is so willing to sell out our values. That's why you're seeing prominent Republicans speaking out against him publicly. They're acknowledging that his brand of politics is divisive, dangerous, and ultimately detrimental to our nation's future. This is a turning point, and Plump can no longer rely on blind loyalty to keep him in power."

The studio's silence deepened as she pivoted, her voice gathering strength. Her hands spread slightly, punctuating her words. "That's why I'm endorsing James Machiavelli. He's the only candidate who can unite this country. He's the only one who can restore America's standing in the world and bring back a sense of dignity to the Oval Office. But Machiavelli isn't just a political outsider. He has the support of the military, the military families, and the American intelligence community at large. These are the people who understand what's at stake. They know that the country is at a crossroads, and they are rallying behind Machiavelli because they see in him the leadership we so desperately need."

Her voice grew firmer. "Unlike Plump, who has surrounded himself with sycophants and corrupt officials, Machiavelli has the backing of people willing to protect the nation from anyone who seeks to destroy it. Regardless if from external threats or from a president who would trample on the Constitution to hold on to power. Because the military and intelligence agencies understand the importance of national security, integrity, and stability, they've aligned with Machiavelli. They won't let Plump hijack this country for his personal gain. And I believe that with their support, Machiavelli will not only defeat Plump, but he will restore the United States to its rightful place in the world."

By the time she finished, her chin lifted, her eyes alive with resolve.

The air in the studio grew even heavier as Haylie's words settled in.

For the first time in years, Fox & Friends had no rebuttal, no spin. Just the quiet, weighty acceptance of a reality they could no longer deny. The tide had turned.

38
POWER VACUUM
PRESENT DAY
OCTOBER 2028 — 6:00 P.M.

Manhattan, NY.

The nation stood on the precipice of an unprecedented presidential debate. With less than a month before Election Day, the political battleground had been transformed by a force neither of the two dominant parties had anticipated: James Machiavelli.

For over a century, American politics had been defined by a binary struggle between Republicans and Democrats, but the past two and a half months had shattered that paradigm. The explosive emergence of Machiavelli, who had not only survived an assassination attempt ordered by President Plump but had provided irrefutable audio evidence of it, had upended the race.

His announcement at the Republican National Convention sent shockwaves through the political world. What began as an anomaly had grown into an unstoppable movement, forcing a total recalibration of electoral strategies.

As of October 7th, the day before the first presidential debate, national polls showed a virtual dead heat: Newtsum at 34%, Plump at 33%, and Machiavelli at 33%.

What made Machiavelli's rise even more astonishing was the voter shift he had ignited. Over 53 million Americans had registered to vote, with over 80% identifying as Independent. An additional 70 million had changed party affiliation, with over 70% switching to Independent.

If either Plump or Newtsum had any chance of winning the presidency, the consensus across all political circles was clear: they would need a resounding debate victory to stall Machiavelli's momentum.

The air was thick with anticipation. Americans across the country consumed endless commentary, debates, and speculation about the upcoming showdown while glued to their screens. Bars and coffee shops buzzed with conversations about what could be the most defining debate in modern history.

Posters, signs, and murals of Machiavelli filled the streets, some portraying him as a revolutionary hero, and others as a dangerous disruptor.

. . .

The Media Frenzy

Mainstream Media Perspectives
CNN: "A Political Revolution or a Dangerous Unknown?"

CNN, while acknowledging Machiavelli's meteoric rise, remained skeptical of his ability to govern. "He has captured the anger and frustration of an America that feels betrayed by its leaders," said host Anderson Cooper. "But beyond his rhetoric, where are the concrete policies? Does he have the experience to lead the most powerful nation on Earth?"

Their panel discussions often focused on Machiavelli's outsider status, warning that his ascendancy could throw the country into instability. Some commentators even compared his rise to other populist movements around the world, arguing that his rapid ascent lacked the institutional grounding necessary to succeed. Despite this, CNN could not deny his overwhelming appeal. Van Jones described him as "a political disruptor with an almost cult-like following," while Jake Tapper pointed out the contradictions in his messaging. "Is he for the working class, or is he an opportunist exploiting discontent?"

However, as the campaign progressed, CNN was forced to acknowledge that Machiavelli was not just a candidate fueled by anger; he was offering clear, structured solutions for many of the nation's pressing problems. His proposals on economic reform, healthcare, and government accountability were resonating across party lines, drawing support even from traditionally Democratic and Republican voters who felt unheard by their respective parties. More than just rhetoric, Machiavelli was empowering people to believe they had a real stake in their government once again.

Fox News: Plump's America Under Siege

Fox News, once Plump's most formidable media ally, found itself fractured. Sean Hannity, who had distanced himself from the former president after the Plump Russian Prostitutes Golden Shower video, called Machiavelli "the only candidate who speaks for real Americans." Meanwhile, Jesse Watters remained staunchly in Plump's camp, dismissing the independent challenger as "a product of liberal media hype and deep-state operatives who want to fracture the Republican vote."

Laura Ingraham, on the other hand, expressed concerns that Machiavelli's rise signaled the Republican Party's loss of identity: "Are we now just looking for the next strongman? Or are we standing by the principles that made conservatism great?"

Yet, as Machiavelli's movement gained momentum, even Fox News could not ignore his cross-partisan appeal. He was speaking directly to disillusioned voters, Plump supporters who felt betrayed, moderates tired of political infighting, and even some progressives who saw in him an unfiltered honesty missing from their own party's leadership. His emphasis on restoring power to the people and challenging entrenched elites made him a force neither conservatives nor liberals could dismiss.

MSNBC: Newtsum's Last Stand

MSNBC painted the race as a desperate attempt by Governor Gavin Newtsum to hold the Democratic Party together against a rising tide of independent voters. "Newtsum is the last firewall between American democracy and an authoritarian future," said Rachel Maddow. "But can he appeal to an electorate that no longer trusts the establishment?"

As Newtsum's approval numbers faltered, MSNBC hosts discussed whether the Democratic Party had underestimated the public's dissatisfaction. Their focus shifted to strategies he might use to break Machiavelli's momentum in the upcoming debate. Joy Reid highlighted Machiavelli's vague policy proposals as a potential weakness, while Chris Hayes examined whether the media's coverage itself was fueling his rise.

Despite their skepticism, even MSNBC had to contend with the reality that Machiavelli was uniting voters in a way unseen in modern politics. His call for direct civic engagement, his rejection of corporate influence in government, and his demand for accountability were energizing Americans across ideological divides. He was not merely a disruptor; he was giving people hope that real change was possible, outside of traditional party lines.

Social Media and Online Discourse

Twitter, TikTok, and Reddit had become breeding grounds for Machiavelli's movement. His followers, dubbed 'The Unshackled,' spread his message with a fervor unmatched by any political campaign in modern history.

Hashtags like #Machiavelli2028, #UnshackledNation, and #EndTheDuoParty trended daily. The virality of his speeches, particularly his infamous line from the RNC, "I survived Plump's bullets, and now I'll take his office," became an anthem for disillusioned voters across the spectrum.

Meme culture played an overwhelmingly pro-Machiavelli role. Supporters flooded social media with videos dissecting his policies, exposing establishment corruption, and showcasing his fiery, no-nonsense rhetoric. Clips of his speeches amassed hundreds of millions of views overnight, with influencers and content creators hailing him as the candidate of the people. Some viral videos depicted Machiavelli as a modern-day revolutionary, a man standing against the corruption of both major parties. Political influencers who had once dismissed him as a wildcard now openly endorsed his candidacy, calling him the only genuine choice for systemic change.

Opponents struggled to control the narrative. Users debunked claims in real time with video evidence and grassroots investigations, countering the mainstream media's attempts to portray Machiavelli as a dangerous unknown. The overwhelming sentiment on social media was clear: the establishment was afraid, and the people were ready to take their country back.

The Talk Show Circuit

The Joe Brogan Experience: James Machiavelli is the Stone Cold Steve Austin of Politics

Joe Brogan's podcast had become one of the most influential platforms in modern political discourse, shaping opinions on everything from health and fitness to culture and, more recently, the explosive rise of James Machiavelli. Though Machiavelli had appeared on *The Joe Brogan Experience* months earlier, this particular episode was different. He wasn't in the chair this time. Instead, Brogan and his guests dissected the political phenomenon that was reshaping the country.

"Dude, this guy is like the Stone Cold Steve Austin of politics," Brogan said, laughing as he took a sip of his whiskey. "He just came out of nowhere, flipped off the establishment, and now he's body-slamming these guys. It's insane."

Mark Cuban, billionaire entrepreneur and outspoken advocate for independent politics, nodded in agreement. "I've been in business a long time, Joe, and I know disruption when I see it. The traditional parties? They're Blockbuster Video. Machiavelli? He's Netflix. He's giving people an alternative they didn't even know they wanted, and now they can't get enough."

The panel, which also included independent journalists and former political operatives, leaned in. "People are done with the system," one guest noted. "They've been watching the same political playbook for decades. Left or Right, it doesn't matter. Machiavelli is breaking the fourth wall, saying what everyone else is too afraid to say."

Brogan, always playing the role of both inquisitor and instigator, pressed Cuban on his involvement. "So, Mark, you're not just a supporter now, right? You're in the trenches with this guy?"

Cuban smirked. "Yeah, I'm in. At first, I was just watching from the sidelines, fascinated like everyone else. But then I realized, this isn't just a moment. It's a movement. So, I'm bringing my resources, my connections, my business acumen, and, yeah, my money, to help Machiavelli take this all the way."

The room buzzed with energy. Brogan shook his head in amazement. "Man, the media is losing its mind over this guy. The attack pieces, the hit jobs—they're throwing everything at him, and nothing sticks."

A journalist on the panel chimed in. "That's because

people don't trust legacy media anymore. Machiavelli has figured out that the real battleground isn't on cable news; it's right here, in the digital space. Podcasts, social media, viral moments. He's meeting voters where they are, not where the establishment wants them to be."

Brogan leaned forward. "So, is this real? Does he actually have a shot at winning?"

Cuban's expression turned serious. "Joe, let me put it this way: if the election were held tomorrow, the two-party system would be in full panic mode. The real question isn't whether he can win. The question is… can the machine stop him before he does?"

Silence hung in the air for a moment before Brogan broke it with a grin. "Well, if Machiavelli is the Stone Cold of politics, I guess that means we're about to see a few Stunners in Washington."

The panel laughed, but there was an undeniable truth in Brogan's words. James Machiavelli wasn't just another third-party candidate. He was a disruptor; a wrecking ball aimed at the very foundation of American politics. And if the establishment thought they could contain him, they were in for one hell of a fight.

Jimmy Kimmel Live! Machiavelli or Machiavellian?

Jimmy took full advantage of the uncanny historical parallel, with Kimmel delivering his signature blend of wit and cultural commentary. "I mean, come on, this guy's literally named Machiavelli. What's next? A challenger named Julius Caesar. Maybe we'll throw in a Brutus for good measure." The audience roared with laughter as Kimmel leaned into the absurdity of it all.

Kimmel's monologue continued to dissect the spectacle, drawing comparisons to reality TV, historical power plays, and even Game of Thrones. "We're either witnessing a masterclass in strategy or the biggest political fluke of all time. Either way, I've got my popcorn ready."

With a mix of biting satire and genuine curiosity, the segment captured the surreal nature of the moment, blurring the lines between history, politics, and entertainment in classic late-night fashion.

But beneath the humor, the show couldn't completely sidestep the serious political undercurrents at play. "At this point, it feels like we're watching a WWE Royal Rumble, and the underdog just suplexed the two big guys out of the ring. But can he actually win? Or are we just setting up for the ultimate heel turn?"

The Final Countdown

As the October 8th debate loomed, the stakes had never been higher. It was more than just a political showdown. It was a moment of reckoning for a divided nation. Three men, each representing a vastly different vision for America, were about to collide in an arena where words cut deeper than swords.

Ronald Plump, the ultimate political brawler, had never faced an opponent who could match his aggression blow for blow. His presence loomed large, a force of nature in the political landscape, unyielding and unpredictable. Gavin Newtsum, the polished politician, had spent his career mastering the art of persuasion, but now he found himself walking a tightrope, struggling to keep the Democratic Party from fracturing under the weight of competing factions. And then there was Machiavelli, an insurgent, a disruptor, a wildcard whose very existence defied conventional wisdom. His rise had stunned the establishment, and now he stood poised to rewrite the rules of the game entirely.

St. Louis, Missouri, the chosen battleground, had become a fortress. Every street within miles of the debate venue pulsed with energy, protesters clashing, supporters chanting, journalists scrambling to capture the chaos. Police barricades and security checkpoints turned the city into a militarized zone, a reflection of the boiling tensions that had gripped the country. Helicopters circled overhead, monitoring the crowd, while armored vehicles stood by, ready for the worst. The air crackled with anticipation, a collective breath held by millions of Americans watching from their living rooms, bars, and packed town halls.

There would be no live audience inside the debate hall. Just three men, the moderators, and the unblinking eye of the cameras broadcasting their every move to the nation. It was a fitting backdrop for a contest that had already shattered expectations. Each candidate knew that this night could be the turning point, the moment when momentum swung decisively in their favor, or when a single misstep could send their campaign into a death spiral.

The stage was set. America was watching. And as the final countdown began, one truth was undeniable: the battle for the future of the nation was about to begin.

39
BACKGROUND NOISE
PRESENT DAY
OCTOBER 8, 2028 — 5:00 P.M

St. Louis, MO.

The atmosphere inside the athletic complex at Washington University in St. Louis was a microcosm of the political battlefield that awaited the nation. Three holding areas, three vastly different approaches, and one stage where all hell was about to break loose.

Inside the Democratic nominee's room, Gavin Newtsum stood before a team of advisors, engaging in a last-minute mock debate. His campaign manager fired off potential questions while a trusted aide played the role of Ronald Plump, mimicking his erratic behavior and Machiavelli's cerebral unpredictability. Newtsum, his brow furrowed, responded with calculated precision, his voice steady. He had spent weeks preparing for this, determined to present himself as the competent alternative to the chaos that had defined the last four years. Every question was a chance for him to prove he was the most presidential figure on stage.

But despite his best efforts, the music infiltrated the room, first, Eminem's *The Way I Am* blared, followed by Rage Against the Machine's *Killing in the Name*, each track an invasive surge of bass that reverberated through the walls like a relentless war drum. Newtsum exhaled sharply, trying to focus, but his irritation was evident. It was designed to be. He rubbed his temple, shaking his head. "Christ, does he think this is a WWE event?" he muttered under his breath. His aides exchanged nervous glances. Machiavelli was already inside their heads.

The room felt tighter, the air heavier. An aide hesitated before speaking. "Do we push back? Ask for it to be shut off?"

Newtsum scoffed, shaking his head. "And let him win before we even get on stage? No. We push through."

Just a few feet away, in another holding area, the scene was pure chaos. President Ronald Plump, red-faced and animated, paced back and forth, gesturing wildly as he vented his frustrations at his aides.

"They're going to come after me with all their lies!" he barked. "Fake news, all of it! Newtsum? Weak. Machiavelli? A joke!" His aides nodded furiously, offering rehearsed lines to counter expected attacks. But Plump wasn't interested in rehearsing. He was preparing the only way he knew how—

by dominating, by attacking, by making the debate about him.

And then there was the music. That goddamn music.

Plump's scowl deepened as another pulse of bass vibrated through the walls.

"What the hell is that?" he snapped, glaring toward the source of the sound.

"Uh, it's Machiavelli, sir," an aide offered hesitantly.

Plump clenched his jaw. "Machiavelli," he repeated, the name like venom on his tongue. "What kind of idiot blasts music before a debate? Who does that?"

A pause. Then, another wave of sound, Tupac's and Snoop Dogg's *2 of Amerikaz Most Wanted* shaking the walls, followed by the bone-crushing riffs of Metallica's *Seek and Destroy*.

"Jesus Christ," Plump muttered. His hand clenched into a fist. "Somebody shut that down."

A different aide cleared his throat. "Uh, sir... we can't."

Plump turned, eyes narrowing. "We can't?"

"It's... it's Machiavelli."

Plump scoffed, shaking his head. "Unbelievable. Total lack of respect. Total fraud. And that music... Horrible! Noise! What is he, a teenager? Ridiculous." He whirled on his closest advisor. "You see what I have to deal with? Is this what they want? This is their guy?!"

He exhaled sharply, then turned toward the mirror, straightening his tie in quick, aggravated jerks. "Fine. Fine.

Let him play his little games. It won't matter when I get on that stage."

But the music continued, a deliberate taunt wrapped in distortion and bass.

In the third room, Machiavelli sat back in a lounge chair, legs crossed, eyes closed, a subtle smirk playing on his lips. Every note was calculated. Every track was chosen with purpose. Rage. Defiance. Anarchy. He wanted them to hear it. He wanted them to feel it.

He pictured Newtsum trying to drown it out with focus, but failing. He envisioned Plump, fists clenching, agitation bubbling. They thought he was an outsider, some unhinged wildcard, but they didn't understand. He wasn't just here to disrupt; he was here to control. To dictate the rhythm before a single word was spoken.

Everything was theater, and tonight, he was the director.

Across from him, seated on a sleek leather couch, was Paola Machiavelli, his wife and closest confidante. She scrolled through her phone, keeping a close eye on real-time reactions from social media. "They're already talking about the music," she said, amusement flickering in her voice. "Plump's camp is furious."

"Good," James murmured without opening his eyes. "Agitation breeds mistakes."

His brother, Giovanni, stood near the door, arms crossed, his expression impassive. "Newtsum's trying to ignore it, but it's working. His people are rattled."

Rachele, Giovanni's wife, was perched on the armrest

beside him, a glass of whiskey in hand. "They still don't understand us," she said, swirling the amber liquid. "They think we're chaos. We're not. We're precision."

Paola smirked, looking up from her phone. "And that's what makes us dangerous. They don't know what to expect."

Giovanni chuckled. "They're expecting a wild card. Instead, they're getting a scalpel."

James finally opened his eyes, smirking. He didn't need to add anything. They were all right. His team, his family, they understood. Let them think he was unpredictable. Let them think he was reckless. That's when they'd be most vulnerable.

Beyond his family, the network was already in motion. A cadre of highly intelligent operatives, media tacticians, the security team, and digital strategists were working in the background, amplifying his presence. On social media, the Machiavelli campaign had already deployed a wave of memes, clips, and out-of-context soundbites designed to dominate the conversation before the debate even began.

He let the next song build, felt the tempo rising with the ticking clock. It wasn't just about the debate. It was about perception. It was about control.

Five minutes to showtime.

A stagehand entered each room, handing out index cards with the candidates' positions. Plump would be in the center. Newtsum to his right. Machiavelli to his left.

The symbolism wasn't lost on anyone.

40
POWER SHIFT
PRESENT DAY
OCTOBER 8, 2028 — 6:00 P.M

St. Louis, MO.

Backstage, the tension was palpable. The three candidates stood at a distance from one another, each radiating their own unique energy. Plump, surrounded by his Secret Service detail, wore his signature smug expression. Newtsum adjusted his tie, exuding the polished confidence of a seasoned politician. Meanwhile, James Machiavelli stood apart, arms crossed, eyes burning with determination.

There would be no live audience inside the debate hall. Just three men, the moderators, and the unblinking eye of the cameras broadcasting their every move to the nation. It was a fitting backdrop for a contest that had already shattered expectations.

The moderator's voice rang out over the speakers. "Now introducing, Independent Presidential Candidate James Machiavelli."

The debate hall's silence was shattered with a deafening crash, the unmistakable sound of glass breaking. In that instant, millions watching at home knew exactly what was coming. A raw, distorted guitar riff ripped through the speakers, its heavy, unrelenting rhythm pounding like the heartbeat of a warrior marching into battle.

The drums hit, driving forward with an unshakable force, each beat a declaration of dominance. The bass snarled underneath, a growling, rebellious undercurrent that sent a surge of adrenaline through anyone listening. As the iconic riff looped, it carried an aura of pure defiance. This was the sound of a man who took orders from no one.

James Machiavelli strode onto the stage with the kind of confidence that made it clear he wasn't just walking; he was making a statement. Every step was deliberate; every movement charged with the energy of someone who thrived in chaos. The pounding beat of the song perfectly matched his stride, amplifying the moment, turning the debate stage into his personal arena.

For those watching at home, the message was clear. This wasn't just another candidate. This was a man walking into battle, ready to raise hell. He ran up to the center podium, gripping it tightly as he perched over it like a king claiming his throne.

The moderator hesitated for a moment, perplexed.

Plump was supposed to take the center podium. But before he could interject, the next introduction came.

"Next, Democratic nominee Gavin Newtsum."

A polished, almost regal air clung to Newtsum as he stepped forward, his stride measured, his expression composed. He adjusted his cuffs with practiced precision, the bright studio lights reflecting off his immaculate suit. For a brief second, his eyes flicked to the camera. He was always aware of the lens, always conscious of his image.

As he moved past Machiavelli, his lips barely moved as he muttered, just loud enough for only one person to hear.

"Gutter trash."

Machiavelli's smirk was instant, razor-sharp. He didn't flinch, didn't even turn his head. Instead, he chuckled, the kind of slow, knowing laugh that made it clear he relished the insult. Then, in a voice dripping with venomous amusement, he fired back.

"Hell yeah, and it must burn you that you're losing to someone like me."

Newtsum's jaw tensed. For the first time, the mask slipped, just a fraction. His eyes darkened as he glanced at Machiavelli, a flash of pure disdain in his gaze. But he said nothing more. Swallowing the moment, he stepped behind his podium, his practiced composure returning, but the air between them had already been poisoned.

The room, already thick with tension, felt heavier. This wasn't just a debate. It was a battlefield.

"And finally, the 47th President of the United States, Ronald J. Plump."

The doors parted, and Plump strode onto the stage, his signature grin plastered across his face. He waved to the cameras, basking in the spotlight, his presence sucking up all the oxygen in the room. His signature confidence was on full display until his gaze met Machiavelli's.

Machiavelli was already staring him down. Unmoving. Unblinking. The smirk was gone, replaced with something colder, more primal. The kind of look a predator gives right before it strikes.

Plump's grin faltered, just slightly. But Machiavelli saw it. Everyone watching saw it.

As Plump approached the center podium—his podium —Machiavelli leaned in, voice low and cutting, but loud enough to carry through the microphones.

"You get your punk ass over there. The center is my spot, bitch. That's right, don't look at me, coward. Keep walking with that dumbass smile on your face."

The room felt like it had frozen. The millions watching at home could hear every word, unfiltered and raw.

For a split second, Plump hesitated. A rare moment of indecision. His eyes darted to the podium, to Machiavelli, to the moderators, searching for something, some sign that he could ignore this moment. But there was nothing.

Without a word, he adjusted course, veering off to the podium that had originally been assigned to Machiavelli.

The shift was subtle, just a few feet, but the impact was seismic.

Gasps erupted online. Social media exploded. The unshakable, unbreakable Plump, punked, live on national television. The aura of invincibility he had cultivated for years had been shattered in a single exchange.

Machiavelli, now standing tall at the center, planted his hands on the podium like a conqueror surveying his domain. He glanced to his left, where Newtsum stood rigid, burning with silent rage. He glanced to his right, where Plump was adjusting his mic, trying to recover.

Then, nonchalantly, Machiavelli smirked.

The debate hadn't even started, and he had already won the first battle.

Back in the holding area, two Secret Service agents exchanged glances before whispering to members of Machiavelli's security team.

"Boy, we hope your guy wins. We can't stand our guy."

The debate officially began.

The moderator, a seasoned journalist with decades of political showdowns under his belt, turned to Plump first. His tone was calm, authoritative.

"Let's get started. I want to begin tonight with the issue voters repeatedly say is their primary concerns are the economy and the cost of living. When it comes to the economy, do you believe Americans are better off than they were four years ago?"

Plump, resting his hands on the podium, glanced at

Machiavelli, expecting him to jump in with some outlandish remark. Instead, the independent candidate remained still, his expression unreadable. Plump decided to play it safe.

"I'll let my opponents answer first," he said, flashing his signature smirk.

The moderator nodded and turned to Machiavelli. "Mr. Machiavelli?"

Machiavelli leaned forward, gripping the sides of his podium, his voice carrying the weight of a man who wasn't here for political pleasantries.

"Forget the last four years. Americans haven't been better off for at least forty, hell, maybe fifty years. Let's cut the bullshit. How can we say we're better off when 60% of Americans live paycheck to paycheck? When 83% of households struggle financially? When have real, inflation-adjusted wages declined for the average worker over the last fifty years?" He let the silence linger, his piercing gaze scanning the cameras, as if speaking directly to the millions watching at home. "The rich keep getting richer while the rest of us keep scraping by. The 1% has never had it better, and yet we're supposed to believe that GDP growth benefits us all?" He scoffed. "Let's ask the people at home: What has the American economy done for you? For your family? For your community? The answer is obvious; it's only getting worse for most of us."

The internet erupted in real time. Twitter, TikTok, Reddit—all of them flooded with reactions.

The moderator turned to Newtsum, who straightened

his tie, schooling his expression into calm authority. His voice was smooth, measured, as he began his response.

"Look, we have to be honest with the American people. The last administration left us in economic disarray. We inherited skyrocketing debt, crumbling infrastructure, and a job market that, frankly, wasn't working for the middle class. Under my leadership in California, we've invested in green energy, raised the minimum wage, and created hundreds of thousands of jobs. That's the kind of leadership America needs."

But midway through Newtsum's response, Plump's patience cracked. He did what he always did—mocked, interrupted, tried to dominate the stage. He threw in sarcastic quips, rolled his eyes, and waved his hand dismissively, making it clear that in his mind, this debate was about him.

Plump snorted loudly, waving a dismissive hand. "Yeah, sure, Gavin. You turned California into a homeless encampment. Great job."

Newtsum barely reacted, continuing, "We can't afford to go backward. If we want to make real progress, we need to…"

Plump cut in again, louder this time. "Oh, real progress? Did you mean like the mass exodus out of your state? Nobody wants to live in California anymore, Gavin. You're running it like a third-world country!"

Newtsum sighed, shaking his head. "Mr. President, you lost California by five million votes."

"I won the real America," Plump shot back.

But Machiavelli wasn't having it.

He turned sharply, taking several steps toward Plump's podium. The movement alone was enough to silence Plump, but then he raised a finger, pointing directly at Plump. His voice, when it came, was sharp as a knife.

"You need to shut the fuck up, or I'll shut you up."

A stunned silence fell over the room. The moderators froze. Even Newtsum, always one to mask his emotions, blinked.

Plump, caught completely off guard, faltered. His mouth hung slightly open, as if trying to process what had just been said to him on live television, with millions watching. For the first time in his career, he didn't have an immediate comeback.

The moderator, regaining his composure, cleared his throat. "Mr. Machiavelli, I must ask you to return to your podium."

Machiavelli lingered for a beat, staring Plump down, then smirked and sauntered back. Newtsum, his expression unreadable, picked up where he left off, but the energy had shifted. The focus was no longer on him.

The moderator, attempting to regain order, turned to Plump. "Mr. President, how about your answer?"

Plump took a deep breath, then launched into his typical speech.

"Look, under my administration, we had the greatest economy in the history of this country. The stock market was at an all-time high, unemployment was at record lows, and businesses were thriving. But then the radical left, the deep-state came in. They rigged the election, and look what happened. Inflation, gas prices through the roof, people losing their jobs. It's a disaster. And I'll tell you, the only reason anyone is even asking this question is because of the total incompetence of these two guys up here." He gestured toward Newtsum and Machiavelli.

Machiavelli, leaning idly on his podium, let out an exaggerated yawn.

Plump's eyes snapped at him. "Oh, you got something to say, tough guy?"

Machiavelli grinned. "Yeah. Hey, bitch, why don't you get Poutine's dick out of your mouth? Nobody can understand what you're saying."

The audience watching at home lost it. The internet exploded. A TikTok clip of the moment gained thousands of likes before Plump even had a chance to respond.

Plump's face darkened. "Oh, real classy. Real presidential."

Machiavelli spread his arms. "What? I'm just saying what everyone else is thinking."

Plump jabbed a finger at him. "You have no idea what it takes to run a country. You're a nobody. You don't have experience, and you don't have a real plan. You're just a loudmouth running his mouth for attention."

Machiavelli's grin widened. "You just described yourself, Donny."

The crowd watching at home erupted again. Twitter was on fire.

Plump, flustered, doubled down. "I built an empire! I am the President of the United States! What have you done? What have you built?"

Machiavelli took a step forward, voice dropping to an almost mocking calmness. "I built this moment. Right now. Where everyone watching can see you for what you really are... a fraud. A coward who backs down the second someone calls you out to your face."

Plump's mouth opened, then closed. For a split second, it looked like he wanted to lash out, but something stopped him.

Machiavelli tilted his head. "What's the matter, Donny? Russian prostitute got your tongue? We've all seen the video."

Plump seethed but said nothing.

The moderator, momentarily stunned into silence, let the tension hang in the air before finally clearing his throat. His voice was measured, but there was no hiding the strain in it.

"Gentlemen, let's take a breath. Tension is high, but we have several more questions left."

He turned to Machiavelli, hoping to pull the debate back from the brink. "Government efficiency and accountability are huge parts of your campaign. How will you maintain a solid working relationship with Congress and the judiciary?"

Machiavelli exhaled slowly, then leaned into the microphone, his voice calm but deliberate, each word carrying weight.

"The real question isn't how I'll work with them; it's how they plan on working with me."

The audience watching at home could feel it. That wasn't a politician talking. That was a man making a declaration of war.

Machiavelli let the moment stretch just long enough before continuing.

"My plan is simple: rip out the rot that has been eating away at this country for decades. That means accountability at every level. That means ending the revolving door between corporate lobbyists and our lawmakers. That means..."

Plump, still fuming from earlier, saw his opening and seized it with a fury. His voice, sharp and agitated, cut through the hall as he threw out his usual barrage of accusations, trying to wrestle the spotlight back onto himself.

"This guy is a joke, folks! A total joke! No experience, no clue what he's doing. Do you think he's gonna fight corruption? Please! He is the corruption! I wouldn't be surprised if he's a plant from the deep state! Probably getting funded by George Soros, the radical left, maybe even China! Yeah, wouldn't that be something? This guy, this nobody, coming out of nowhere, trying to act tough?"

Machiavelli didn't even blink.

Instead, he moved.

With a slow, measured stride, he walked straight to Plump's podium, closing the distance between them until they were standing just inches apart.

Plump, certainly not used to being physically confronted, took a half-step back before catching himself. But the cameras caught it. The internet caught it.

Machiavelli tilted his head; eyes locked onto Plump's. The room was dead silent; the tension crackling.

Then...

SMACK.

41

FALL FROM GRACE

PRESENT DAY

OCTOBER 8, 2028 — 6:30 P.M

St. Louis, MO.

Not a punch. Not a shove. A forehanded smack so vicious, so sudden, that the sound of it rang through the silent auditorium like a gunshot. The world seemed to pause as Ronald Plump's knees buckled, his balance faltering, and then, just like that, he was on his ass.

The moderator gasped, his breath catching in his throat. Gavin Newtsum's eyebrows shot up so high they nearly vanished into his hairline. Plump's mouth hung open, his signature pout gone, replaced by a perfect expression of pure shock and terror, frozen in time like a grotesque wax figure. But it wasn't just the people in the room who were stunned.

The internet detonated.

Clips of the moment spread at the speed of light, hashtags flooding every social media platform within seconds. #PlumpSlapped, #MachiavelliReigns, #Orange-KnockedOut, #BitchMade, all variations trended globally. Commentators, influencers, and politicians scrambled to react, some laughing in disbelief, others gasping in horror. News outlets went live within minutes, hurried anchors struggling to maintain journalistic neutrality as they replayed the footage on an endless loop.

And at the center of it all stood Machiavelli.

His stance was unwavering, his body a coiled spring of controlled violence. His eyes burned with a lethal intensity, cold and unforgiving. The entire room felt the shift in power, the tectonic plates of political dominance cracking beneath their feet. He wasn't just standing over Plump. He towered over him. His presence swallowed the stage whole.

When he finally spoke, his voice was a terrifying whisper, steady and deliberate, the kind of voice that promised nothing but ruin.

"I told you to shut the fuck up."

The words sliced through the silence like a blade, each syllable a scalpel peeling away the last scraps of Plump's invincibility.

And then, in a single deliberate motion, Machiavelli gestured with his hands, challenging Plump to rise.

"Get the fuck up! Get the fuck up, you fuckin' coward! You ain't nothing but a BITCH!"

But Plump didn't get up. He didn't even speak. The bravado, the bluster, the unchecked arrogance that had carried him through scandal after scandal; gone. What was left was something small. Something pathetic. He scrambled backward on his hands and knees like a cornered animal, his eyes darting wildly, seeking refuge that wasn't there. For the first time in his life, Ronald Plump looked terrified.

The entire scene lasted no more than fifteen seconds before chaos erupted.

Secret Service agents stormed the stage, their movements swift, mechanical, trained for moments of crisis. The first agent crouched next to Plump, shielding him with his body. The second placed himself between Machiavelli and Plump, his hand hovering near his holster, unsure of what the next move would be. The air thickened with tension, the entire stage vibrating with the weight of an unspoken war.

Machiavelli's security team moved just as quickly, their presence a declaration in itself. They weren't just there to protect him. They were there to ensure dominance. Like a pack of wolves, they encircled him, silent, waiting, their expressions unreadable behind their dark sunglasses. Their tailored suits didn't hide the sheer brutality they carried with them.

For a moment, it seemed as if the world teetered on the edge of something uncontrollable.

And then, just as quickly, Newtsum's security detail took action. The California governor was swept off the stage, disappearing into the wings before things spiraled even further. For a brief moment, it seemed as if the chaos would settle. The debate hall, once electrified with tension, now crackled with the lingering aftershocks of raw fury. An agent helped Plump to his feet, dusting him off, trying to restore some semblance of dignity. His suit was ruffled, his tie skewed to the side, and the orange hue of his face was flushed a deep, angry red. But then, Plump lost it.

Red-faced and fuming, he started spewing venom at Machiavelli, his voice a shrill mix of rage and desperation. "That was a cheap shot! You're a fraud! A coward! You're nothing without your little goons protecting you!"

Machiavelli didn't hesitate. He roared back; eyes locked onto Plump with a look that could burn steel. His posture was relaxed, but his body was coiled, ready for another round if necessary.

"Funny how tough you get when there's fifteen body-guards between us. You were a little bitch when it was just the two of us. I gave you every opportunity to stand up for yourself, and you lay there like the punk-ass bitch you've always been and always will be."

Plump's face twisted with rage. His fists were clenched. He lunged forward, but his own agents held him back, their grip firm against his flailing arms.

"You think you're some kind of tough guy?" Plump spat. "You're a joke! You couldn't win a fair fight if your life depended on it!"

Machiavelli smirked. "Fair fight? Do you mean the one

where you curled up like a baby and whimpered? That fight?"

Plump's eyes bulged. "I had to let my men handle it! I'm the President! You think I'd waste my time on trash like you?"

Machiavelli scoffed. "You waste your time on Twitter tantrums and whining about ratings. Face it, coward, you were born on third base and still can't make it home without someone carrying you."

Plump's lips quivered with fury. "You'll regret this! I have power! You're nothing! **NOTHING!**"

Machiavelli threw his head back and let out a sharp, mocking laugh before deliberately raising both middle fingers at Plump, his smirk widening as he locked eyes with him.

Plump was still cursing, still seething, when another player entered the chaos.

Ronald Plump Jr.

No one had seen him coming. He slipped in from the opposite side of the debate hall, moving like a snake in the grass. His eyes were dark with intent, his jaw clenched so tightly it looked like he might break his own teeth. Before anyone could react, he was behind Machiavelli, arms locking around his neck in a tight chokehold.

For a split second, it looked like Plump Jr. had the upper hand. But only for a split second.

Machiavelli's instincts took over. He didn't panic. He didn't flail. He reacted with deadly precision honed over months of calculated conflict. He reached behind him, grabbed the backs of Plump Jr.'s legs, and with one explosive motion, jumped backward. The force sent both men crashing to the stage floor, but Machiavelli was ready. He rolled, shifting his weight, and before Plump Jr. could react, Machiavelli was on top of him.

Three brutal elbows to the face.

Crack. Crack. Crack.

Plump Jr.'s head bounced off the floor. Blood erupted from his now-broken nose, the crimson stark against his pale, stunned face. His limbs twitched, his body stiffening as if his nervous system had short-circuited. His breath came in ragged gasps, his eyes fluttering with shock.

Then, the world seemed to catch up.

A mix of black suits and earpieces clashed as agents scrambled to contain the chaos. Two guards yanked Machiavelli back, their grips ironclad, but his face remained stone-cold, unshaken.

The stage devolved into pushing and shoving, Secret Service agents barking orders, security teams squaring off. It was a scene out of a political apocalypse, a moment so surreal it would be dissected for decades. But amidst the madness, one voice cut through.

The head Secret Service agent's voice was sharp and final.

"Get President Plump out of here. Now."

Plump thrashed, screaming curses at Machiavelli, his face contorted with a desperate fury. But his agents obeyed.

He was dragged off the stage, his shoes scuffing against the polished wood, still shouting, still trying to salvage his ego.

Then, the agent turned to his men. "Stand down."

Finally, he pointed to Plump Jr., who lay supine, his body stiff, blood pooling beneath his nose.

"Get medical help for him. Now."

The smack had been heard around the world. But what had started as a single moment had now become something much, much bigger. The footage was already spreading, the internet ablaze with theories, memes, and furious debates. The political landscape had been shattered in an instant, a fault line splitting right down the middle.

42
DEMONSTRATING DOMINANCE
PRESENT DAY
OCTOBER 8, 2028 — 7:00 P.M

St. Louis, MO.

C haos. That was the only way to describe it. Every news station, every social media feed, every live podcast was consumed by the shocking moment that had just unfolded on the presidential debate stage. The world had just witnessed James Machiavelli smack Ronald Plump. Live. Unfiltered. Raw. The replay looped endlessly, analyzed from every possible angle. Was it staged? Was it real? What did it mean?

Then, amidst the confusion, a new development. Anchors paused mid-sentence as their producers handed them urgent messages. Notifications flooded the screens of journalists, influencers, and political commentators alike.

James Machiavelli's campaign had just released a video recorded months earlier on June 28th, 2028. Within moments, every major news outlet was airing it. Social media exploded, with accounts from both ends of the political spectrum sharing the link.

The video opened to a dimly lit conference room. A long table was covered with documents, strategy maps, and whiteboards filled with flowcharts detailing the downfall of Ronald Plump. The camera panned over the table, zooming in on folders labeled 'Debate Strategy: Phase III,' 'Psychological Triggers,' and 'Weak Points: Plump's Breaking Threshold.'

Standing at the end of the table was James Machiavelli himself, alongside his wife Paola, his brother Giovanni, and his sister-in-law Rachele. Just at the far edge of the camera view was his core team of advisors. They looked calm, methodical, like generals plotting the final stage of a war.

Paola leaned forward, scanning the documents before speaking. "He will be primed for an explosion. You will see his outbursts become more frequent, more erratic, especially after we release the video showing Plump receiving golden showers from Russian prostitutes and releasing a series of documents, emails, and transcripts detailing that he has been getting blackmailed by Poutine this whole time. We don't need to create a moment. We just need to direct him into it."

Rachele nodded, tapping a highlighted section on the whiteboard. "His biggest weakness is perception. The moment people see him as weak, his entire persona crumbles. If we make him feel trapped, humiliated, he'll lash out. That's when we strike."

Giovanni smirked, flipping through a dossier. "We need to keep him on edge. Every calculated jab, every strategic leak—it all serves one purpose, making him feel cornered. His whole life, he's been able to spin things, talk his way out. But not this time. This time, we control the board."

Machiavelli leaned forward, hands clasped. "We know who he is. We know how he reacts. And we know exactly what will push him past the breaking point."

A strategist gestured toward the screen at the front of the room, which displayed clips of Plump at rallies, interviews, and debates. Each clip was paused and analyzed, with Machiavelli's team dissecting his body language, his speech patterns, and his moments of hesitation.

"He thrives on control," Giovanni noted. "Take that away, and he spirals. The key is escalation. We push, we prod, and then…"

"We hit," Machiavelli interrupted, standing. "Not just metaphorically. Physically."

Silence fell over the room.

"You mean?" one of his advisors began.

Machiavelli nodded. "Yes. At the debate, in front of the entire world. When the moment is right, I will strike him. And in that moment, he will show them all how weak he truly is. He will sputter, he will rage, and in his desperation, he will prove what we've been saying all along. That he's unfit. That he's a fraud. That he's all bark and no bite. A complete pussy."

Paola leaned in, her tone cold and measured. "And the beauty of it? He won't even see it coming. He thinks of himself as untouchable, beyond consequences. That's why he won't be able to process it in real time. He'll be stunned, vulnerable. And the entire world will witness it."

An advisor asked, "What happens if you hit him too hard and knock him down?"

Machiavelli replied, "I hope I don't knock him down because he will say that he tripped or I sucker-punched him. I want him on his feet so the world can see him cower."

Giovanni interjected, "If you knocked him off his feet, it wouldn't be the worst thing in the world. You will have about ten to fifteen seconds before the Secret Service gets out there. Give him the opportunity to stand up for himself."

Rachele chuckled. "And we all know he won't. He'll flail, he'll scream, but he won't fight back. That's the moment we'll burn into history. The moment the world stops seeing him as a strongman and starts seeing him for what he really is… a scared, pathetic fraud."

A strategist looked around the room. "And what if they call it assault? What if it backfires?"

Machiavelli smirked. "Let them. By then, the narrative will already be ours. The world will have seen what they needed to see. And that moment? It'll define the election.

They won't be talking about me hitting him. They'll be talking about his reaction, his weakness."

Paola crossed her arms. "So, we go through with this, and when the footage rolls, the world will see this wasn't an accident. It wasn't reckless. It was a demonstration."

A slow zoom-in on Machiavelli's face.

"Everything we do leads to that moment. And when it happens, the world will see it was never about chaos. It was never about impulse. It was planned. Controlled. Calculated."

The screen faded to black. Then, a single phrase appeared in bold white letters: "We were always ahead. Now you understand."

As the video ended, the reaction was immediate. News anchors sat in stunned silence before scrambling to respond. Social media ignited with debates, theories, and endless replays. The Machiavelli campaign had not just struck first; they had proven beyond a shadow of a doubt that they had orchestrated the entire thing from the very beginning. And in doing so, they had turned a moment of apparent chaos into the ultimate display of strategic dominance.

43

IRONY ON DISPLAY

PRESENT DAY

OCTOBER 9, 2028 — 5:00 P.M

St. Louis, MO.

T he afternoon sun cast long shadows across the tarmac as James Machiavelli's campaign prepared to depart St. Louis. The energy from the previous night's debate still lingered, electrifying the air around the candidate and his team. Luggage was being loaded, final calls were being made, and security personnel stood alert as the convoy prepared for departure.

Then, the unmistakable wail of sirens shattered the relative calm. Three police vehicles sped onto the scene, their blue and red lights flashing ominously. The sight sent a ripple of unease through the campaign staff, some exchanging nervous glances while others naturally moved toward Machiavelli for reassurance. Doors swung open in near-unison, and uniformed officers stepped out with a purpose. The air grew tense as Machiavelli's security team moved instinctively, forming a protective barrier between their charge and the approaching law enforcement officers.

The lead officer, a tall, no-nonsense man in his late forties, held up his hands in a calming gesture. "James Machiavelli, we have a warrant for your arrest. You are being charged with assaulting a federal official." His tone was firm but respectful. "President Plump is pressing charges."

A murmur spread among the campaign staff. Some gasped; others muttered in disbelief. Reporters nearby scrambled to capture the unfolding scene, cameras flashing and microphones being thrust forward.

Machiavelli's expression remained unreadable as he slowly exhaled, his mind processing the absurdity of the situation.

His security detail—well-trained and fiercely loyal—did not budge. A few shifted, hands resting near their holsters, waiting for a command. The tension was razor-sharp.

Machiavelli raised his hand, signaling his team to stand down.

"Gentlemen, I appreciate your concern," he said, his voice smooth but edged with steel. He turned his gaze toward the officer. "I assume you understand the irony of this moment?"

The officer hesitated before responding. "Sir?"

"I am being arrested for smacking a man who ordered

the assassination of me and my family." Machiavelli's eyes locked onto the officer's, waiting for a reaction.

The officer sighed, his lips pressing into a thin line. "I'm very sorry, Mr. Machiavelli. We're just doing our jobs. If it's any consolation, my family and I have already voted for you."

A smirk tugged at the corner of Machiavelli's mouth. He shook his head slightly, almost amused at the absurdity of it all. "Then let's keep this peaceful. I will surrender myself in person. My team will bring me to your precinct."

The officer gave a curt nod. "That will work. Thank you, Mr. Machiavelli."

With a final glance at his team, Machiavelli stepped forward. The tension eased marginally, but the weight of the moment lingered. His security team flanked him as they made their way to the convoy, now bound not for another rally, but for a police precinct.

At the precinct, Machiavelli moved with the same commanding presence he had on the debate stage. The booking process was expeditious but thorough. Cameras flashed as he took his mugshot, the resulting image capturing a man who looked less like a desperate politician and more like a cerebral mafia don, exuding restrained power even in the face of adversity. His eyes were sharp, piercing, as if challenging the world itself to come at him.

The media frenzy outside the precinct had already begun. News channels ran breaking reports, pundits debated the implications of his arrest, and social media exploded with reactions from supporters and critics alike. The narrative was already being shaped, and Machiavelli knew this moment would be more than just another headline. It would define the coming weeks of his campaign.

Once processed, he was escorted to a holding cell. The heavy door clanked open, revealing its current occupants, two homeless men who reeked of cheap booze and urine. The stench was nearly overwhelming, but Machiavelli barely reacted, merely stepping inside with measured control.

A moment later, two members of his security detail positioned themselves just outside the cell, their postures rigid and alert. A lone officer was assigned as police protection, though he seemed uneasy about the whole situation.

One of the homeless men stirred, blinking bleary-eyed at Machiavelli. "You one of them big shots?" he slurred.

Machiavelli smirked, leaning against the cold, unyielding wall. "Something like that."

The other man chuckled to himself, taking another swig from a crumpled paper bag. "Guess even the rich ain't safe from the law," he muttered.

Machiavelli said nothing, letting the words settle. He wasn't a man prone to unnecessary conversations, especially now. His mind was already racing, calculating his next move, preparing for what was to come.

44

REALLY, AGAIN

PRESENT DAY

OCTOBER 9, 2028 — 8:00 P.M

St. Louis, MO.

James Machiavelli leaned back against the cold cinderblock wall of the holding cell, exuding an air of calm defiance. The acrid stench of urine and stale alcohol wafted from the two homeless men slumped nearby, their ragged coats doing little to shield them from the chill of the precinct's fluorescent-lit purgatory. Across the room, the iron bars rattled as another prisoner was escorted in, a behemoth of a man whose presence alone seemed to shrink the space. The officer leading him said nothing as he uncuffed the giant and stepped out, securing the gate with a dull metallic clang.

Machiavelli assessed the man as he sat down in the farthest corner, separated only by the reeking bodies of the homeless men. His security detail, standing just beyond the cell, bristled as an officer approached.

"The chief's orders," the officer declared. "Your men have to leave."

The protest was immediate and fervent, but Machiavelli raised a hand. "It's fine," he assured them. "I'll be out in less than an hour."

Reluctantly, they obeyed, though one subtly placed a bag on an officer's desk before leaving. Unbeknownst to anyone else, the small camera inside the bag blinked to life, capturing everything in its frame—the entirety of the holding cell, with Machiavelli closest to the lens and the imposing newcomer lingering in the background.

Minutes passed before the last remaining officer at the cell was called away to assist with the media frenzy outside. He hesitated. "I should stay here."

Machiavelli leaned forward slightly. "Go help your officers," he said smoothly. "I'll be fine."

The officer wavered but eventually nodded. "Alright, if you're sure."

As the door swung shut behind him, the silence stretched, broken only by the slow, amused chuckle of the mountain of a man.

"I wouldn't have done that if I were you."

Machiavelli smirked. "I imagine not. But then again, you don't intend for me to leave here alive, do you, Mikhail Volkov?"

Volkov's expression flickered with surprise before settling back into a grin. "How did you…"

Machiavelli interjected, "You arrived this morning on Plump's private plane under an alias, but we've been monitoring flights. And anyone in intelligence would recognize one of Poutine's favorite assassins." Machiavelli's smirk deepened. "I had a feeling we'd be seeing each other."

Volkov's chuckle returned, a low rumble of amusement. "What's your plan then? I'm not some old man you can just smack around."

Machiavelli shrugged. "Oh, I have no illusions about that. That old man never dirtied his own hands. But I do intend to leave here alive. The only question is, are you working for Poutine, Plump, or someone else?"

Volkov stretched his massive shoulders, his smile widening. "Plump, but he needed Poutine's permission." He continued, "And how do you think you're going to survive an hour, if I don't plan on letting you survive the next ten minutes?"

Machiavelli remained seated, his expression relaxed, almost amused. "That depends. On whether I incapacitate you or kill you first." He paused, then added with a smirk, "Whenever you're ready, Suka."

Volkov's expression darkened instantly. Rage flared in his eyes at the insult, but what unsettled him more was the man before him, grinning in the face of death.

A movement. One of the homeless men stirred and

shuffled closer to Volkov. The stench of booze clung to him as he mumbled, "Hey, you know Drago?"

Volkov barely spared him a glance. "Shut up, silly man, and stay out of my way."

It was the last thing he said before the two ragged figures sprang into action. In a blur of trained precision, they struck like coiled vipers, their movements too swift for the lumbering assassin to counter. One delivered a brutal chop to Volkov's throat, momentarily cutting off his air, while the other pivoted behind him, yanking his arms into a lock that even his brute strength couldn't break.

Volkov bucked wildly, his massive frame thrashing as he attempted to shake them off. He swung an elbow, missing by inches as one of the disguised operatives ducked beneath the blow and drove a knee into his ribs. The other twisted his captured arm at an excruciating angle, forcing a pained grunt from Volkov's lips. Before he could fully recover, the soaked chloroform rag was clamped over his face. His struggles became sluggish, his furious growls turning into muffled gasps before his body finally went limp, crumpling to the floor in an unconscious heap.

Machiavelli stood, brushing off imaginary dust from his sleeves as he stepped toward the fallen assassin. He crouched beside Volkov, his gaze cold, calculating. Then, without breaking eye contact with the camera's lens, he smirked and murmured, "That's the second time you missed, Plump. At least this time, you left my family out of it."

The silence was shattered as the doors burst open, a flood of officers rushing into the room. Weapons were drawn, orders barked, and confusion reigned until someone noticed the blinking light of the hidden camera. Outside, the roar of the media dimmed as screens across the country broadcast the foiled assassination attempt in real-time.

The Chief of Police shoved his way through the chaos, his face a mask of realization and guilt. "Release them," he commanded, his voice brooking no argument.

As Machiavelli walked toward the exit, the Chief caught his arm. His grip was firm, yet there was a weight to it.

"I owe you an apology."

Machiavelli nodded. "I appreciate that, Chief. And by the way," he added, his voice calm but deliberate, "the CIA has a hefty bounty for Volkov's capture. Turn him in. Use the money to give your officers a well-earned bonus."

With that, James Machiavelli strode into the storm of flashing lights and shouting reporters, a knowing smile still playing on his lips.

45

THE COLLAPSE

PRESENT DAY

OCTOBER 2028 — 8:30 P.M.

St. Louis, MO.

The seismic impact of the smack heard around the world was still reverberating through the political landscape when another shocking event rattled the nation: another assassination attempt on James Machiavelli. But rather than shaking the confidence of his supporters, it solidified his standing as the dominant political force in the country. Machiavelli's poll numbers soared to an unprecedented 62%, while Ronald Plump's support cratered to a humiliating 13%. Gavin Newtsum, once seen as a serious contender, saw his numbers slip to 23%, with a mere 2% of voters still undecided.

The media, once beholden to their respective partisan narratives, could no longer ignore the reality unfolding before them. Networks that had spent years shaping public perception—CNN, Fox News, MSNBC—were now forced to acknowledge Machiavelli's inevitability. Stories once buried were now being broadcast to millions; the relentless efforts of both the Republican and Democratic establishments to disqualify Machiavelli through legal and procedural warfare. Republicans worked to challenge his eligibility in multiple battleground states, leveraging obscure technicalities in election laws to argue that he failed to meet certain requirements. Lawsuits were filed at an unprecedented rate, seeking emergency rulings to remove his name from ballots. Election officials aligned with the GOP attempted to stall certification processes, delaying the printing of ballots in crucial states.

On the Democratic side, the DNC poured resources into legal challenges, arguing that Machiavelli's campaign had violated campaign finance laws and procedural deadlines, all in an attempt to discredit his candidacy before voters had their say. Liberal-leaning states pushed restrictive regulations targeting independent candidates, aiming to limit their access to debates and public funding. At the grassroots level, efforts to register new voters were hampered by sudden changes in voter ID requirements and the purging of registrations tied to Machiavelli's demographic base. The lengths to which both parties went made it impossible to deny that the two-party system had conspired to prevent the rise of a true outsider.

In the aftermath, traditional Republican allies turned

against Plump with stunning speed. Once-loyal supporters, including some of his closest confidants, publicly distanced themselves. Former allies, such as Senate Minority Leader John Thune and former Secretary of State Michael Pompeo, began openly criticizing him.

"The party has been hijacked for too long," Thune declared on a Primetime CNN interview. "It's time for real conservatives to reclaim our values. Plump has led us into chaos, and now we are seeing the cost."

Pompeo, who had served under Plump, was even more direct. "The man is unhinged. We ignored the warning signs, and now he's dragging the entire party down with him."

The calls for aggressive investigations into the latest assassination attempt on Machiavelli grew louder, with members of the Senate Intelligence Committee confirming there was credible evidence linking the attack to individuals within Plump's inner circle. The FBI launched an official probe, and leaks suggested that Plump himself may have been involved in orchestrating the hit.

Headlines across the nation reflected the growing outrage.

Shocking Links Between Plump and Machiavelli Assassination Attempt Emerge

—The Washington Post

Republican Exodus: Allies Abandon Plump in Wake of Machiavelli Attack

—*The New York Times*

FBI Investigating Plump Inner Circle for Ties to Machiavelli Hit

—*NBC News*

The GOP's Reckoning: Plump's Fall from Power Has Begun

—*The Wall Street Journal*

On social media, the reaction was immediate and unforgiving. Hashtags like `#PlumpTheCoward` and `#GOPRevolt` trended worldwide, with former supporters sharing videos of Plump's terrified expression from the debate, now juxtaposed with clips of Machiavelli standing tall in the face of an assassination attempt. Editorials questioned whether Plump had ever truly been the strong leader he claimed to be, or if he had merely been a manufactured persona protected by those around him.

The whispers turned into a deafening roar, and the headlines ignited a firestorm of national outrage.

Meanwhile, the Democratic establishment, facing its own reckoning, quietly conceded that Newtsum had little chance of victory. Panic rippled through high-level DNC meetings as strategists scrambled to make sense of Machiavelli's unprecedented rise. It wasn't just that he was winning. It was how he was winning. He had not only conquered Plump but done what Democrats had spent years and billions of dollars failing to achieve: he had shattered the myth of Plump's strength, exposing him as nothing more than a manufactured figurehead, a pampered nepo baby propped up by handlers and enablers.

In closed-door discussions, DNC officials begrudgingly acknowledged Machiavelli's brilliance. His network operated with military precision, infiltrating key social media platforms, crafting viral narratives, and ensuring that every revelation about Plump's weakness was timed for maximum impact. A leaked strategy memo circulating within Democratic circles detailed Machiavelli's months-long campaign to methodically dismantle Plump's public persona, culminating in the smack heard around the world. His operatives had studied Plump's every weakness, every moment of hesitation, every crack in his bravado, and exploited them masterfully.

"He didn't just defeat Plump," one senior Democratic strategist admitted in a secretly recorded conversation leaked to independent media. "He rewrote the rules of engagement. We threw everything we had at Plump for years, and Machiavelli took him apart in a couple of months, spending a fraction of the cost. And now we're the ones playing catch-up."

Newtsum, desperate to reclaim momentum, publicly challenged Machiavelli to a one-on-one debate, hoping to reframe the election as a choice between stability and chaos. But behind the scenes, his campaign was unraveling. High-level meetings at the DNC headquarters were marked by shouting matches, desperate strategy revisions, and a sense of impending doom.

"We're not fighting to win anymore," one senior campaign official admitted in a leaked audio recording. "We're fighting to make sure we don't come in third. If we let Plump beat us, we lose all credibility."

The realization was sobering: if Newtsum secured second place, the Democratic National Committee could continue its efforts to disqualify Machiavelli through relent-less legal challenges, even after the election. Lawyers worked around the clock, combing through decades-old case law to find obscure constitutional loopholes. Pressure was put on state election boards to delay certifications, citing unverified claims of financial improprieties and technical disqualifica-tions. Media surrogates were deployed to cast doubt on the legitimacy of Machiavelli's meteoric rise, portraying him as a destabilizing force rather than a populist champion.

"This is a hostile takeover of American democracy," one DNC spokesperson argued on MSNBC. "If we allow someone like Machiavelli to seize power unchecked, we are inviting chaos into our institutions."

But even within Democratic circles, the tide was shifting. Younger, progressive voices in the party saw Machiavelli as an unstoppable force, a once-in-a-generation disruptor who had done the impossible. He'd crushed Plump in a way Democrats had failed to for years. A growing faction within the party believed that opposing Machiavelli was futile and that the DNC needed to adapt rather than resist.

"He's already changed the game," a prominent Democratic strategist confessed in a private roundtable discussion. "We either evolve, or we die."

Plump's campaign, however, was in freefall. Every move he made reeked of desperation. He ranted on Truth Social at all hours, raging about conspiracies, blaming Machiavelli, the Democrats, the deep state, even Poutine for his predicament.

```
"Rigged! The whole thing is
rigged!"
```

He posted at 3 a.m., only for his words to be met with mockery rather than outrage. He even tried holding smaller rallies on consecutive days. A couple of days after the debate, once overflowing with diehard supporters, had become ghost towns. The people who once cheered his every word now booed when he spoke. When he tried to play the victim over the debate slap, his own audience heckled him. "You let him punk you out!" a man shouted during a rally in Georgia, only for Plump to sputter in frustration and storm off stage.

Former allies turned against him in droves. "He's finished," said Steve Bannon on his podcast. "We backed a fighter, not a whiner." Even Fox News, which once defended him at all costs, had shifted its tone. "Plump has become his own worst enemy," declared Jesse Watters. "He's lost control of the narrative, and frankly, he looks weak."

His campaign war chest, once an untouchable fortune, was now a black hole of legal expenses. Instead of funding ads or ground operations, every cent went into lawsuits aimed at disqualifying Machiavelli. Donor confidence collapsed. Billionaire backers refused to throw good money after bad.

Inside Plump's inner circle, paranoia ran rampant. "We need a nuclear option," an aide was caught saying in a leaked audio recording. "We can't let him lose like this." The words "martial law" were uttered in hushed tones, though even Plump's most devoted advisors knew that declaring it before the election would lead to open revolt.

The walls were closing in, and for the first time in his life, Plump had no escape route.

Meanwhile, the cultural zeitgeist embraced the spectacle with an almost obsessive fervor. Talk shows, late-night comedians, and viral podcasts dedicated entire segments to dissecting the "smack heard around the world." Jimmy Kimmel opened his monologue with the now-iconic footage playing on loop behind him: "Folks, I have to say, I never thought I'd see the day where a presidential debate turned into a WWE SmackDown event, but here we are!" The audience erupted in laughter as he added, "And you know Plump knew it was bad because for the first time in his life, he didn't get up and start yelling at the ref."

Over on The Daily Show, Jon Stewart, back in the host's chair for a special election series, held up a side-by-side comparison of Plump's horrified expression post-slap and a still from The Godfather's infamous restaurant scene. "This is the face of a man who just realized he ain't the Don anymore," Stewart quipped. The segment went viral, racking up millions of views overnight.

Podcasts also seized the moment. Joe Brogan, in a three-hour special, brought on political analysts, former military strategists, and even renowned fight commentators to break down the moment in forensic detail. "I don't care what side you're on," Brogan said, shaking his head as the infamous clip played on a loop behind him. "That was a dominance display. That wasn't just a smack; that was the moment the alpha of the room was reestablished. Plump's base always thought he was that guy. Turns out he was just pretending."

His guest, UFC commentator Joe Schilling, leaned forward, analyzing the clip like a fight breakdown. "Look at Plump's body language. The moment before the hit, he's puffed up, shoulders squared, trying to play big. But as soon as Machiavelli makes contact, BOOM, he collapses. The fear in his eyes? That's primal. He wasn't expecting it, and worse, he had no response."

Political strategist Tim Dillon chimed in, laughing. "The GOP built this myth of Plump as the brawler, the counter-puncher, the guy who never backs down. And in two seconds, Machiavelli shattered that illusion. Watch the way Plump hits the floor. He looks around like a confused kid who has just been embarrassed in front of everyone. Where's the bravado? Where's the toughness? Gone."

Brogan nodded; his expression was a mix of admiration and disbelief. "And that's the key moment, right? Not just the smack, but the aftermath. Look at Machiavelli. He's standing there, stone-faced, no hesitation, no fear. It's like he owns the room. It's one thing to take the stage. It's another to completely reframe the power dynamic. He just sent a message: 'I run this now.'"

Schilling jumped in again, emphasizing the strategic brilliance of Machiavelli's move. "He didn't just punk Plump with that move; he punked him the whole time. Taking the center podium was a calculated move. That's where the real power lies in a debate setting, and Machi-avelli just took it. He forced Plump to move to the left, like a peasant trying to find his place in the room. The whole debate after that? It was all on Machiavelli's terms."

Brogan watched the clip once more; his face lit with a mixture of awe and respect. "That's why his numbers skyrocketed after the debate. People respect power. And Machiavelli just proved he's the one calling the shots. This isn't just about politics anymore. It's about who has the authority, the guts, and the control. And right now, Machiavelli owns that stage."

Even conservative media struggled to contain the narrative. Tucker Carlson, now hosting his own independent show, hesitated before addressing the incident: "Look, I'm not saying Plump lost the debate because he got hit. But let's be honest here, how do you come back from that? You can't call yourself a strongman and then… fall on your ass on live television."

Social media exploded in an unprecedented frenzy. Within seconds, meme pages were churning out endless variations of the infamous moment, remixing the slap with all the creativity the internet could muster. Fans turned it into a pop culture phenomenon, with edits ranging from dramatic anime-style music that intensified the already tense moment, to slow-motion sequences reminiscent of Western duels. Over-the-top sound effects, everything from lightning strikes to dramatic orchestral swells, accompanied the images, adding to the growing aura of absurdity and brilliance surrounding the slap.

A viral post captioned "The emperor has no clothes!" spread like wildfire, juxtaposing the image of Plump sprawled out on the debate stage with the stunned look of a man who had lost all pretense of invincibility. His eyes were wide with shock, as if the weight of his decades of political persona had collapsed in an instant. The phrase, a historical reference to the truth being exposed, perfectly captured the sheer humiliation Plump was experiencing in real time.

On TikTok, the incident took on a life of its own. A new trend emerged where users passionately reenacted the moment, adding absurd sound effects like a booming "KA-POW!" or the iconic "wrestling bell" chimes. Others used exaggerated visual effects, turning the slap into a slow-motion explosion, with sparks flying, and even 'Comic Book-style' sound bubbles like "BAM!" and "ZAP!" This was no longer just a political moment. It was an internet earthquake that rattled the very foundations of how people viewed not just Plump but the entire political establishment.

The memes were relentless. GIFs created of Plump recoiling in shock, often with hilarious audio overdubs, like a whip crack or the shriek of a cartoon character. The internet had fully embraced this moment of absurdity, turning it into a statement not just on the political climate, but on the ridiculousness of Plump's fall from power. It was a digital manifestation of the broader cultural shift, one that no one could have predicted.

Machiavelli's slap, once a singular political gesture, became the modern-day equivalent of an iconic cultural event. It was meme-ified, dissected, and endlessly shared, making it impossible for anyone to forget. The internet had turned it into something that transcended politics—it was now a symbol of defiance, a moment of ultimate triumph over the man who had long been untouchable.

Machiavelli's strategic takedown of Plump, now documented in viral videos and in-depth analysis exposing his meticulous plan, was hailed as nothing short of political genius. Experts and commentators alike marveled at how each of Machiavelli's calculated moves had chipped away at Plump's public persona, until the former president was left exposed, vulnerable, and seemingly powerless. "This wasn't just a moment," said a popular YouTuber in a breakdown video that amassed millions of views. "This was a meticulously crafted psychological coup. Plump was dismantled, piece by piece, and we all watched it happen in real-time."

The analysis of Machiavelli's strategy became a case study in political brilliance. Podcasts dedicated entire episodes to dissecting how Machiavelli used every tool at his disposal, timing, media manipulation, and psychological warfare. One viral video on Twitter aptly compared Machiavelli's rise to that of a chess grandmaster who, instead of rushing for checkmate, made calculated moves that put Plump into a position where he had no choice but to surrender. "Plump didn't lose this battle in one moment," the video narrator explained. "He was strategically ground down over time until, when that smack hit him, there was nothing left to protect him."

For those watching, it was evident Machiavelli didn't just attack Plump's policies; he attacked his identity. The clip that circulated widely on Reddit revealed Machiavelli taunting Plump before their debate even started. Machiavelli's voice was smooth and controlled, drawing out every word. The footage was shared millions of times, with commentators praising how Machiavelli had effortlessly broken Plump's most guarded defenses.

Then came the botched assassination attempt, captured on a live-streaming camera, turning what was already a political earthquake into an unstoppable tsunami. The footage spread like wildfire: Machiavelli, standing his ground, his expression unflinching, his stance unwavering. The chaos around him only seemed to amplify his presence, making him appear larger than life. Meanwhile, the internet wasted no time in juxtaposing this moment with Plump's most humiliating failures. Side-by-side clips flooded social media: Machiavelli staring down danger versus Plump recoiling from a protester at a rally, Machiavelli remaining resolute versus Plump crawling away from Machiavelli on the debate stage. The contrast as stark as it was damning.

The perception was undeniable; Machiavelli wasn't just winning; he was rewriting history. Political commentators scrambled to grasp the magnitude of what had transpired.

"We've never seen anything like this," said Nate Silver on a special election panel. "Machiavelli has turned an assassination attempt into the ultimate display of strength, and the effect on the electorate is immediate. His numbers are soaring; this is myth-making in real-time."

Social media detonated. Memes, reaction videos, and minute-by-minute breakdowns of the assassination attempt flooded TikTok and Twitter. A viral super cut, edited like an action movie trailer, racked up millions of views in hours: Machiavelli's stoic response, the crowd's panicked screams, the sound of Volkov hitting the ground reverberating, all set to Hans Zimmer's "Time." The final frame? Machiavelli adjusting his black button-up dress shirt, brushing off a fleck of debris. The caption: "UNBREAKABLE."

The internet didn't just react; it erupted. This was more than a moment; it was the moment. The event that cemented Machiavelli's image as an unshakable force in American politics. It was no longer just about winning an election; it was about reshaping the very foundation of power in America.

The internet erupted in a frenzy unlike anything seen before. Within twenty-four hours, three major events—the debate smack, the leaked Machiavelli strategy tapes, and the failed assassination attempt—had rewritten the narrative of the election. The establishment was powerless to stop the tidal wave of change, and for the first time in modern political history, the American people were witnessing the collapse of the old order in real time.

And at the center of it all stood Machiavelli, the man who had turned the impossible into the inevitable.

46
BURNING THE RULEBOOK
PRESENT DAY
OCTOBER 2028 — 7:00 P.M

San Antonio, TX.

The studio hummed with anticipation. Joe Brogan leaned forward in his chair, his signature grin spreading across his face as he adjusted his mic.

"Alright, folks, welcome back to the podcast. We have a hell of a show today. First up, my regular guest and radio legend, Harold Stern."

Harold smirked, flicking his dark curls back. "Oh, it's gonna be a good one, Joe."

"And," Brogan continued, "we have a very special guest commentator joining us. The man who doesn't pull any punches, literally and figuratively, Bill Matter."

Matter chuckled, nodding. "I'm just here to make sure we keep things civilized. You know, like the debates."

The trio shared a knowing laugh before Brogan turned to the couple sitting across from them. "And now, the man of the hour. Independent Presidential candidate, the guy who just had the most insane week of any politician in modern history; James Machiavelli, along with his badass wife, Paola."

James leaned in, flashing a confident smile. "Joe, Harold, Bill, thanks for having us."

Paola, poised and composed, offered a small nod. "Always a pleasure."

Brogan leaned back, shaking his head in amusement. "I don't even know where to start. I mean, James, you absolutely punked Plump in that debate. That slap? The world saw it. Man, you knocked his ass clean to the ground."

Harold burst into laughter, practically gasping for breath. "Dude, I have never seen Plump look that shocked. He went down like a sack of expired McRonald's nuggets. I mean, the guy looked like he'd seen the ghost of every bad business deal he ever made."

Bill Matter interjected, rubbing his temples. "The funniest part was the look in his eyes. Like he just saw all his unpaid debts flash before him. For a second, I thought he was about to start calling his accountants from the floor."

James shrugged, feigning innocence. "What can I say? The man had it coming. He ran his mouth, he pushed his luck, and he learned real quick that actions have consequences."

Brogan laughed, leaning forward. "And the best part?

He didn't even try to get up right away. He just sat there, looking around as if someone had unplugged him from the Matrix."

Harold smirked. "And then you just stood over him, staring down like some final boss in a video game. That was some cold-blooded shit."

James smirked. "I wasn't trying to intimidate him. I was trying to give him a chance to get up and stand up for himself, but you all saw how that played out."

Brogan, still laughing, wiped a tear from his eye. "By the way, entering the debate stage using Stone Cold Steve Austin's entrance music was pure genius. I jumped out of my seat and thought, 'Shit is about to go down!' It was like watching WrestleMania, but with real-world consequences."

Paola smirked and leaned in. "Then you'll love this even more. A few of the members of our network heard you calling my husband the 'Stone Cold Steve Austin of Politics' the day before the debate, and that gave them an idea. They actually reached out to Stone Cold himself and asked if it would be all right if we used his entrance music for the debate. Not only did he give the green light, but he told our team that he's a fan of Machiavelli's politics and to give all of us a big ol' 'Hell Yeah!'"

Harold burst out laughing. "Wait, wait, wait; you're telling me that Stone Cold personally endorsed the move? That's legendary. I mean, Plump knew he was about to get politically body-slammed."

Bill Matter chuckled and turned to Machiavelli. "And then you just took it to another level. The way you walked right up and stole Plump's center podium spot? Man, that was brutal. You punked him in front of the entire world. And when you told him, 'Get your punk ass over there. The center is my spot, bitch. That's right, don't look at me, coward. Keep walking with that dumbass smile on your face' Jesus, I nearly fell out of my chair. I don't think I've ever seen Plump look so unsure of himself."

James grinned. "He had it coming. He spent the entire campaign acting like he owned the stage, like he was untouchable. I just reminded him that respect isn't given, it's earned. And that night, he earned himself a one-way ticket to the corner podium."

Brogan's eyes lit up. "And then, because apparently, the universe was bored, you catch your own assassination attempt on a live stream while locked in a holding cell. How the hell did that happen?"

Paola sighed, gripping James's hand tightly. "That was terrifying. But James? He just kept his cool, like he always does. We knew after he slapped Plump that there would be retaliation. Plump plays dirty, and pressing charges was just the first step. But when our sources picked up chatter that Volkov, a known Poutine mercenary, had landed in St. Louis on a private plane linked to Plump, we knew something bigger was coming."

James nodded. "It wasn't paranoia. It was pattern recognition. These people don't accept losses gracefully. They cheat, they intimidate, and when that fails, they resort to violence."

Paola continued, her voice steady but laced with anger. "So, we planned ahead. We had a couple of our security guys get themselves arrested as 'homeless drunks' and placed in the same holding area as James. That way, if anything went down, he wouldn't be alone."

Harold whistled. "Jesus. That's some next-level espionage."

Bill Matter shook his head in disbelief. "And people say politicians aren't interesting anymore. Meanwhile, you're out here running a campaign like it's a goddamn spy thriller."

Harold whistled. "And if that wasn't enough, a few days later, a new video drops showing what really went down after the debate went to break. Let's talk about Plump Jr."

Matter winced. "Oh man. Junior tried to be the tough guy, but… well, you tell it, James."

James smirked, leaning back as he recalled the moment. "All I felt was an arm locking around my throat. He was coming in for the chokehold, thinking he was slick. But I knew better. I let him get just enough leverage to feel confident, then I went with it. Reached back, grabbed his legs, and with one explosive motion, I threw both of us backward. He hit hard. I hit harder."

Brogan clapped his hands together, eyes wide with excitement. "And then those elbows; Crack. Crack. Crack. I mean, that dude was leaking like a busted pipe. Blood everywhere. He looked like someone had dropped a bottle of ketchup on the stage."

Harold snorted, shaking his head. "Plump Jr. looked like he just realized his trust fund doesn't come with a health plan. The way his arms stiffened, the twitching... He got knocked into another tax bracket."

Paola shook her head, her expression firm. "Honestly, it wasn't just about self-defense. It was a message. These people think they can intimidate James, that they can strong-arm us into submission. But we're not backing down. Not now. Not ever."

Matter leaned forward, his gaze sharp. "That's the question on everyone's mind. You're dominating the polls, the race is practically over, and unless something crazy happens, you'll be the next President of the United States. After a week like this, how do you move forward?"

James exhaled, his expression unwavering. "Simple. We keep pushing. The work doesn't stop just because the numbers are in our favor. We're still holding town halls, still engaging with people, because this campaign was never just about getting votes. It's about igniting something bigger, a movement of Americans taking back control of their government. People need to understand that casting a ballot isn't the end of their responsibility. If they want real change, they have to stay involved long after election day."

Paola nodded decisively. "This campaign isn't built around James alone. It's built around the people who believe in us and what we stand for. That's why we don't see this as a victory lap. We see it as a call to action."

Harold leaned in, intrigued. "But let's be real, after a week where you slapped the sitting president to the floor, survived an assassination attempt, and laid out Plump Jr., you're not just running a campaign. You're rewriting the rulebook. Are you ready for what comes next?"

James met Harold's gaze head-on. "I was ready the moment I decided to run. This isn't about playing nice with the establishment. It's about breaking the cycle of corruption and fear. So yeah, I'm ready. And so is America."

The room fell silent for a moment, the weight of everything that had been said hanging in the air. Then, slowly, Brogan's signature grin spread across his face. He leaned into the mic, eyes gleaming with excitement.

"Ladies and gentlemen, James Machiavelli. This campaign isn't just interesting… it's legendary. We are witnessing history in real time."

47

THE FINAL STRETCH

PRESENT DAY

OCTOBER 2028 — 5:00 P.M.

Undisclosed Location

The last few weeks leading up to Election Day had been a whirlwind of energy, controversy, and shifting dynamics that none of the candidates could have fully anticipated. For James Machiavelli and his wife, Paola, the campaign was a relentless journey across the country. Instead of hosting grand rallies filled with spectacle, they chose a more personal approach. Town halls with live streaming. These intimate gatherings allowed them to engage directly with voters, answering unfiltered questions with a rare candor that resonated deeply with the public.

What made their approach even more remarkable was the lack of a safety net. Unlike the carefully curated events of traditional politicians, Machiavelli and Paola embraced spontaneity, often allowing audience members to challenge them directly on difficult topics. Their ability to respond confidently and authentically only strengthened their appeal. Every event felt less like a campaign stop and more like an open conversation with the American people. In contrast to the rigid scripts and polished performances of his rivals, Machiavelli's transparency became his greatest weapon.

It was an unconventional strategy, but it was working. People saw them as accessible, honest, and willing to take on tough issues without hiding behind rehearsed soundbites. The movement surrounding Machiavelli wasn't just political. It was personal. Each town hall was a testament to the growing disillusionment with the establishment and the hunger for a leader who would break the mold.

Meanwhile, Gavin Newtsum ramped up his campaign efforts, crisscrossing the country in a desperate bid to regain momentum. His rallies were well organized, filled with enthusiastic supporters, but something was missing. No matter how hard he tried, he could not shake the overwhelming sense that the people had already made up their minds. In a last-ditch effort to revive his numbers, he repeatedly called out Machiavelli, challenging him to a one-on-one debate. Yet Machiavelli ignored the bait, staying focused on his ground game. Newtsum's frustration grew as his pleas for a debate went unanswered.

For President Plump, the landscape had turned hostile. Following a disastrous debate performance and a subsequent rally where he was booed and heckled, he made a drastic decision. He would no longer hold public rallies. The risk of facing further public humiliation was too high. Instead, he retreated into private meetings with America's elite, weaving elaborate conspiracy theories about how the election was rigged against him. However, his audience was dwindling. Even the most powerful figures in the country had grown tired of his rants, and his claims failed to gain traction among the public. What was once a political force of nature had become an isolated figure, speaking to an echo chamber that no longer cared to listen.

As the days inched closer to the election, Machiavelli's numbers surged. In national polls, he reached an unprecedented 71%, a level of dominance rarely seen in modern electoral history. Reports from early voters further confirmed what the polls suggested, an overwhelming majority were casting their ballots for Machiavelli. Even in the five states where his name had been removed from the ballot due to court rulings fought by the RNC and DNC, voters were undeterred. Write-in campaigns gained incredible traction, and political analysts speculated that Machiavelli had a real chance of winning those states regardless of the roadblocks set before him.

The media landscape has also undergone a dramatic shift in these final weeks. Networks that had once thrived on sensationalism and partisan narratives now found themselves struggling to maintain credibility in the face of overwhelming public support for Machiavelli. Fox News and

CNN, long considered ideological opposites, surprised many by abandoning their usual biases and instead committing to providing honest election coverage. Their analysts acknowledged the unprecedented nature of Machiavelli's rise and begrudgingly admitted that attempts to disqualify him were failing to gain traction with the public.

For the first time in decades, election coverage became less about pushing political agendas and more about hard facts. Panel discussions shifted from speculative fear-mongering to analytical breakdowns of polling data and legal rulings. Even veteran anchors, who had spent years defending their respective party lines, appeared to adjust to the new reality. Machiavelli's rise was undeniable, and the public was demanding straightforward reporting.

At the same time, smaller independent outlets and social media influencers played a crucial role in countering the establishment's legal maneuvers. Citizen journalists, armed with smartphones and an unyielding sense of determination, reporting on court rulings and election board meetings in real-time. Their coverage often exposed the coordinated efforts by political operatives to delay certifications and suppress the will of the voters. Viral videos of backroom dealings, leaked internal memos, and whistleblower accounts flooded the internet, making it impossible for mainstream media to ignore what was happening. The American public, more engaged than ever, refused to let their voices be silenced, amplifying the truth through grassroots networks that rivaled the reach of traditional broad-casters.

Desperation gripped the political establishment as the RNC and DNC doubled down on efforts to disqualify Machiavelli, pouring hundreds of millions into relentless legal challenges. Teams of elite lawyers worked around the clock, scouring decades-old case law to unearth obscure constitutional loopholes that could be weaponized against his candidacy. Every technicality was explored, no matter how far-fetched, in a bid to undermine his overwhelming support. Pressure mounted on state election boards to delay certification, with legal filings citing unverified claims of financial improprieties and administrative disqualifications. The legal battlefield was as fierce as the campaign trail, but despite these efforts, Machiavelli's supporters remained undeterred, ensuring that his momentum carried forward into Election Day.

Election Day loomed, and the political world braced for what was shaping up to be one of the most historic and unconventional elections in American history. The people had spoken in the polls and early voting numbers. Now, all that remained was to count the votes.

48

A NATION AWAKENS
PRESENT DAY
NOVEMBER 7, 2028 — 7:00 P.M.

Washinton D.C.

7:00 P.M. EST—The First Returns

The energy in the room was electric, a mixture of tension and sheer disbelief. The highest voter turnout in American history. Two-hundred-fifty-two million ballots cast, shattering records. The first numbers trickled in from the East Coast, and already, something unprecedented was happening.

"Florida called for Machiavelli," the anchor on the screen announced, his voice faltering for just a moment. The crowd at the campaign headquarters erupted. A state that had swung back and forth between red and blue for decades had gone Independent.

The returns continued. New Hampshire, Vermont, Virginia, all lighting up for James Machiavelli. The write-in votes were showing up in overwhelming numbers. Even in states where his name had been removed from the ballot, Americans had refused to be silenced.

8:30 P.M. EST—A Political Earthquake

Pennsylvania. Ohio. Michigan. The Rust Belt was his. The numbers weren't even close. The networks, usually hesitant to call battleground states early, were forced to acknowledge reality: this was a landslide.

CNN cut to a stunned panel of analysts. "This is beyond a wave. This is a political tsunami," one of them managed to say. A veteran political strategist shook his head in disbelief. "We knew Machiavelli had a following, but this? This is rewriting American politics as we know it."

Texas, strongly Independent. California, solidly Independent. The most populous states in the country were delivering massive victories for Machiavelli. The trend was undeniable. County after county flipped in ways no one had predicted. Rural voters, suburban households, urban centers, everywhere, his name had overwhelmed the ballot.

9:45 P.M. EST—The West Watches in Shock

As the Central and Mountain Time Zones reported, the reality of the night set in. The write-in votes had poured in at unprecedented levels. Even in the eight states that had attempted to remove him from the ballot, the people had spoken.

Wyoming, the first real deviation from the script, stayed in Plump's column, just barely. And in Washington, D.C., Governor Gavin Newtsum eked out a win, though Machiavelli's performance in the deep blue district left commentators speechless. "Never in my career have I seen anything like this," a stunned MSNBC anchor admitted. "This is not just a political movement... this is an outright revolution."

10:30 P.M. EST–Maine and Nebraska Split

The unique systems in Maine and Nebraska created slight outliers. Maine's four electoral votes split evenly, two for Newtsum, two for Machiavelli. Nebraska, typically a Republican stronghold, saw Machiavelli claiming four of its five districts, leaving one for Plump.

But the outcome was already clear.

11:15 P.M. EST–The Inevitable Declaration

"Ladies and gentlemen, we are witnessing history." The broadcaster looked directly into the camera. "With 80% of the national vote and an electoral map never before seen in American politics, we can now project James Machiavelli as the next President of the United States."

The eruption from the streets of New York, Chicago,

Los Angeles, and even smaller towns across America was deafening. Fireworks exploded in the night sky. Spontaneous parades formed in cities nationwide. For the first time in modern history, an Independent had shattered the two-party system.

11:45 P.M. EST–The Aftermath

The cameras panned to the losing candidates. Ronald Plump, visibly fuming, stepped up to the podium, his expression hard as stone. The room was silent for a moment, the tension thick as he adjusted the microphone. Then, he let loose.

"This election was a disgrace," he thundered, his face turning red with fury. "A total fraud! They rigged it against me, against the American people! James Machiavelli should have been disqualified from day one, and yet here we are, watching one of the biggest election scams in history unfold before our very eyes. This was an organized coup by the corrupt establishment, and they think we're just going to accept it? No! We're not going to take this!"

Boos erupted from his gathered supporters, chants of "Stop the steal!" filling the air. "Stop the steal! Stop the steal!" The room shook with their rage, their fists pumping in the air. Plump raised a hand, calling for silence, his voice defiant. "We are not conceding. We will fight this. We will challenge every illegitimate vote, every fraudulent write-in, every crooked election official who let this happen. I have never backed down from a fight, and I am not starting now!"

His voice grew sharper, cutting through the roar of his supporters. "The courts will hear our case. The American people deserve the truth. This isn't about me; this is about YOU! This is about YOUR country being stolen right in front of your eyes. We will not go quietly. We will not surrender! This battle is just beginning!"

Meanwhile, Gavin Newtsum's speech took a very different tone. He strode confidently to his podium, flashing a brief smile before addressing the nation. "This was a hard-fought race," he admitted. "And while I had hoped for a different outcome, let's be clear, I beat Ronald Plump. The American people rejected his extremism, and that is a victory in itself."

Cheers erupted from his supporters. He let them carry on for a moment before raising a hand to quiet them. His voice became more measured, his eyes narrowing. "But now, we face an unprecedented situation. If James Machiavelli is to be disqualified, and let's be honest, there are legitimate legal questions surrounding this election, then I will be ready. I am the next rightful candidate in line to assume the presidency. We cannot let chaos overtake our democracy. We must ensure that the transition of power happens lawfully, and I will fight to protect the integrity of our system. We need stability now more than ever."

Newtsum straightened his tie, looking directly into the camera. "The American people have spoken. But if the courts decide otherwise, we must be prepared. I stand ready to lead."

12:30 A.M. EST—The Hard Part Begins

James Machiavelli took the stage. The chant from the massive crowd was deafening: "MA-CHI-A-VEL-LI! MA-CHI-A-VEL-LI!" He raised his hands, signaling for calm, before he spoke.

"Tonight, history has been made. Not by me, but by you… the American people." The cheers rose again. "For too long, they told you that you had to choose between the lesser of two evils. That you had no other option. That an Independent could never win. Well, you proved them wrong. The people of America just showed the world that there is strength in numbers! We are a network of hundreds of millions of individuals working together to achieve a common goal. A collective American dream, where all Americans are given the education and resources to succeed in our society."

He took a deep breath, and his face grew serious. "But the easy part is over. Now the real fight begins. Our network is here to clear the obstacles preventing the American people from reaching their potential, but it will be up to every American to do their part. This is not just our victory; it is a mandate for real change. And rest assured, there will be those who try to undermine it."

He leaned forward, gripping the podium. "We are

already hearing the voices of resistance. We knew they wouldn't go quietly. But we promise you this, we will not falter. We will not be intimidated. And we will not let the will of the people be overturned."

The crowd erupted again, their chants growing louder. He let the roar wash over them before finishing.

"The establishment will fight tooth and nail to cling to their power. We still face legal obstacles and deep-rooted corruption within the judicial system. And mark my words, at some point, the coward President Plump will try to impose martial law. But remember this: the night is darkest before the dawn.

They have underestimated you. They have underestimated us.

But they forget, this nation does not belong to the powerful. It belongs to the people.

Together, we will rise. Together, we will rebuild. And together, we will fulfill the true promise of America, for every citizen, in every corner of this land."

Because as much as the people had spoken, the battle was only just beginning.

Thank you for reading *American Machiavelli*. If you liked it please leave a review so that others can find it.

ACKNOWLEDGMENTS

A heartfelt thanks to Samara Cove, for her guidance, knowledge, and insight from the very beginning of this journey.

And to my editor, your sharp eye and steady hand helped shape these words into what they are today.

ABOUT THE AUTHOR

If knowledge is power, then education is everything.

But true education is not measured in grades or titles. It lives in questions, in shadows, in the quiet spaces where the world often tells you not to look. It calls you to uncover what others overlook, to listen for truths hidden beneath the noise, and to walk paths that may at first feel uncertain.

This page is not about me, it is about us. Every story, every idea, is a mirror, inviting reflection not only of the self but of our shared human struggle. What you find here is meant to awaken curiosity, summon courage, and remind you that growth is never a solitary act, we rise strongest when we rise together.

Because in the end, it isn't the author who matters. It is the readers, bound by a hunger for truth and a refusal to look away, who dare to confront the unknown, seek what is real, and rise strong, unified on the other side.

ALSO BY F. YEW

American Machiavelli

American Maciavelli—Bonus Content